HOOFBEATS AT WINDSONG

June Whyte

A Shadow Creek Romance
Book 1

Miraflores Nights
Press

HOOFBEATS
AT
WINDSONG

✠✠✠✠✠✠✠✠✠✠✠✠✠✠✠✠✠✠✠✠✠✠✠✠✠✠✠✠✠✠

June Whyte

This edition published by Miraflores Nights
An imprint of Misti Media LLC
https://www.mistimedia.com
Available in both Paperback and eBook Editions
1 2 3 4 5 6 7 8 9 10
Text Copyright © June Whyte 2023
Cover design by *GetCovers*
Paperback ISBN: 9781963479140
eBook ISBN: 9781963479041

Dedication

Dedicated to my friend, June Diehl's brave little dog, FRANKLIN, who, after spinal surgery, has been attending rehabilitation at VRSVA almost daily and has now been fitted with a cart to maximize his mobility.

Go Franklin!

ONE

Kiah Jayne Stanton, gripped the hard plastic steering wheel in both hands and swallowed bile threatening to upchuck in her throat. Her chest cramped. Dread, with its snake-like tentacles, played Ring-a-Rosies in her stomach. She couldn't do it. Couldn't face the tea-drinking, sandwich munching mourners back at the house. All wearing their fake sympathy like a badge, all rabbiting on about what a good, loving, hardworking husband and brave, well-respected policeman Richard Stanton had been; expecting her to break down and cry rivers of tears for the dearly departed when she was actually waving coloured balloons and blowing joyful party poppers inside her head.

Kiah's grip on the steering wheel tightened. Conflicting thoughts, like fish in a pond, darted through her brain. The road ahead looked much more inviting…

Heart in her throat, she made a decision. Instead of steering Richard's ball-breaking Range Rover SUV up George Street, around the square and then into the driveway of the luxury two-bedroom apartment they'd shifted into the day after their wedding, with a decisive wrench of the wheel, she chose the main road out of town. Stomped on the accelerator. Gave a fist-pumping *whoopee* and kept on driving.

A bubble of laughter pressed against Kiah's chest. If only Richard could see her now. His precious and untouchable Range Rover had always been completely off limits. Her finger marks on the exterior once resulting in a week of the silent treatment, one of his favourite punishments. And yet here she was now, crouched behind the wheel of his precious status symbol like a race-car driver, the middle finger of her left hand raised to the sky.

As Kiah exploded onto the South Eastern Freeway, the judder, the deep growl of the V8 engine under her was both terrifying and freeing. Terrifying, because she'd never driven a vehicle so big, so powerful, so exhilarating. It was a blast. A full-on power trip. She jammed her foot on the gas, taking the first step to freedom, to becoming the woman she aspired to be — a cross between Xena the Warrior Princess and a souped-up joyful Mary Poppins.

Strong and happy.

She could barely remember the last time she'd been either. Maybe in her late teens, early twenties, when she used to parade in the streets wearing holey jeans and slogan-bearing tees, chanting and waving banners stating, *Say No to Sow stalls*, or *Save the Dingos* or whichever animal they'd decided to save that week. Or when she was astride her favourite riding-school horse, Queenie, cantering along a country path with like-minded friends. But twelve years was a long time to be married to the late Chief of Police's son, himself already a Police Lieutenant. A big-bodied, pompous man, who became cold and angry if she didn't jump to his commands. Kiah's arms prickled, the fear of him touching her like a ghost tiptoeing across her skin. Strangely, she'd always found Richard's coldness far worse than his anger. The icy blue eyes that stared right through her. And over the years she'd learned it was far easier to do as she was told, to walk on eggshells whenever Richard was in one of his moods.

And wondered, not for the first time, if she hadn't decided to leave him that fateful night a week ago today, whether he'd still be alive.

After driving non-stop for close to four hours, leaving the hills behind, passing through regional towns where she had no inclination to stop, Kiah took stock of her surroundings. She'd been driving off the main roads, for the last hour and now appeared to be in the middle of nowhere. Red parched earth disappeared into the distance on both sides of the road. Spinifex grass and thick stunted clumps of silvery green mulga, with their thin black trunks and needle-like drought-proof leaves, the main vegetation.

Had she unknowingly driven through a time zone and landed on the moon?

When she had to slow down behind a big rumbling orange tractor that took up most of the road, she also realized, if she didn't stop for a toilet break within the next few minutes, she'd be in more trouble than a Sphinx cat stuck in a rose bush.

The tractor turned into a run-down petrol station and rattled to a stop at the nearest pump. Kiah followed and parked at the second of the four petrol bowsers that looked to be circa 1960, a combination of red dirt and cobwebs ingrained on each. Other than the petrol station, the only other structure for miles around was a tumbledown skeleton of a house set in the middle of the scrub, a hundred yards back from the road, the remains not much more than three blackened brick chimneys, half-strangled by the ravenous spinifex.

Legs crossed, she almost fell out of the Range Rover and immediately opted for toilet first, petrol second.

The restroom was around the side of the building and the door was locked, a sign indicating she needed to procure the key from the tall gangly teenager with the bad haircut she'd seen propped up behind the till inside the main building.

She blew out a breath of frustration, squeezed her legs together another notch. What were they afraid of? That she'd steal a roll of their crappy toilet paper?

"Key for the rest room, please?" She held a hand out to the teenager, her teeth and stomach in a clench of desperation. "Now," she added when he didn't look up from his phone.

"Two dollars deposit," he droned, still scrolling.

"You're joking."

"Company policy. We've had three drive-offs within the last six months."

While scrounging a two-dollar piece from the bottom of her bag, Kiah pushed aside the bizarreness of his words, then snatched the key from his outstretched hand. Would she make it in time? After procuring the key, she jogged back around the building, unlocked the door and slowly, and blissfully, did her thing.

Absolute heaven…

Finished, she washed her hands at the sink, and checked herself out in the spotty restroom mirror. A pale-faced, slightly overweight red head dressed all in black, right down to tights and shoes, stared back at her. *She so didn't look good in black.* Most women believed a little black dress in the wardrobe was a must. Not Kiah. Made her look washed out and dumpy. She shifted the fluffy black beret to a different angle, tipped her head to one side for a better appraisal. Nope. Didn't suit her at all. She dropped the headwear into the battered pedal bin on the floor beside her. If only she'd brought some everyday jeans and a tee, she'd change, then stuff the rest of the morbid funeral attire into the bin along with the beret.

Kiah studied her reflection in the mirror one more time. Almost forty, and she looked every one of those years. Why was it women were made to worry about wrinkles and sagging body bits as they grew older, yet men didn't give a hoot about their wrinkles, double chins and beer bellies? When a man's hair started to go grey, he thought of himself as a 'silver fox'. When a woman found one grey hair, she immediately rang her hairdressers and booked in for an emergency dye job. Kiah sighed. Stress hadn't been a friend to her complexion; her eyes looked tired and the wrinkles across her forehead appeared cemented in place. Another reason to become a new person, a woman who stood up for herself and didn't give a damn about the consequences.

She added a quick slick of lipstick, tugged her long bushy hair out of its restraining ponytail and then, head held high, marched out of the restroom, locking the door behind her.

After filling the Range Rover with petrol, Kiah went looking for sustenance. Even though it seemed like particles of red dust had worked their way into every crevice of the lone building squatting in the middle of nowhere, the goods on display inside looked fresh and inviting.

"Where am I?" she asked her new friend, the gangly, ginger-haired beanstalk lounging behind the till, hair in one of those spiky updos popular with kids of his age.

His eyebrows shot up so fast they almost bounced off his hairline. "You're standing right here in front of me, just like you were a few minutes ago. You're like, at a petrol station."

Kiah rolled her eyes before swiping her credit card across the terminal. Maybe scrolling continuously on his phone had dimmed his senses. "What's the *name* of this place?"

"You're at the Cowji service station, lady." His voice, too loud, and with a distinct pause between each word, indicated that in his opinion females over 30 were *way old*, and way beyond his comprehension.

As the attendant passed her receipt across, Kiah glanced at a small notice board attached to the side of his little cubicle. The board was covered in fly speckled notes and coloured adverts for events long since passed, like a dance at the United Church Hall three months ago, and a dog show held at the Showgrounds late last year. But one notice, fresher than the others, stood out. She leaned closer to read the small spidery printing: 'Wanted urgently: Groom and exercise rider for Windsong Racing Stables. Basic pay plus accommodation. Shadow Creek. Phone 0402989777 and ask for Jack Sullivan.'

When she was younger, Kiah had been horse-mad. She'd read every pony book she could get her hands on at the library, looked forward to weekly riding lesson at the local stables, dreamed of one day owning her own horse, but before that could happen, she'd said, 'I do', and *belonged* to Richard Stanton, and he hadn't approved of useless fripperies, like horses.

"How far to Shadow Creek?" Kiah pointed to the notice on the board.

Giving her a quick up and down assessment, the young attendant's lips quirked. "Can you *ride?*"

"Would I apply for the job if I couldn't?"

He lifted one expressive eyebrow. A know-it-all kid not long out of high school assessing the attributes of a slightly overweight, tired looking woman approaching or already in the middle of middle-age country. "Just sayin', lady."

"If you could give me the directions to Shadow Creek, I'll get out of your hair."

He ripped a sheet of paper from a nearby pad and began scratching out a rough map. "It's like, another three hours on from here."

Slipping the map into her pocket, Kiah frowned. *Can you ride?* Guess that was a fair enough question and the first one this Jack Sullivan would ask. She drew in a deep breath, let it out slowly. Had she taken leave of her senses? How was applying for a job at a racing stable going to find the 'new Kiah Stanton'? All it would do was make her feel even more useless when this Jack Sullivan guy laughed in her face, or if he did give her a go, say, 'I told you so', when she landed in hospital with two broken arms and a busted head before the end of the first day on the job. She hadn't ridden a horse for twelve years and even then, they were only riding-school horses. Not hot, flighty, thoroughbred racehorses.

Funny, she'd always had a way with horses, with most animals, actually. They responded to her touch. Like the skittish stray cat only she could handle. The poor thing had hung around the neighbourhood for weeks, until Richard came home early one day and found her feeding it one of the lamb chops intended for his dinner. The following day, two council-employees had rocked up, chased and caught the terrified cat in a net and taken it away in their van.

Straightening her shoulders, Kiah strode towards the Range Rover and swung herself into the driver's seat. Sinking into the comfort of the soft leather, she tugged the map with directions to Shadow Creek out of her pocket, screwed the paper in a ball and tossed it on the floor — just because she could. A sense of calm settled over her as she fastened her seat belt. Today was the beginning of her new life. She was looking for freedom, for fulfillment, not some bossy racing guy with bad breath and bowed legs bellowing in her ear, cursing her, because she didn't know the difference between the conformation of a stayer and a sprinter.

No, she'd push on, enjoy her freedom, maybe even wind up in the top end of Australia, somewhere tropical, like Cairns. Or what about Byron Bay? She could see herself lying on a sunbed on the beach, sunscreen slathered over her body, sipping something sweet and alcoholic and reading a Mills & Boon romance about a millionaire playboy and his feisty housemaid, who was only cleaning his toilet to help pay for her younger sister's medical bills.

After all, she could go anywhere, do whatever she liked and there was nothing, or no one, to stop her.

Kiah had switched her mobile off during the funeral service and forgotten to turn it back on. Snaffling her phone from the depths of her tote, she powered it up ready to log onto Google Maps, see where to head next, when about ten missed calls and fifty texts came through, one after the other, in one long ding.

Two from the funeral director with an invoice attached, but all the rest from Beryl Stanton, her cold, judgmental, lying-through-her-teeth mother-in-law. The woman who never had a kind word for Kiah, even on that awful day, a week ago.

The first text listed items Beryl insisted Kiah pick up for her from the chemist, the next half dozen furious because Kiah still hadn't arrived, and the rest seemed to be either demanding to know where Kiah was or complaining that she, Beryl, couldn't be expected to take care of the guests and pour teas. She was chief mourner.

Kiah switched the phone off and buried it deep inside her bag. Even from the grave Richard had continued to control her. His will stated that although the apartment was now in Kiah's name, she couldn't sell it until his mother died. Until then, Beryl, a young sixty-year-old, could live there, rent free and be cared for by her daughter-in-law. Richard's mother, who already owned her own home, had promptly put it on the market, shifted into Kiah's apartment, and taken over.

Her movements jerky, Kiah pressed the ignition button to start the engine and tossed her bag on the floor alongside the screwed-up map.

The open road was looking more and more inviting…

TWO

After spending the night at a country pub, in a little town she didn't bother to learn the name of, Kiah woke the next morning to the unearthly crow of a bronchial rooster welcoming the day while in the midst of a coughing fit.

According to the analogue clock squatting smugly on the bedside cabinet to her right, it was 5 am. *Damn rooster — should be in a bucket of KFC!* Rolling onto her back Kiah tugged the fringed powder pink candlewick bedspread up higher around her chin and contemplated the dark ceiling.

No way would she get back to sleep now. Not with the forebodings, the doubts, and the anxieties that were rattling around like loose screws in her head.

5 a.m. The devil's play time. When all confidence and dignity hit rock bottom and splattered like a carton of eggs on the pavement. When grand ideas and schemes and resolutions disappeared into the gloom.

Why hadn't she stood up to her monster of a mother-in-law and told her she'd fight the ridiculous terms of Richard's will? Kiah let out a sigh that felt like it came from the tips of her toes. Because she'd forgotten how to fight. That's why. Years of being married to Richard had leached all the fight out of her.

She stared at the room's narrow window, where an old-fashioned roller shade, complete with scallops and fringing, hung at half-mast, letting in the lingering remnants of night. Dark unknown shadows that flittered and slid across the shade. The mournful howl of a lonely dog. The disquieting *skritch* of something — or someone — scraping dead fingernails against the window glass.

Tremors of panic bubbled in her stomach, moving in rapid waves up to her chest, forcing the muscles to tighten, and ice to solidify in her veins. Was that *skritching* sound caused by the rustle of the wind? A leafy branch from a nearby tree? Or was it Richard, scrabbling to get in? Blaming her for his death?

She tried to suck in a deep calming breath but all she could manage were rasping gasps that sent sharp pains across her chest.

Richard can't get to you any more…

Gradually her breath returned to normal and the leaden weight pressing down on her chest eased. Kiah closed her eyes. Would she ever escape Richard's hold over her?

Was she strong enough, resolute enough, to stand up for herself in her new life? Or would she end up curled in a ball on the side of the road, a mental wreck waiting to be taken into care? Her bottom lip trembled. No…she wasn't going to cry. Nothing ever helped by crying — only made things worse. She'd found that out barely two weeks into her marriage.

Kiah switched on the bedside lamp, and, pushing away all negative thoughts, lay back on the lumpy single bed and watched the ceiling fan go through its final juddering death throes. It whirred, it clunked, it groaned, until finally the yellowing fan, fly dirt its only décor, gave one last shudder and jerked to a stop.

Immobile, the fly detritus on the fan became even more evident. Kiah let out a strangled giggle as a fast fact she'd read on *Quora* popped into her head: a housefly defecates about 300 times in a single day — once every 4-5 minutes. Her lips twitched. Was it any wonder the poor ceiling fan had finally given up under the weight of all that fly poop?

Rolling back the bedclothes Kiah sat up, back straight, legs crossed and began to meditate. She drew in a deep breath, held it for five seconds, and slowly exhaled to the count of ten. And again. And one more time. Much better. Just for a moment she'd let herself to become overwhelmed — or if she was going to be honest — turn into a woos, a chicken, a yellow-bellied scaredy cat. But somehow, giggling at the thought of that poor overloaded ceiling fan, had successfully kicked her panic to the curb. Allowed her Xena-wannabe persona to sneak back in.

Scrambling out of bed, Kiah decided to have a long hot shower, change into the comfortable jeans and skivvy she'd bought from a late-night shopping mall on the way to the-town-with-no-name, and get an early start to the day. The sooner she was back on the road, the sooner she'd find out where it was leading.

First stop was at an all-night service station where she breakfasted on a truckie-sized meal of fried eggs, crisp bacon, sausages, and fried tomatoes — who counted calories after the age of 35 — plus two large mugs of sweet milky coffee.

Couldn't get a better start to the day than that.

Sipping on her second coffee, Kiah sat back, switched on her phone, and waited while it whirred and buzzed and spewed up a bevy of missed calls and texts. All from Beryl. Refusing to be drawn in by the woman who had never listened or cared for her, she dealt with the situation by adding her mother-in-law's number to her blocked sender's list. There. Mission complete. The only other text she'd received was from the physio reminding her of a visit she'd missed the day before and demanding payment. Also, a missed call from a telemarketer. Not one text from anyone concerned, worried about where she'd gone. Richard wouldn't allow her to have friends, and as for family, her heart sighed and cracked a little more at the memory; both parents had been killed in an auto crash nineteen years ago, when she was 20. She had no siblings, no aunts, no uncles, no cousins. She was on her own now. And that was fine. With no dependents, Kiah was free to do whatever she liked and travel wherever the road took her.

Dropping the phone back in her bag, Kiah added an extra spoonful of sugar to the last of her coffee and watched as another double-B snorted and steamed its way into the petrol station and pulled up beside five other road trains. Truckie-sized breakfasts were in high demand this morning.

By 8 o'clock, Kiah was back on the open road, the Ranger Rover powering along, transporting her through big and little country towns, past painted silos, sweeping paddocks dotted with grazing sheep, their necks stretching to the ground and their little fluffy tails juddering each time they stepped forward.

On the way through one country town, sporting nothing much more than a general store, a pub and a petrol-station-cum-fodder store, she came across a painted sign propped up on the side of the road — 20 KMS TO CHESTERTON HORSE MARKET — SALE STARTING AT 8 AM TODAY — and an arrow pointing out of town. Horses for sale at a market? The only items Kiah had ever seen for sale at a market were fruit and veg, second-hand books, hot dogs, homemade cakes, and pre-loved clothing — never horses.

After following more signs pointing her in the direction of Chesterton market, Kiah pulled into the carpark between a large horse truck, paint peeling off both sides, and a small daffodil-yellow hatchback. She had no idea why she was here. Maybe to inhale that addictive horsey smell she'd loved in her younger years? Or for the serenity, the slowing of the heartbeat when caressing an animal's fur? Whatever. She certainly wasn't there for the sale itself. She had her own life to sort out before attempting to sort out the life of another living creature. Especially a large dependent animal that couldn't be squeezed into the back seat of a Range Rover.

Colourful flags and banners fluttered in the light breeze, inviting her down the cement steps and into the marketplace itself. With dust floating up her nostrils and the mixed sounds of horses snorting and stamping and marketgoers calling out to each other, Kiah stood at the top and soaked up the scene. This was a different world. No fruit-and-vegetable stands, second-hand books or trestles loaded with homemade sponges and lamingtons on sale here. Instead, everything was equine related. There were rows of portable yards housing horses and ponies of all shapes and sizes, horse floats, saddles, bridles, rugs, horse-feed, equestrian clothing, and even, at the bottom of the steps, some budding teenaged entrepreneur who was selling horse-shaped pink fairy floss on sticks from a gaudily painted kiosk.

She couldn't wait to investigate.

However, after half an hour of wandering along the horse yards, Kiah decided she'd rather be at a fruit and veg market, where the worst that could happen was to slip on a squashed mango and maybe lose your cool. She shivered in the warm air, wrapped both arms around her waist. Okay, at first, she'd been happy to inhale the almost forgotten smells, the sounds, and the visuals of all these horses waiting with numbers stamped on their rumps to be sold. She even got to pat a couple of the friendlier ones. But the overall picture was one of despair. Too many bewildered horses roared up and down their yard, rolling the whites of their eyes in fear, while others were so tired and skinny, so cowed by ill-treatment, they stood in the far corner of their yard, shaking, their heads almost touching the ground.

Kiah had made a mistake coming here. A huge mistake. Time to get back onto the open road and continue looking for her own future.

On her way back to the carpark, she passed the auctioneer, a weaselly guy constricted by a too-tight white shirt and a gaudy tie. He was standing on a raised dais taking bids on item number 12 — in his words, 'a quiet, unflappable child's pony, going by the name of Sweet Sue'. However, the 13hh grey mare under the hammer was flinging herself from one side of the yard to the other, rearing, screaming out to the other horses, and proving him to be a liar.

The whole sale-yard scene had turned from exciting to stomach-achingly sad. It seemed tawdry, unfeeling, to subject these beautiful creatures to this environment.

As she passed the last stall and turned to climb the cement steps leading back to the carpark, a rough voice, loaded with menace, brought her to an abrupt halt.

"Bite *me*, ya bloody mongrel? I'll show ya! You'll be first for a bullet in the head when I get ya back to the meatworks."

Kiah whirled around in time to witness an overweight, red-faced man in dirty khaki overalls slam his fist into the face of a black horse in the last stall. The horse, so thin its ribs pushed against the skin, shook his head, but stood his ground.

Oh, you poor darling, she thought, her chest flooding with instant love. *You are so much braver than me...*

When the man raised his fist again, all the hurt she'd endured with Richard exploded to the surface, momentarily blinded her, sent her scrambling over the portable fence and into the yard, a human shield between man and horse. "Punch this horse again," she growled both fists up in front of her, "and I'll, I'll..."

"Slap me?" A coarse grin, revealing a row of broken teeth, crawled across the sweaty face now inches from hers. A pock-marked, cruel face, with marble black eyes that were brazenly undressing her, making her feel dirty.

Kiah took a shaky breath, felt her heart stutter in her chest. The man was so close his sour breath made her want to gag. So close, she could count the thick ugly hairs up his nose. She licked her lips. Oh, God, he looked a lot bigger, nastier, more dangerous than from the other side of the fence. She tried to stop her hand from shaking as she ran it up and down the horse's thin neck, calming him, letting him know she was trying to be strong for him. She really was...

"G-get away from me."

His cruel laugh sent prickles down her spine. Her breath caught in her throat. She couldn't breathe…

"You deaf, Cockroach?" A rich chocolatey voice, a voice that could have its owner starring in the next James Bond movie, came from outside the stall. "The lady said to get away from her."

Afraid to take her eyes off 'Cockroach' for more than a couple of seconds, Kiah slotted a quick glance at the face belonging to the chocolatey voice and couldn't help the tiny *mmm* of pleasure that escaped her lips when her eyes collided with high cheek bones, strong jaw and dark curly hair caressing a set of shoulders that knew hard work. The man was leaning against the gate of the stall, outwardly relaxed, but blue-grey eyes sparking fire.

The slimy grin slithered off Cockroach's face. He lurched a step backwards. Wiped at his thick wet lips. "Bloody nag took a bite outta me."

Kiah felt the other man's eyes leisurely assessing her, a scrutiny that had her heart speeding up and a warmth spreading from her face down her neck. He shook his head before answering. "So that gives you the right to threaten a woman at least eight stone lighter and a hundred times prettier than you?"

Pretty? Kiah's heart gave a double hitch. Even with the scary horse-beater turning her legs into limp celery, Kiah felt her spine stiffen. It had been so long since that word had been directed at her.

Cockroach spat on the ground. "She got in my way."

"And I'm telling you to get *out* of her way. Right now."

A soft warm muzzle snuffled at the base of Kiah's neck, tickling her. She turned to run fingers through the black horse's matted forelock, stroke his soft nose, whisper in his ear, assure him he'd never go without food or be beaten again because he was coming home with her — wherever that might be — and when she turned back, the angry horsemeat man had disappeared.

And so had the guy with the rich chocolatey voice.

Kiah's shoulders slumped. She'd frozen when challenged by the bullying Cockroach. Made to look needy when rescued by the hunk with the blue-grey eyes. She let out a shaky sigh and scratched behind the black horse's ears. What did she expect? To turn into a warrior princess after one day of freedom?

*****

Jack Sullivan stepped away from the battered Ford Premier and lifted a regretful thumb at his favourite client. "Hey, worth a look, Andy, but with that boxy hoof, there's always the risk of him going lame the day before a race.

Give us nothing but heartache."

And Andy didn't need any more of that. Manager of the *Best Pals* syndicate, a group of young owners who'd pooled their money to buy an unraced three-year old for Jack to train last year were on the lookout for another racing proposition. Their three-year old had proved too slow for racing and was now Andy's sister's future eventer.

"I know, Jack," he said. "Should have guessed. Why else would a 2-year-old with proven staying bloodlines be here at a lowly market sale, hey?" Andy lifted his lips in a rueful grin. "Owner trying to reel in another sucker."

"Just keep looking, mate." Jack slapped his hand on top of the car roof as Andy revved the engine. His chest prickled at the disappointment. A potential stayer by So You Think, would have been a handy addition to his racing stable. Especially as most of his present team were only country prospects, while the others, past city winners, were almost ready to collect their pensions. What Jack really needed was a slew of rich owners banging on his door, but the catch-22 — rich owners had a tendency to entrust their million-dollar horses to proven group-winning trainers. He lifted his chin at the man in the car. "Maybe talk a few more mates into joining your syndicate, Andy. Double your money and I'll find you something that might win a low-grade race in the city."

Jack watched Andy drive toward the exit gate and shook his head. By the roar of the exhaust and the stutter of the engine, he should be spending his money on another car instead of a horse, but Jack knew how addictive racing could be. Nothing beat the thrill of seeing your horse compete on the track. Especially when your mates, all co-owners, were jumping up and down beside you, cheering him on. Jack loved giving his owners that longed for win, but competition in the sport was stronger than ever now.

Losing sight of the beat-up Ford, Jack rammed his Akubra down over his too long hair that should have been cut months ago but he hadn't the time and raked his eyes over the saleyard. The crowd had dwindled by now. All that remained was nose-clogging dust, dogged flies homing in on steaming manure and a few die-hard stragglers gathered to witness the last two sales of the day. He could hear the auctioneer's clear voice urging bidders interested in Lot 74, a handy pony club type, to go higher and higher — the higher the price the better the commission — until the gelding was eventually knocked down for $3,000.

Time to go…

But before he could leave, there was one last thing Jack had to do.

As he strolled toward the auctioneer's podium, he could see her standing there. The woman who'd stood up to Cockroach. She was shifting from one foot to the other, waiting for the last sale of the day, Lot 75. Damn. He was right. She was going to bid for that skeletal black horse. A horse she knew nothing about. A horse that'd already attacked Cockroach, although, to be fair, who wouldn't want to take a bite out of that piece of excrement. Still, there was no future in buying a horse that would take a wad of money just to make it *look* like a horse again.

He shifted his eyes to the red plastic crate over to the side where Cockroach usually sat waiting to bid on any horse no one else wanted. He'd get them for next to nothing and make a profit by selling the horsemeat to kennels. Jack blew out a breath, frowned. Cockroach wasn't squatted toadlike on his box, like normal. Instead, he was upright, hairy arms folded over his bloated beer belly, the smirk on his face meaner than a hungry snake stalking its dinner. Just as he thought…Barry Cochran, alias Cockroach, was making this sale personal.

For a moment, Jack hesitated. What the heck was he doing? Why had he let his protective nature hijack his common sense? And how come he wasn't in his truck on his way home right now? His eyes settled on the woman waiting for the bidding on Lot 75 to begin. Okay, she was pretty, and he respected the way she'd defended the horse, but that wasn't the reason he wanted to protect her. So, why? And then it hit him in the gut. Sent a sharp pain strafing across his chest. This woman with the haunted eyes, determined to save the world, reminded him of Bianca…

When he'd spotted her standing up to Cockroach's bullying, the scene brought back memories of the first day he'd set eyes on the love of his life. Ten years ago. He'd just turned thirty, single and determined to stay that way, and Bianca was in her mid-twenties. Tiny, barely 5'2", her long silver-blonde hair streaming in the breeze, she'd been berating this giant of a guy who was dragging two skinny, worn-out ponies along the sand at the beach, giving children rides. Bianca bawled the guy out in front of everyone. Threatened to get the RSPCA down if he didn't look after his ponies. Said she'd check on him every day.

"I know where you live, and I'll be that persistent bug you can't swat."

Hands on hips, head tossed back, she'd taken his breath away. "Either retire your ponies in a good grassy paddock, or feed and care for them like working animals."

He'd stood there transfixed. Couldn't take his eyes off her and when he'd moved to join her, her smile, wide and fully centered on him, had sent his heart into free fall...

And he'd married the woman three months later.

Jack closed his eyes at the memory. Felt his throat go dry. Sometimes, usually late at night when he couldn't sleep, it scared him that one day he might forget Bianca's face; the color of her eyes, the dimples in both cheeks, the cute way she'd wrinkle her nose when she disagreed with him. Barely able to breathe, he'd upend the box of old photos at the bottom of his wardrobe so he could study her details, draw in her memories, savor each one like a fine wine.

By now, the bidding for Lot 75 had reached $1000. Already double Cockroach's usual limit. Jack straightened his shoulders and tugged at the brim of his hat. Yep, seemed like our beloved horsemeat dealer was in this for payback.

He sauntered up beside her. Leaned closer. "You seem determined to buy that horse," he growled, his voice gruffer than he intended.

She looked up and a shy smile of recognition lit her face. A smile that made his breath hitch. He hadn't realized she'd taken notice of him earlier, what with Cockroach's foul dragon breath blasting in her face. "Yes," she said, her smile widening. "And I've decided to call him Jet."

Oh, God, what hope did he have of changing her mind now? She'd already *named* the damn horse. "Look...you'd be crazy to buy that horse. You know nothing of his history."

The smile slowly slid off her face leaving her with a look of such vulnerability, he wanted to wrap her in his arms, tell her life didn't suck — well, not all the time. It was as though she had something in common with the neglected horse she was out to save. "I'm not crazy."

"I'm sorry, that came out wrong." He could kick himself as he watched her flick her thick dark red hair out of her eyes and blink up at him. "I'm just trying to talk you out of doing something you'll regret later."

She shook her head, gaze going back to the dejected looking animal hunched up in the corner of the stall, eyes dull. "You're only seeing the outside of this horse," she told him, her voice soft. "Underneath, he has a beautiful soul."

"But what if he's a killer?" He blew out a frustrated sigh. She seemed to have switched off, stopped listening to him, but he had to give it one last go. "Come on, there's plenty of nice horses out there. Why him? Why don't you buy yourself a nice-looking show horse?"

She turned her back on him, rigid shoulders telling him to go away, mind his own business, and lifted one finger for the auctioneer. "I'll make it $1200."

Jack growled deep in his throat. Stubborn. Just like his Bianca. Okay, he couldn't talk the woman out of buying the horse, so the only thing left was to have a word in the other bidder's ear. Stop Cockroach from turning this into a three-ring-circus.

The rancid smell of dried blood and stale sweat threatened to make Jack gag as he approached his second target. How long since the man had showered? Changed his clothes? Jack and the horsemeat dealer were actually old foes. They'd been in the same class way back in high school. And even then, Barry Cochrane was as mean as a fox with its tail caught in a trap. Running scams, stealing, bullying anyone smaller than himself. Jack snapped to a stop beside the man, folded his arms. "What's the high bid all about, Barry?" he asked. "That horse hasn't got enough meat on his bones to feed a chihuahua for a week."

"Get lost, Sullivan."

"Not going to happen, Cochrane." Jack moved deeper into the man's space. "So…unless you walk away now, forget about putting a bullet in that horse's head because he figured out what a creep you were and bit you, I'm going to the authorities. You're on your third warning, so if I report you for abusing another horse, there wouldn't be a sale-yard in Australia that'd let you within a hundred meters of them."

Cockroach's face turned into one big ugly sneer. "Oh yeah…out to impress the crazy lady, Jack? Get into her knickers?" He shoved his face so close, Jack had to hold his breath for fear of asphyxiation. "Your word against mine. *Mate!*"

While slowly shaking his head, Jack dragged his phone from his back pocket, pressed, scrolled, and held the phone up for Cockroach to see. "Well, then, isn't it lucky I recorded this little film clip. With you as the leading man."

As he stared at the video, Cockroach's thick lips twisted, and his face went a brilliant shade of postbox red. "And if you watch it a little longer," Jack crooned, "you'll find the movie gets even more entertaining. Not only do you punch a horse in the face but also threaten a bystander — the lady currently in a bidding war for the horse — when she tried to stop you."

"I'll get you for this, Jack…" Snatching up his battered plastic crate, Barry Cochrane stormed off in the direction of his large horse van, already crammed with horses too old, too wild, or just plain too neglected by their human owners to have a future.

Arms folded across his chest, Jack watched until the man climbed into his van, slammed the door behind him and juiced up the engine.

Right, his work here was done.

With a nod to the woman who'd bought herself a horse she'd probably regret by the end of the week, Jack tugged the brim of his hat down over his eyes and walked away.

THREE

Three hours later, as Kiah drove through the rustic town of Shadow Creek, a cloud of pink and grey galahs, disturbed from their task of stripping the stringybark gum shading O'Leary's Shoe Store, rose into the air, their harsh shrieks blotting out all other sounds. On the seat beside her lay a crumpled map drawn the day before by the teenager at the Cowji service station. Luckily, she'd tossed the paper on the floor of the SUV and not out the window, because now, being the brand-new owner of a horse, she needed a stable to put him in. And the only stable Kiah could think of was the one she'd seen posted on the servo's notice board. The one advertising for a track-rider and groom. And according to the map, Windsong Racing Stables were 2 kms. on from Shadow Creek.

Before leaving Chesterton horse market, Kiah had to not only buy Jet a new wardrobe — summer and winter rugs, plus fly veil, hay net, and leather halter — but also a horse float to hook onto the back of the Range Rover. The chatty seller of the second-hand horse float had helped her load Jet and filled his hay net with oaten hay, so he'd have something to keep him quiet while on the road.

Kiah's heart gave a sudden twist and thumped against her chest. A horse of her own? A real live flesh and blood horse? Not part of her new life-plan when she'd hit the open road yesterday — but she had no regrets. Jet needed her. She let out a shaky breath and smiled as the thumping in her chest eased, slowed to its regular rhythm. And maybe *she* needed *him* even more.

Two kilometres on from the town, Kiah eased the Range Rover to a halt, the unfamiliar horse float swaying precariously as its wheels drifted onto the uneven siding in front of the gateway. If she was going to keep her newest acquisition, towing a horse float was only one of the new experiences she'd need to master.

A sign over the gate swung gently in the breeze, informing her she'd come to the right place, *Windsong Racing Stables*. Under the bright yellow signage there was a painting of a magnificent chestnut horse in full flight, jockey dressed in green and white racing silks crouched on top, urging him on.

She stared at the painting. Was the horse, Windsong? Were the stables named after him? And if so, what was the story behind it?

In smaller lettering at the bottom right-hand corner she read, Proprietor: Jack Sullivan. Ph. 0402989777.

Climbing from the car, she opened the gate and stepped onto a narrow dirt roadway that snaked its way toward a sprawling homestead with a shady veranda wrapped all the way around, like a protective bandage. She shaded her eyes with one hand to see a trial track at the rear of the property and a long red-brick stable block with outside yards, spreading outwards to the right of the house. A typical country training set up. If she didn't get the job, she could ask to agist Jet here. She hitched herself back into the SUV and drove through the gate. That's if this Jack Sullivan wasn't a horse snob and kicked them both off the property after taking one look at poor Jet's bony back and overgrown hooves.

Even a city slicker like her knew leaving a gate open where animals were concerned was a cardinal sin, so she climbed down once more, closed the gate, and then drove slowly toward the house. White-fenced paddocks lined the driveway. Half a dozen mares with their long-legged gangly foals in one, a couple of cavorting youngsters in another and what looked like several retired racehorses in the paddock closest to the house, all toasty in canvas rugs, their greying muzzles and arthritic gait giving away their ages. A warm feeling swept through her. If he kept his horses after their racing days were over, this mysterious Jack Sullivan must care for his horses.

As she rumbled up to the house and parked under the sprawling shade of an oak tree, a long shrill whinny resounded from inside her trailer, the call immediately answered by two of the bored-looking thoroughbreds trudging around on a nearby horse walker. The horse-float swayed slightly as Jet, evidently tired of being cooped up, stamped his feet.

Should she knock on the door? Go across to the nearest stable block? Unload Jet from the float in case he hurt himself? Before she could make up her mind, the front door of the house clattered open and a girl of about eight or nine, blonde pigtails flying, eyes dancing with mischief, spilled out, closely followed by a heavy-set woman in her early sixties waving a feather duster.

"Bring that back, Angel! It's for your dad's afternoon tea!"

Kiah's grin widened as the girl, a cream cake held high in the air, leaped off the veranda onto the gravel in front of her.

"G'day," the girl said, taking a large bite out of her trophy while studying Kiah. "You here with our new horse?"

Kiah blinked. Was Jack Sullivan expecting her?

"We're going to win the Kangaroo Downs Cup with him," Angel continued. "Dad said he could even win in the city."

Jet? Win in the city? In the condition he was in, he'd be lucky to beat a three-legged dog to the water trough.

Kiah shook her head. "No, sorry, I'm Kiah Stanton. I'm here to apply for a job." She flicked her head toward the float. "And to hopefully agist Jet in one of your stables. He's a rescue horse and needs lots of love and good feed. He also needs somewhere to live because he can't stay in that float forever."

"Can't he live at your place?"

"Um…not really."

"Why?"

"'Cos if I don't get the job, I'll be renting a room at the Shadow Creek pub and I don't think the landlord would approve of a horse sharing a bathroom with the other tenants."

"Be a bit squashy." Angel let out a giggle. By now the cream cake had completely disappeared — except for the blob on her nose — and so had the woman with the duster. Probably decided there was no way the cake was going to be saved so had gone back inside to find something else for afternoon tea.

Angel clambered up onto the side of the float and peered through the window. "He has a kind eye," she said, her voice serious. "And a nice sloping shoulder."

Kiah wanted to hug the girl. Instead of commenting on the ugly scar running down one side of Jet's neck or turning that cute little cream-dotted nose up at the bag of bones sagging inside the float, Angel had found two positives.

She could get to like this kid.

"Want me to take you to my dad?" Angel jumped off the side of the float and, like a ballerina, twirled around on one foot, both arms in the air. "He's holding Betty for the farrier. She's a real mare. Can't stand still for five minutes."

Kiah's lips twitched. Betty and Angel had a lot in common.

"Is your dad Jack Sullivan?"

Angel nodded and danced in the direction of the red-brick stable block. Kiah followed. If Jack Sullivan was as friendly as his daughter, maybe he'd let Jet stay. She couldn't let herself think what she'd do if he refused. Maybe that hot guy at the horse sales was right. Maybe she was an idiot for buying a horse when she didn't even have a home for herself. But with the vicious dogmeat guy hovering around, what else could she do?

Entering the stable block, Kiah, eyes slowly adjusting from the bright light outside, spotted a burly guy in a leather apron, nails sticking out from his mouth. His muscles flexed as he bent to hammer a horseshoe onto the hoof of a big-boned bay mare. A second man, tall, dark curly hair brushing his shoulders, his back to them, stood holding Betty's lead rope, one hand resting on the mare's neck.

"Dad, this is my new best friend, Kiah." Angel flopped onto a bale of hay, arms spread out dramatically. "She wants to work here and she's brought her own horse."

The tall dark-haired man slowly turned around, his welcoming smile faltering the moment his eyes fell on Kiah. He tipped his head to the side and regarded her with a questioning frown. "What are you doing here?"

"I…" Kiah gasped, tried to swallow, but her throat was too dry. Jack Sullivan, the owner of Windsong Racing Stables, was the interfering, know-it-all guy from the saleyard. The knight-in-shining-armour who'd rescued her from Cockroach's slimy clutches and then, before she could thank him, told her, no punches pulled, that she was crazy. That buying an emaciated horse with no papers and no known history from a dodgy horse sale could only lead to disaster.

*****

Words rarely failed Jack Sullivan. He blinked at the petite woman with the flaming red hair awkwardly shifting from one foot to the other, her face and neck suffused with color, her green cat's eyes accusing him of God-knows-what. And found himself strangely disconcerted.

What was she doing here? Had she followed him? Last time he'd set eyes on the woman she'd just bid top dollar for a horse that was worth less than a night out at the movies. Yet, here she was, a few hours later, his daughter's new best friend, and not only asking for a job at his stables, but to agist the radish-on-four-legs she'd saved from certain death.

He rubbed his fingers across the back of his neck. Was this payback for getting involved, for poking his nose into something that didn't concern him? For letting this woman infiltrate his mind and his senses back at the saleyard?

Taking advantage of his loss of concentration, Betty, the flighty bay mare he was holding for the farrier, tossed her head high in the air, and, giving a three-legged leap forward, tried unsuccessfully to tug her fourth leg out of the blacksmith's large, calloused hands. Damn mare. Gorgeous looker, but with a brain the size of a pea. Jack quickly settled her down, took a firmer hold of the lead rope and turned back to his intriguing visitor.

"So…," he began, adopting his most professional tone, "you're here after the job of groom and track-rider?"

She nodded, and Jack smothered a grin when he caught her surreptitiously crossing two fingers on her left hand before hiding the evidence behind her back. "I'm good with horses."

"Had much experience?"

"I've ridden a lot and I remember—um—I *know* how to groom and clean stables and I'm willing to do whatever it is the job entails."

"But have you actually worked in registered racing stables as a—"

"Dad…!" Angel bounced up off her hay bale and danced across the aisleway. She tugged on his arm. "Kiah has a horse called Jet and I saw him through the window of her float."

"Angel, not now."

"But he's a rescue horse, Dad, and he needs lots of love and good food." She clasped Jack's hand and looked up at him with that special smile that always won his heart. "If Kiah works here, we can help her make Jet look all beautiful again, can't we?"

"Well, that's not really..." He looked over his daughter's head at the woman — Kiah — who was giving him an identical big-eyed look. "I don't think..."

"But Dad...we got lots and lots of horse food and a spare stable and a vet on call and you know so much about horses, you can help Kiah with Jet. Please say she can stay."

Jack rolled his eyes. She did it to him every time. Bending down, he placed a kiss on Angel's forehead. "Okay, we'll see how it goes. Now, poppet, Betty's getting restless again, so why don't you take Kiah and show her where she'll be living. There's a small, enclosed paddock behind the caravan where she can turn Jet out for now. Okay?"

Angel threw her arms around Jack's waist and squeezed. "You're the best dad in the whole world and I wouldn't trade you in for anything — not even for a new BMX bike."

Jack almost choked trying not to laugh. Was that a hint for what she wanted for Christmas? "You wouldn't?"

"Nah. Love you lots, Dad."

"Love you more."

"Love you most!" Angel giggled. "I always win that one, don't I?"

Kiah, watching the exchange between father and daughter, cleared her throat. "Does that mean...?"

Jack flicked his eyes across to her. She was biting her bottom lip, her eyes wide and uncertain. There was something about the woman Jack couldn't put a handle on. She'd been feisty, like a modern-day Boadicea, when standing up to Cockroach, yet she had this vulnerability about her that tugged at his protective side, made him want to keep her safe. Exactly how she'd affected him at the sale yard — and look where that got him — agreeing to let her try out as his new groom and track rider. What was he thinking of?

"It's only a trial," he reiterated, lifting his chin and glaring at her. "At the first sign you're not competent to look after my horses, you're out. Clear?"

She straightened her shoulders and glared right back. "As crystal."

"My other workers live locally, but you can shift into the caravan at the rear of the big house and live onsite. My housekeeper, Marg, filled the caravan's cupboard and refrigerator with food two days ago, when the successful applicant for the job was *supposed* to arrive. Lucky for you, she changed her mind at the last minute and left us hanging." He frowned at the memory of the woman informing him, by text, that a job at a better stable had come up, so she'd taken it. "When that's gone, you'll have to shop for your own food. Right?"

She shrugged one shoulder. "Of course."

"You'll find there's a working stove, shower, all necessary facilities in the caravan, but if there's anything else you need, just ask me, or my housekeeper. You'll most likely find Marg inside the house."

She smiled up at him, a smile that seemed to light her face from within, made her look younger. "Thank you, Mr. Sullivan."

"It's Jack. But most of my staff just call me, boss."

"Okay, boss."

"Right, well, I have a cranky horse to look after here, so I'll see you back in the stable block, at 4.30 tomorrow morning. Riding helmet in hand."

"F-four thirty?" Her voice sounded like chalk on a blackboard.

Jack turned away to adjust Betty's halter so she couldn't see his grin. "And not a second later."

FOUR

First day on the job and Kiah was running late.

After his initial surprise yesterday, Jack Sullivan — a man who tangled her brain in snarled knots — had offered her a month's trial, plus free accommodation and agistment for Jet. It was now up to her to prove she was worthy of his trust.

But why such an early start?

Feeling much like the White Rabbit in *Alice in Wonderland*, Kiah moved up a gear in her race to the stable block; her almost forty-year-old body testifying that the bed in the 1980's caravan, her new home, was every bit as hard as it looked.

How could she be late? How could *anyone* be late for work when the sun was still stretching its arms and yawning, half an hour off making an appearance? When civilized members of the human race were still tucked in bed, doona up under their chin, dreaming of money, holidays, and that gorgeous guy or gal they'd flirted with last night at the bar.

And then her thoughts switched to Jet, who, only minutes ago, she'd left in the paddock behind her caravan. His ears had pricked when he'd seen her coming. His eyes lighting up when she attached a hay net full of sweet-smelling hay to the fence and carefully brushed his stark coat, chatting to him all the while. That's why she was here…to gain experience and earn enough money to make her horse whole again. To give Jet a safe home. She straightened her shoulders, grabbed a steadying breath, and stepped through the open doorway into the brightly lit stable block.

Immediately, all noise ceased. All eyes focused on Kiah. Damn. Where was Harry Potter's invisibility cloak when she needed it?

She could see six riders, three females and three males, all gathered around a large whiteboard attached to the end wall of the stable block. Directly in front, whip slapping rhythmically against his leg, stood Jack Sullivan, and like yesterday, he was dressed in hip-hugging moleskins, but today, instead of a checked shirt, he wore a black ribbed-knit jumper and a glint in his eye that spelt trouble…for her.

He nodded, his eyes narrowing further. "Nice of you to join us, Kiah."

"Sorry, had to feed Jet," she mumbled, slipping in between a young guy with freckles across his nose, and a girl in her early-20's who flashed her a quick grin and a sympathetic wink.

"In future, look after your horse on your own time, Kiah. Four-thirty, here, in front of the daily schedule, means four-thirty, on the dot." Jack pointed his whip at the whiteboard. "As you would know if you'd been here on time, I've put you up on Lofty for the first string. He's the big ugly horse in stable 10."

Kiah's stomach did a long, low, thunderous growl, and she felt an embarrassing warmth slowly creep up her neck into her cheeks.

Just kill me now…

Worried about riding a horse after so many years, she'd been too on edge to eat breakfast. Or it could have been the unearthly hour of 4.00 am when her alarm woke her with an ungodly shriek that put her off her toast. She stared at the ground. Not that she'd managed much in the way of sleep; what with the family of mutant opera-loving crickets she swore had taken up residence in the roof of her caravan keeping her awake.

"Lofty's a lazy sod," continued Jack, and she swore she saw his lips twitch, "but he's been known to put in the occasional buck, so keep your wits about you."

Just what she needed — an occasional buck to keep her from wetting her pants with fear. She toed the ground with her left boot and vaguely wondered where they kept the spare parachutes. With a name like Lofty, she'd probably need one on that long trip down.

"Slow work for the first three laps, and then build to a medium gallop on the fourth lap, finishing off strongly over the last hundred metres. And Belle," Jack's eyes moved to the girl who'd winked at her when she'd first sidled in; his don't-mess-with-me stare demanding she pocket her phone immediately or said phone would end up as landfill under his R.M. William's boots. "Stick with the new girl. Make sure she keeps pace with your horse all the way around. I'm relying on you to bring her back in one piece." His eyes flicked to Kiah and the corners of his lips definitely twitched. "After all, she has two more horses to work, stables to clean, feed to prepare, yards to rake, and six paddocks to muck out — all before lunch. No time to stop for first aid."

Kiah's mouth gaped like a landed fish. She opened her mouth to object, thought of her malnourished rescue horse, happy in his paddock behind her caravan, and slammed her lips shut again.

"Sure, boss. No worries," said Belle, flipping one blonde plait over her shoulder, while giving Kiah a discreet wink and pocketing her phone with a grin.

When Kiah pushed open the door of stable 10, it took all her self-control to stop from running to her Range Rover and driving far away from Windsong Racing Stables.

The horse inside stable 10 was ginormous. Descended from a tyrannosaurus.

Her stomach cramped as she dumped her gear on the straw and closed the stable door behind her. That son of a bitch had allotted her this horse on purpose. He *wanted* her reaching for her car keys and high tailing it out the gate. But he'd only made her more determined to prove she could do this, that she wasn't weak, ready to buckle at the first sign of conflict. That she wasn't the same woman who'd stayed in a bullying relationship for twelve years because she was too scared to leave.

The big horse was dozing, ears twitching, bottom lip drooping. Would he be upset if she disturbed him? She moved closer. "Hey, big fella, I'm your new exercise rider. I know it's still considered night-time in civilized society, but we all need to make a living."

The horse opened his eyes and snuffled at her open palm, inspecting the carrot she'd brought as a bribe. She ran a hand up his neck and while he was occupied with crunching the treat, she stood on tiptoe and slipped a halter over his head then led him to the tie-up rail to saddle up.

"Righto! Everyone outside!"

The cold morning air brushed her face as, crash helmet fastened under her chin, Kiah led the big bay along with the other six horses through the open doorway of the stable block onto a sandy path that led to the training track.

"Ready, Kiah?" Jack was standing so close behind her, she could smell his aftershave, something minty and fresh with a hint of lemon. "Let's get you on board." His fingers fastened around her left leg, and in one fluid upward movement, she was in the saddle clutching for Lofty's ratty mane, like it was the last cold beer in the fridge.

"Leg forward." Jack tightened the girth two notches and frowned up at her. "Unless you're a trick rider who likes to keep us entertained by riding upside down, always check your girth before mounting. Rule number one at any reputable training establishment. Now, feet in the stirrups and off you go."

The horse leading the group, a pretty grey mare ridden by Steve, a bow-legged sexagenarian who looked to have been around racing stables since the day he was born, moved off, prancing, snorting at a magpie preening itself on the fence. As Lofty lurched forward Kiah jammed her feet in the stirrups and picked up the reins. The ground seemed a long way down, the saddle so small it was barely there, but it felt amazing to be astride a horse again. Her hips moved in sync with Lofty's long relaxed strides, and she grinned down at the now warbling magpie as they passed. Maybe her first experience on a racehorse wouldn't be so bad after all.

And that's when Lofty shied at the magpie and she lost both stirrups and ended up on his neck. "Woah!" Using his mane and neck as a fulcrum, Kiah pushed herself back into the saddle and reunited her feet with the stirrups.

She heard a cheer behind her. "Good save, Kiah. Lofty's a sweetie really, but he always tries out a new rider." It was Belle, riding behind her astride a pretty, lightly-built bay mare. "The big goof thinks it's a huge joke if he can unseat his rider before we reach the training track. Give him a kick in the ribs and let him know you're onto him. "

Not only was the horse testing her, but so was Jack Sullivan.

Taking a stronger grip of Lofty's mane, along with both reins, Kiah sat up straighter in the saddle. So…Lofty was up to his old tricks…and she'd survived. Her chest swelled and a strange sense of accomplishment lifted her spirits. Made her feel as though maybe she was in the right place after all.

On reaching the training track, merely a well-graded, wide, sandy track on the inside of the back paddock, Belle moved up alongside Kiah. "We'll trot the first lap to warm up, then move into a canter for the next two laps. Right?"

Her focus wholly centred on not falling off, Kiah nodded.

"And don't let the boss get to you," Belle added. "He's a bit like Lofty. All bark and no bite. Hard on those who do the wrong thing by his horses — they're his babies — but under that gruff exterior, he's nothing but a pussycat."

Pussycat? Kiah almost fell off her horse trying not to laugh as an image of Scar from *The Lion King* sprang to mind. "Um…good to know."

Due to Lofty's huge, ground-covering strides, Kiah kept losing her balance and consequently, getting left behind, bumping in the saddle. Not good. One wrong move by this massive dinosaur of a horse and she'd be eating dirt. A quick glance across at Belle, who made rising to the trot look so easy on her short-striding bay mare, and Kiah decided imitation was the best form of survival. Eyes on Belle, she let her weight drop into her stirrups and tilted her body slightly more forward. Eureka! Immediately she felt Lofty's body swinging rhythmically and balanced beneath her.

Just as Kiah was starting to enjoy the trot, Belle spoilt it all by yelling, "Okay, let's up the pace."

Nooo…

"Watch him," Belle warned. "The big galah sometimes tries to take off the moment you switch up a gear. Ease him into a canter and keep a strong hold of the reins. Act like you're the boss."

"Riiiight."

Belles' amused laugh grated on Kiah's ears. "Don't worry," she said, moving into a canter. "Lofty's a milksop, really."

Don't worry? Kiah's heart slipped a gear. Not only was Lofty a goof who liked to dump his rider on the way to the track, he was also a milksop who thrived on taking the bit between his teeth and bolting.

With Belle already cantering sedately alongside and another horse ranging up on the other side, Kiah tentatively squeezed her legs against Lofty's sides. His head shot up, he dragged the reins out of her hands and the feel of his haunches bunching beneath her came close to making her scream.

And then he took off, his long strides powering forward, the wind whistling past her ears.

Grabbing at the reins, Kia leaned back, but the harder she pulled, the faster Lofty galloped. They were passing one horse after the other. *Ohmygod, I'm going to die.* Then she remembered a riding instructor from years ago telling her to use her body and her voice, not her strength, to stop a horse. Pushing her weight down further into the stirrups, she crouched over Lofty's neck, going with him instead of against him, and giving short sharp tugs on the reins in rhythm with his stride. "Woah. Easy…easy, boy."

Gradually, bit by bit, Lofty's mad gallop slowed to what in contrast felt like a rocking horse canter. Mouth drier than an outback creek in summer, Kiah licked her lips. Her hands trembled on the reins. Her heart hammered so fast she swore it was trying to rip through her chest and leave the scene of the crime.

"Like, where did *you* learn to ride horses? On a merry-go-round?"

With no voice to answer the snooty teenager she'd seen back in the stables, now riding beside her on a sweaty chestnut horse with a white blaze, Kiah shook her head.

"Don't listen to Olivia. She's snarling at everyone today. Her crappy boyfriend dumped her by text last night." Belle, eyes wide, rode up beside Kiah and leaned closer. "You, okay?"

"Think so."

Belle frowned across at Olivia. "If I remember rightly, you didn't handle Lofty any better when the boss made you ride him on your first day. Just because you're upset with Dunderhead, doesn't mean you can go around making others feel like crap too."

By now they'd brought their horses back to a walk, cooling them off, bringing their heartbeat back to normal. Olivia screwed up her nose, making it look like her silver nose-ring actually shrugged. "Yeah, sorry, Kiah. Lofty can be a little shit. Boss always throws new riders up on him, like, just to see if they're tough enough to join our team." She scrubbed at her eyes with her fist. "A little shit — just like bloody Alex. Didn't even, like, have the balls to dump me to my face."

"In which case, he's not worth one more second of your thoughts." Kiah found herself empathizing with the angry teenager. "Forget him — plenty more saucepans in the cupboard."

Olivia spluttered and burst out laughing. "Alex looks more like a cheese grater than a saucepan, you know, like, with a face full of acne."

"Or a garlic grinder," put in Belle, giggling.

"How about a flat frypan — just like his *ugly* nose?"

Kiah let out a sigh and switched off momentarily while the two youngsters continued denigrating the hapless Alex. Made her feel ancient. She patted Lofty's sweaty neck, astonished at how relaxed the big horse was now. She let out the reins and he dropped his head and ambled along like a kid's pony; like he'd done his bit to determine Kiah's toughness and was now reverting to his normal, laid-back, goofiness.

"Hey, Kiah, why don't you come with us to The Creek after work tonight?" Belle interrupted Kiah's thoughts. "Have a few drinks, let your hair down. We'll show you the ropes and you can get to know the rest of the team."

"Hmm…maybe." Except for grizzled old Steve, Kiah already felt old enough to be the team's surrogate mother-figure and couldn't imagine herself 'letting her hair down' at the pub with a mob of kids only a few years out of high school.

"It's like, Josh's turn to be designated driver, so we'll, like, pick you up at seven," said Olivia with a grin. "And don't wear anything too fancy. It's your initiation night."

"Initiation night?"

Belle's grin was as feral as Olivia's. "Consider yourself honoured. We don't usually put newcomers through our special inauguration for at least two weeks after they arrive."

Kiah's heart sank. Not only was she going to the pub with a grumpy sexagenarian, a recently dumped teenager, and four twenty-something party-goers, now she had an 'initiation ceremony' to look forward to.

Probably end up being dunked head-first in a toilet bowl before the night ended.

FIVE

It was 6 pm, and instead of getting ready to go out, all Kiah wanted to do was collapse on her bed, boots and all, and die. Preferably after watching the crows pick holes in Jack Sullivan's liver.

While returning Lofty to the stable block after his workout that morning, she'd passed Jack perched on a shooting stick beside the gateway leading onto the track, observing the gallops, taking notes on his iPad. He'd raised one quizzical eyebrow at her, and it had taken great restraint not to present him with her middle finger — to show what she thought of his 'evaluating' techniques.

Then, after hosing Lofty and scraping him dry, Kiah had barely finished settling the horse down in his stable with a small hard feed, when Olivia came scuttling in, yelling for her to hurry, the second string was outside waiting to go.

And she wasn't even saddled up.

According to the whiteboard on the wall, her next ride was on a horse called Zipper, who she quickly discovered was a biter. Precious minutes were wasted dodging flashing teeth while saddling, which made her even later and resulted in smirks from the other riders and a scowl from the boss.

So, by the time Kiah had dismounted her third horse for the day, a chestnut mare with a poor work ethic and faulty springs, she'd been struggling to stand upright. Being unable to stand was not an option, however, in this establishment, because she had six stables to clean, six water troughs to scrub, and just when she thought she could flop onto a hay bale and pass out, Jack had sent her off into the paddocks armed with a pooper-scooper and a wheelbarrow with a flat tyre.

Was it any wonder her rock-hard bed was looking more and more like a fluffy cloud? But she'd promised to get to know the team by having a few drinks with them at *The Creek*, the local pub, so, giving the bed one last wishful gaze she reluctantly kicked off her boots, stripped, and padded into the shower alcove. A space so small the soap holder dug into her ribs and the edge of the toilet seat kept buckling her knees.

At seven on the dot, a car rattled to a halt outside the caravan, music blaring at a decibel set to deafen penguins in Antarctica. Still attempting to tame her wild bush of hair into something more suited to nightwear, Kiah twitched the gingham curtains to one side and peered out. The cavalry had arrived. Josh's beat-up Holden squatted like a dying dragon at the end of the path, coughing and spluttering consumptively, smoke billowing from its back end, while Belle, Olivia, and Taylor, a slightly more mature member of the team in her late twenties, leaned out their open windows, waving.

It was only a five-minute drive to *The Creek*, a hostelry typical of all country watering holes dotted across Australia, where everyone from the town's resident drunk, to shopkeepers, white-collar workers, farmers, travellers, housewives and the local youth, could let their hair down and enjoy, not only a drink, but entertainment, companionship, and a good night out.

"I can only have one drink," Kia warned as they pulled up outside. "Any more and I'll be rubbish at work tomorrow. Can't hold my liquor and I can't afford to get the sack."

Bella, wearing little more than a long shirt and boots that came up to her thighs, eyeballed Kiah with a grin as she opened the car door and swivelled out onto the pavement. "One drink on a Saturday night is forbidden at *The Creek*."

"But—"

"Don't worry," chimed in Olivia, giving her a reassuring pat on the shoulder. "It's like, *Sunday* tomorrow. Our day off. Jack does the rugs and feeds and puts the horses on the walker, while a casual girl comes in really early, to like, clean the stables."

"Yeah," Belle continued, doing an exaggerated twirl followed by a sexy shimmer that accentuated her youthful body. "Saturday night is fun night for the *Windsong* slaves. And on Sundays, we sleep 'til noon."

"Yesss!" Kiah said to the car roof. "There *is* a God!" Her aching body gave a fist-pump of relief as she pictured a day with no mad gallops, no lifting, no bending, no stretching, no pushing a sluggish wheelbarrow around acres of paddocks — just her, Jet, chocolate, and a good book. However, not having drunk alcohol since the night she'd had her stomach pumped after attempting to drink herself to death due to Richard's reaction the *first* time she'd tried to leave him, Kiah wasn't so sure that having more than one drink would be *fun*.

But she'd give it a go.

The Creek likely hadn't changed much since it was first built in 1920. Weathered wooden poles topped by latticed wrought iron decorations held up the front veranda of the two-story building, and as Kiah stepped from the car, she spotted a kid-sized blackboard propped up on the pavement waiting to be brought in; its chalked lunch-menu giving diners the choice between sausages and chips, fish and chips and steak and chips. And pasted across the quarry-stone walls were the usual array of hotel billboards, spruiking VB Victorian Bitter, XXX Gold, and Bundaberg Rum.

Following the others, Kiah pushed through the swinging double wooden doors that reminded her of all those old Western movies she used to watch with her dad as a kid. There was always a black-hatted baddie making a dramatic entrance through the saloon doors, guns blazing, demanding a showdown with the white-hatted good guy. On the nights her mum went off to run Bingo for the local Aged Care centre, she and her dad would curl up on the lounge in front of the television, Kiah in her pyjamas and slippers, a bowl of popcorn and a giant-sized bag of chocolate frogs between them. They'd watch shows like *Fury at Showdown, Butch Cassidy and the Sundance Kid,* and of course, all those old John Wayne westerns, *The Spoilers, Oklahoma Kid* and *Rio Bravo.*

Music, laughter, and overloud voices descended on her, quickly dispelling warm childhood memories as the girls led her to a large wooden table that already seated four. Two members of the team, Grumpy Steve, who looked to be wearing the same clothes he'd been in all day, and Dillon, a young jockey who was doing his apprenticeship at *Windsong,* with Jack as his employer. The other two, a man and a woman, were unfamiliar faces.

"Hi!" Belle, looking more grown-up with her schoolgirl plaits wound up around her head, took over the introductions. "This is Kiah Stanton. She's here tonight to be welcomed into the *Windsong* team — the best racing stable in country South Australia."

"Bloody rookie newcomers," Steve mumbled into his half-full glass of whisky. Judging by his glazed eyes and the fact that he was still in his work clothes, he'd been sitting there ever since he'd knocked off.

"Glad you could make it, Kiah," said Dillon, his friendly smile making her feel welcome. "And this is my fiancé, Jen. She's not into horses, says they're smelly and dangerous, but don't hold that against her." He let out a laugh as he punched Jen lightly on the arm. "She's a good egg anyway."

The stick-thin woman sitting next to him rolled her heavily made-up eyes. "Don't *listen* to him, Kiah. I *love* horses — but only from a distance. They're *much* too big and scary close up. I prefer *cats*."

"I like cats too," Kiah agreed. "Very independent, but when they do allow you to cuddle them, they can be really sweet. Do you have a cat of your own?"

"Oh, *no*, they leave *hairs* all over the place." She gave a tinny laugh that accentuated her puffy red lips and thin wobbly neck. "But I watch cat *videos* on my *phone*."

While Josh took drink orders and made his way to the bar, everyone else found a seat around the table and Kia was introduced to Taylor's fiancé, Caleb, who worked as a barman, but was currently on a fifteen-minute break.

Up on the makeshift dais in the corner of the pub a raggle-taggle band, consisting of an ancient bandy-legged trumpet player, a skinny teenager, her psychedelic pink hair standing on end as she thumped on the piano, and a drummer of indeterminate age, due to the long scraggly beard and hair covering most of his face. According to the name emblazoned across the drum set they were called *The Head Blasters*. A perfect moniker.

Half an hour later, feeling like a typical wallflower, Kiah took in the happy faces around her. Olivia, laughing at her own jokes, Belle, rocking with Taylor on the miniscule dance floor, and Dillon and Jen, chatting with a group of friends. This lifestyle was all so new to Kiah — or maybe not *new* as she'd been a bit of a social butterfly before marrying Richard — but it had been years since she'd met friends for a drink or partied with the girls.

A dull heaviness settled in her chest making it hard to breathe. She was too old, too jaded, and had too many barriers to knock down to ever be part of this scene again. Instead, it made her feel like an ancient shrivelled up lemon in a tray full of fresh yummy strawberries.

Josh came lolloping towards their table, his jeans at half mast, both hands juggling glasses, beer slopping over the sides. "Hey, I need some help here!"

Olivia, a wide grin wrinkling the freckles across her nose, unwound herself from the jockey she'd flirted with and captured the moment he'd walked in. "Way to go, Josh! You're carrying, like, one more glass than Dillon's record."

Dillon rolled his eyes as he dropped back into his chair. "Doesn't count when you spill more than you deliver."

"That's not a rule," said Josh. "You just made that up."

"Did not."

"Did so."

With Olivia's help, Josh managed to set all the glasses down on the table without losing more than half their contents.

Kiah dragged her glass towards her and shook her head. It was like sitting on the side of a sandbox at the local kindergarten watching the toddlers play grown-ups.

What felt like three hours but was probably not even one hour later, Belle, red faced from dancing with the local off-duty policeman, a mountain of a man she laughingly called Tiny Tim, sashayed over and placed another glass of icy beer on the table in front of Kiah, who'd been sipping slowly on her previous glass, hoping to make it last the rest of the night. She really didn't want to wake up in the morning, not only too stiff to move — but with a hangover from hell.

"Thanks."

"'S' okay, Dillon's shout. And he couldn't beat Josh's new record." Bella slid into the seat beside Kiah. "You having fun?"

Kiah nodded.

"Don't look it."

"Just tired."

Belle took Kiah's hand and squeezed. "I know the boss worked you hard today, but he's an okay guy. He does that with any newcomer. Has to make sure they're good around his horses."

"I can understand that."

"He really tested you, though. Put you up on the three most difficult horses in the stables. So, now you're one of us, he'll ease up. You'll see, he'll allocate easier rides for you on Monday."

"Maybe."

Belle gave a smirk. "Bit of a hunk, our boss, don't you think?"

Kiah answered with a non-committal shrug and another sip of her drink. She might have agreed that he was a hunk first thing this morning, but by the end of the day, he'd grown horns, a Machiavellian moustache and fiery devil eyes.

"Especially for an old guy," added Olivia. She'd gone back to hanging off her new jockey friend who was busy licking the inside of her ear. Kiah wanted to tell Olivia to stop acting easy and throwing herself at the guy. Anyone could see he was a player and she'd get hurt again.

"But a word of warning," said Belle. "It's no good getting interested, 'cos Jack doesn't *do* relationships."

A small twinge of something akin to disappointment, flickered through Kiah's head, quickly replaced by a virtual middle finger. *Well, that makes two of us,* she thought, taking another sip of her beer. As far as she was concerned, she only needed one male in her life right now, and he had four legs, a long nose, a ratty tail, and answered to the name of Jet.

Belle leaned closer, as though keen to let Kiah in on the stable secrets. "The story I heard from Steve, and he worked at the stable way back when Jack's uncle owned it, was that Jack's still not over his wife, Bianca's, death." Like an actor on the stage, she paused before the punch line. "And that was eight years ago."

"Eight years?" Kiah had guessed there was no wife on the scene, presuming he was divorced. But eight years was a long time to grieve. "He must have loved her very much. How did she die?"

"Giving birth to his daughter, Angel."

Kiah's breath caught in her throat. Oh, God, poor Jack, poor Angel. Her heart went out to the little girl who'd never known her mother. If that was the case, Jack should be proud of the way she'd turned out. The kid was a sweetheart.

"Thought it best to warn you." Belle stood up and looked around. Likely hunting for her next dance partner. "A couple of female track riders in the past tried to use their wiles to hook the boss, but they didn't last long. Other than his daughter — Jack's horses are his life." Belle grabbed hold of Josh as he drifted past. "Hey, let's go, Joshy boy. Your turn to dance with me."

Kiah took another sip of her beer and closed her eyes in thought. What a love story that must have been between Jack and Bianca. Like the script of a blockbuster movie. To be in love with someone so deeply, so fully, you couldn't share a piece of your heart with another woman, not even eight years after losing your lover…Kiah swallowed…God, she'd have thrived on just 10%

of Richard's love — but he wasn't even capable of that.

As for horses being Jack's life now — maybe horses could be her lifeline too.

Kiah finished off her beer and went back to people-watching, but it didn't take long for the loud thumping music to skewer her brain, turning it into molten toffee. When another glass of beer landed on the table in front of her, she gulped it down, then squirming in the hard wooden chair, contemplated how to escape without hurting anyone's feelings. Olivia, evidently over being dumped by her texting boyfriend, was still latched onto the five-foot-nothing jockey from another stable, a guy at least ten years her senior. She was draped across his lap, arms wound around his neck, sucking on his lips, while Belle was dancing with whoever she could entice onto the pub's miniscule dance floor. They were partying hard and wouldn't miss her if she slipped into the restroom, called a cab and made her way outside to wait. But did they have cabs in country towns? She sighed. Probably not. Should have insisted she drive herself here. Kiah shifted on the chair again. At this moment she'd give her next pay for padding on the seat. She'd stood under the shower for a good ten minutes, letting the hot water pound into her poor aching body, but was still one big ache. Especially that part of her anatomy used for sitting.

After three more beers, Kiah decided if there were no cabs she'd walk back to the stables. She pushed back her chair and looked up, only to find a grinning Belle, and a bright-eyed Olivia standing beside her.

"It's time!" said Bella.

"Time for what?"

"For your initiation ceremony, of course," said Olivia.

Kiah held one hand up in the conventional stop sign. "Look, guys, I appreciate your sentiments at wanting to welcome me into the team, but hey, I'm too old for this. Let's just forget it."

"No way!" Belle wrapped one hand around Kiah's left arm while Olivia fastened onto the other arm. They hoisted her up out of the chair, while a whooping Taylor waved a black and white bandana in the air.

"Don't worry, Kiah," Taylor said, eyes dancing. "Our initiation ceremony hasn't killed anyone, yet."

"Yet...," echoed Olivia, putting on a deep spooky voice like a villain in a horror movie.

"You'll be okay," said Belle. "It's fun."

"Especially for us," added Olivia, still using her evil Boris Karloff voice.

Kiah gritted her teeth until they hurt. Damn. She knew when she was beaten, but if she was going to survive whatever childish prank the team had planned for her, she'd need more Dutch courage. Leaning across the table, she pulled free from Olivia, snaffled Josh's full glass and downed the contents in five gulps.

"Just give up and go along with us," advised Taylor, as she moved in behind Kiah. "It's much easier."

"For who?" Kiah held her breath as Taylor tied the bandana across her eyes, eliminating all light.

God, she hoped they weren't going to do anything ridiculous — like stripping her naked and making her do the walk of shame, with all her elderly bits flopping.

Her two custodians, fingers digging into her arms, led her forward. She bumped into a chair and heard it topple over.

"Look where you're going, Olivia. You're supposed to be guiding Kiah away from the furniture, not into it."

"Don't be a wet blanket," Olivia replied with a giggle. "Like, this way's much more fun."

Once again…for who?

"Kiah," said Belle in her ear, "we're going up three steps now. You can count them if you like. That way you won't stumble. Ready?"

"No."

"Okay, here we go… One. Two. Three."

After bumping her ankles on both step two and three, Kiah gave in. Putting on the brakes wasn't working. At the top of the steps, she heard the hollow sound of wood beneath her feet.

"And now for the unveiling."

Kiah heard a snap of the fingers before the bandana was suddenly whisked away from her eyes. She blinked, reorientating herself to her new surroundings. She was up on the stage with *The Head Blasters*, while Josh had morphed up beside her holding an open bottle of beer in each hand.

Oh-Uh! Olivia's words on the track that morning— *don't wear anything too fancy* — suddenly made sense.

Kiah stared down at the wooden stage floor, riddled with stains and pock marks. Beside her left foot was a large brown spot in the shape of an emu, its one eye staring back at her. Gloating.

"Let's get started," said Taylor.

"Yay," said Olivia.

"Okay, Kiah," said Belle, crossing her arms over her chest. "What's your favourite song?"

"Um…" Kiah slowly released the tight ball of muscle that had formed in her neck and at the base of her stomach. She took a breath. Let it out on a deep sigh. Maybe this juvenile initiation ceremony would merely consist of answering a list of personal questions. If she kept her wits about her, she could do that without revealing anything too personal.

Favourite song? Um…singing hadn't been part of her life during Richard's reign. She thought back to her late teens when she and her best friend, Shelly, used to go out on the town on Saturday nights. Shelly Jarvis, who she'd met on the first day of kindergarten and, after fighting over a red coloured pencil, became best friends forever. A forever that only lasted until she'd married Richard. Kiah forced her mind back to life B.R. — before Richard — and smiled as the happy memories filtered in. She and Shelly would get three-parts tanked on white wine and invariably end up dancing on a tabletop and singing out-of-tune duets. What was that song they always finished their routine with? Always got the mob going.

Ah, yes. "My favourite song is, 'Who Let the Dogs Out', by the Baha Men."

A snigger hit from both sides.

"Never heard of it," said Belle.

"That's, like, *ancient*!"

Kiah shrugged. "Sorry, you asked for my favourite song."

Olivia scratched her head and frowned. "But the band won't, like, know what to play while you're singing."

Oh-uh! Kiah closed her eyes. They didn't only want to *know* her favourite song — they wanted her to *sing* her favourite song! No way…

"Hey, I think I know that one," said the elderly trumpeter, picking up his instrument and playing a few bars of something that sounded more like six cats fighting than, 'Who Let the Dogs Out'.

"Me too," said the hairy drummer banging wildly on his drums.

"Sorry, never heard of it," said the pink haired piano player. "I'll sit this one out."

"Well, you can't expect me to sing without the piano for backing." Kiah swallowed a grin. "In which case, I declare this initiation ceremony, null and void."

"Not happening," said Olivia in a sing-song voice. "'Cos the alternative is Josh, like, emptying both bottles of beer over your head." Her grin was pure evil. "Your choice."

Oh, yes, Olivia was loving this, but there was no way Kiah wanted to stink of beer for a week. Why hadn't she walked back to the stables when she had the chance? With a growl of frustration, she snatched a bottle out of Josh's hand and, upending it, glugged down half the contents. Then, blinking at her gaolers, let out a very un-Kiah-like giggle and wobbled slightly. She blinked again, then upended the bottle and skulled the rest.

The alcohol hit like a hammer — a soft hammer with a powder-puff head. Her body loosened and she grinned at Belle, then Olivia. She could do this. Back in the day, she and Shelly used to get the pub crowd stamping their feet, swaying along, and joining in with their singing.

"When you're ready, maestros," she said turning to her two-man band and smothering another giggle.

Who was a shrivelled up old lemon now?

With the trumpeter blasting in her left ear and the drummer crashing away behind her, Kia let loose — even adding a few tricky dance steps to embellish her singing.

Whoohoo!

In the middle of an intricate dance step that required her to shimmy, wave her arms, and nod her head, all at the same time, she glanced up to see Jack Sullivan at the back of the room, arms folded, watching her…

And that's when her legs tangled, and she fell flat on her face off the stage.

SIX

Kiah woke in her hard narrow bed inside the caravan wearing the same clothes she'd worn the night before, no memory of how she'd got there, and a bump the size of a walnut on the back of her head. Harsh daylight blasted through the window effectively incinerating both retinas. She winced. Even her teeth ached. And her tongue, thick and coated with something metallic and slimy, filled her mouth, making it hard to swallow. Had a bee stung her tongue while she'd been sleeping? And how the heck did she even get here?

She remembered getting drunk and making a fool of herself up on the stage at Shadow Creek pub. She remembered Jack Sullivan picking her up off the floor and another man, older, shining a torch in her eyes and asking her name and what day it was, and Jack carrying her out to his car…

After that everything was blank.

Had Jack driven her back to the caravan? Put her to bed? Thought about undressing her and decided against it after removing her shoes? Oh, God, the embarrassment. She wanted to curl up and die…

Inside her aching head, several pitchfork-brandishing red devils danced in a circle, banging away on their drums — or was the banging coming from outside the caravan?

Whatever. She wished they would stop.

"Okay, if I come in?" Jack Sullivan's housekeeper, Marg, who she'd briefly met the day before, poked her head around the doorway, her pepper-and-salt hair tied back in a bun, her voice too loud and hearty for Kiah's exploding head.

Kiah tried to say, '*No, go away! I'd rather have my toenails yanked out with red-hot pliers than talk to anyone,*', but she was having trouble forming the words. Her thick slimy tongue kept getting in the way and the dancing devils in her head had swapped their drums for pneumatic drills. Giving up, she grunted, hoping that conveyed her wish to be left alone.

"Mr. S. asked me to check in on you. He had to leave you a couple of hours ago to go look after the horses." Marg bustled into the caravan, a slice of what looked like tablets in one hand and a carton of eggs in the other. She selected a glass from the cupboard, filled it with water, and poked two tablets from the foil.

Jack had to leave her? Kiah scowled, cringed at the after-effects of a cannon going off in her head, and immediately ironed out the painful wrinkles. What did Marg mean? Had Jack Sullivan spent the night in her caravan? And if so — doing what? Watching her drool in her sleep? Listening to her drunken snores? Kiah's brain, already hot-wired to a faulty toaster, went looking for a bucket of water to drown in.

"Here," said Marg, slipping an arm under Kiah's shoulders to help her sit up. "Take two paracetamols, drink a full glass of water, and you'll feel marginally better. Then I'll cook up a couple of fried eggs and bread for your breakfast. Best hangover cure known to woman."

The thought of greasy fried food and the act of sitting up sent Kiah's stomach into free fall. The room spun. The housekeeper's face went blurry. And she gagged. "I-I think I'm going to be—"

"—sick?" Marg finished, while snatching up a plastic bucket from under the sink and placing it in the direct line of fire.

Kiah's body bucked and her stomach did a three-point-eight somersault ending up somewhere in her throat. She wiped her mouth with the back of her hand and groaned. "Ohmygod, I'm never going to drink alcohol again."

"Good plan," said Marg, hiking both eyebrows. "Now, while I empty this, how about you get out of those stinky clothes and into the shower. I've met sweeter smelling farm-yard animals in my travels. And while you're under the shower, I'll cook a good fry up for your breakfast. Might be some tomatoes and sausages in the fridge to go with the eggs."

"Can't eat," Kiah moaned, head in her hands. "And I'll be sick again if

I move."

"Stiff bikkies!" Marg spoke over her shoulder, her voice abrupt, no-nonsense. She emptied the bucket in the toilet, flushed, squirted it with disinfectant and filled it with hot water. "Time to get your engine into gear, 'cos Mr. S. has enough to do on a Sunday without looking after you and your horse."

Oh, my God…Jet. A hot stinging sensation gnawed behind Kiah's eyes. She sniffed. Wiped her nose. As a new horse owner, she'd fallen at the very first hurdle. No wonder she'd been a failure as a wife. She was useless, pathetic, as a human being. Couldn't even look after herself, so how did she think she could take care of a horse? Remembering Richard's words, *crying is for losers*, she forced the tears back, biting down hard on her bottom lip until she tasted blood.

Marg turned with one hand on her hip, her expression forecasting more 'tough bikkies'. Then, spotting Kiah's shaking shoulders, she bustled forward, both arms outstretched, her expression concerned. "Hey, don't listen to me, sweetie," she said placing a comforting arm around Kiah's shoulders. "I've got a way of putting both feet in my gobby mouth and speaking out of turn." She ran a hand over Kiah's hair, smoothing sweaty strands off her forehead. "My Mam, God bless her soul, always used to tell me I had no filter. 'Margaret Elaine Sheehan,' she'd say, 'that mouth of yours is going to get you into more trouble than you can poke a stick at'." She shook her head. "You see, I'm used to jazzing up Mr. S., giving him the tough bikkies routine to keep him firing."

"I-It's okay." Kiah dashed one escaping tear from her cheek and grabbed a quick breath. She gritted her teeth, forced herself to think of playful kittens and baby ducks all in a row — a therapy she'd mastered to keep crying at bay.

"Go on, let it all out, love. No good hanging on to bad juju. It's like a toxic weed that spreads and coils around in your guts, slowly choking everything in life that makes you happy. You've gotta rip it all out and bury it in the green waste bin that gets collected every second Thursday." The older woman's arm tightened around Kiah's shoulders. "You know, I'm not one to pry, but there's something about you that says you've been treated as badly in life as that skinny horse of yours standing head down in the corner of the paddock. And don't worry, I should have told you when I first came in, Mr. S fed him a couple of hours ago."

Like a dam bursting, Kiah let go. Tears that her narcissistic husband had bullied her into keeping locked away for twelve years, flooded her wet cheeks, ran down her neck, buried themselves in the collar of her crumpled red and white striped top. She sobbed, she hiccupped, she howled. And as Marg held her, the poison strangling her emotions finally released.

Eventually, Marg wiped Kiah's tears with the corner of a tea towel. "Hush now, girl. Mr. S will have my tongue in a mincer if he finds out I've made you cry."

"N-not you, Marg, it's me. Sorry, I'm a bit of a wreck, but I'm working on getting stronger by the day." Her bottom lip trembled, and she hooked it with her teeth. "Today's just not one of them." She sniffed, wiped her nose on the tea towel, before dropping it on the floor beside the bed, to wash when she felt more human. "It's-It's your kindness…it-it got to me. No one has been kind to me for such a long time."

"Well, if you're looking for kindness you've come to the right place. We're like family here at *Windsong* and you can talk to me any time. Okay?"

Unable to speak in case the tears started up again, Kiah nodded.

"And, in case you were wondering how you got home from The Creek, you fell over drunk last night, and Mr. S drove you home. He thought you might have suffered a concussion which is why he slept in here on the chair." She stepped back and rolled her eyes. "Which reminds me, I'm supposed to keep asking you your name and what day it is."

Kiah tried a tentative smile. Marg's sweet vanilla perfume reminded her of her beloved Grandma Fraser who she spent her holidays with as a child. Even Marg's voice had that same brusque, no-nonsense, but comforting quality to it. "I'm Kiah Stanton, it's Sunday morning, and it's my day off." She pushed a grin through her dry lips and suddenly felt like a heavy weight had been batted off her chest. As though she could breathe fully for the first time in twelve years. "But I'll get up, shower, eat your horrendous female hangover cure and go brush Jet and clean his paddock." She took hold of Marg's work-calloused hands and squeezed. "And thank you, Margaret Elaine Sheehan, for being you."

*****

As Kiah rounded the corner of the caravan, a hessian grooming bag slung over one shoulder, her stomach performing tentative flip-flops after Marg's greasy fry up, she spotted Jet mooching in the corner of the paddock, his head between his knees.

Her heart constricted, a small chunk breaking off and speeding across the paddock to comfort him. How many people had he trusted in the past and they'd failed him? Treated him like an inanimate object that could be stashed in a corner cupboard and forgotten? Life as a horse was a lottery; so much depending on who was in charge. Although Jet was already responding to Kiah, ears tipping forward when he spotted her, he was far from committed. And why would he be? How did he know she was any different to his previous owners? He'd been fed today — but would he be fed tomorrow?

Latching the paddock gate behind her, Kiah called out and watched as the black horse's head slowly lifted and turned in her direction. His ears pricked, and even from the gate she could see his body soften, but he didn't move.

"So…you want me to come to you today?" she said, pulling a carrot from each pocket and walking towards him. "Decided to become Crown Prince Jet overnight?"

Spotting the treats, Jet gave a soft whinny, shuffled forward, and met her in the middle of the paddock. Kiah held out her hand, feeling his prickly whiskers graze her palm as he crunched into the first treat. Bliss, and something akin to wonderment settled across his face, as carrot juice bubbled from both sides of his lips. Was this the first time her horse had tasted a carrot?

"Come on, let's get you out of those rugs and give you a good brush." Once he'd finished eating, Kiah clipped a lead rope onto his halter and led him back to the paddock gate, where she'd dropped her grooming bag beside the tie-up rail.

Kiah was glad the heavy-duty canvas rug and detachable hood covered Jet's washboard ribs and scrawny neck. It wasn't that she was ashamed of her horse — just worried anyone passing by might blame her for his neglect. She blew out a frustrated sigh. If only she could fatten him up overnight.

After undoing the fastenings, Kiah dragged the rugs off, dumped them at her feet, and studied his ribs and backbone with the intensity of an examination paper. *Was he looking as skinny as yesterday?*

"It'll take time…"

The deep voice behind her had Kiah spinning around, her feet tangling in the rugs in her haste. "Boss?"

He quirked one eyebrow. "It's okay to call me Jack away from work."

Kiah's cheeks turned into two small bonfires. The fry up in her stomach shifted uneasily. This man, her boss, his grey-blue eyes seeming to see inside her head, had brought her home last night — she forced herself to keep breathing in and out at the thought — he'd put her to bed, slipped off her boots, contemplated removing her vomit-enhanced clothes. And then, because she might have concussion, had spent the night sitting on a hard plastic chair in her caravan, watching her sleep.

Ohmygod, she'd never be able to look him in the eye again…

She snatched a soft body brush from her grooming bag and ran it over Jet's stark coat, being wary not to bang any bones in the process.

"I've had horses like Jet come through before," Jack told her, leaning his elbows on the fence and watching her. "You feel like you want to feed them up, put weight on quickly, but it's dangerous for the horse. Slowly, slowly, wins the race, as they say." He chuckled deep in his throat; a sound that made Kiah's heart bang a little harder. "Although, I guess that wouldn't be the best plan in an actual horse race."

Kiah kept brushing, hoping the rhythmic movement would calm her nerves. She could feel Jack's eyes on her. Burning through the sloppy tee-shirt she'd grabbed after her quick shower. Was he thinking of the way she'd been throwing herself around on the stage, acting like some teenage bimbo, before splattering on the floor, skirt up around her waist? Or how disgusting she'd looked asleep, drool running down her chin?

She had to say something. At least thank him for bringing her home. Squashing down the nerves that were making her tongue tie in knots, she turned around. "Thanks for last night."

He spoke at the same time. "You sure you're okay to be out here?"

"Umm…" A bubble of nervous laughter tickled her throat as she watched his lips move upward into a grin.

And then he laughed. A deep belly-laugh that set Kiah off too. "Sorry," he said, still chuckling. "I keep thinking of you up on the stage singing that hilarious dog song."

Kiah groaned. "Me too."

"I'd just popped into *The Creek* to tell Steve he'd better get on home 'cos his wife had rung me, and she was on the warpath, and there you were up on the stage, dancing and singing and having a ball." He pulled a face. "That is, until you lost your footing, went splat, and banged your head."

She automatically rubbed the bump on the back of her head.

"Sorry, I should have warned you about the kids and their initiation ceremony, but they don't usually induct newcomers until they've been here at least a couple of weeks." He flicked one hand at her. "It mightn't seem like it, what with having a sore head and the hangover from hell, but they must like you. And those dance moves. Hey, you really had the pub crowd going — all yelling and dancing and singing along with you." He quirked an eyebrow at her. "Shame you missed your footing."

"You mean, shame I was so drunk, I fell off the stage?"

His grin widened. "Well, that too."

Kiah, determined to change the subject, went back to brushing Jet, using the soft brush to untangle his matted tail. "Any idea how long before Jet can be ridden?"

"Depends how quickly he responds to your tender administration," he joked, ducking under the fence to study the horse more closely. "Seriously, it will probably take six to eight weeks before he'll be strong enough for light work."

"That long?"

"Maybe even longer. Anyway, our vet, Greg Channing's due here tomorrow. My advice is to let Greg examine him, see what he suggests."

Kiah stretched up to scratch Jet behind the ear. Something he loved, if the way he seemed to smile at her and tip his head closer so she could get better access meant anything. Yes, a vet check was a definite. "Thanks, Jack…that'd be great."

"For a start, this horse has been in a paddock with next-to-no-feed, for the last six months, so his stomach will be full of sand. Probably need tubing."

"Tubing?" Kiah stopped scratching Jet's ear to gape at Jack. "What's that?"

"The vet administers oil via a stomach—tube."

She screwed up her nose. "Can't see Jet agreeing to that."

Jack laughed and smoothed Jet's forelock down over his eyes. "Don't worry, Greg is good at his job. He'll worm him, tube him, give him a shot of vitamins and advise you to build him up slowly. Lots of small feeds to start with."

"But he's so skinny…"

"Remember, he hasn't had good solid food for a long time, so if he eats too much at once, he'll colic." Jack rubbed his hand over the horse's thin neck. "And in Jet's condition, that could be fatal."

There was so much more she needed to learn about horses. Kiah stared across at the eight thoroughbreds attached to the mechanical walker near the stable block. All lumbering around in a never-ending circle to nowhere. A laugh bubbled in her chest. Even from here, she could see her nemesis, Lofty, attempting to stop the walker by digging his hooves in the sand and applying his brakes. He was such a goofball.

A large gooseneck-style horse trailer turning in through the gateway, distracted her. Looked like one of those interstate transports, an 8-berther, where the horses could see out through the openings at the side.

"You expecting a new horse?" she asked, watching the vehicle lumber down the driveway towards the house, spitting gravel in its wake.

"Probably Magnifico, the new horse that was supposed to arrive on Friday. The driver rang yesterday to say he got held up coming down through the floods in New South Wales."

"Ah…that's the horse Angel was expecting when I rocked up. She said he was going to win some big Cup, and maybe even a race in the city." Kiah laughed. "And then she looked in the float, saw Jet, and kindly told me my horse had a nice sloping shoulder."

Jack shrugged. "Hey, who knows what Jet's capable of once he's strong and healthy? What say I check his brand on the computer for you, see what I can find. Might even be able to get hold of his papers and transfer ownership. Worth a shot." He opened the paddock gate, but before leaving, dredged up his serious 'boss' face. "Now, don't overdo it out here," he warned. "You'll need to be fit for work tomorrow, 'cos I've put you up on the same three horses you rode yesterday."

"Same three horses?" Her voice squeaked like a rusty gate hinge. She was going to kill him. Drown him in the water trough, smother him in the manure pile and then stake him with a pitchfork. "But Belle said—"

"And by the way…," he interrupted, his grin pure evil. "Might pay to sleep with a peg on your nose. You snore like a hippopotamus."

*****

Jack smothered a grin as he closed the paddock gate behind him and set off in the direction of the horse transport parked outside the stable block. His quip about Kiah snoring had hit its mark. She looked ready to throw a hard-backed horse brush at his head. Good. She needed some fire in her belly to make it through the rest of the day.

When he'd left her caravan early this morning, she'd looked like she'd be lucky to crawl out of bed before Christmas, which is why he'd been surprised to see her head pop out of her caravan door, face pale, hair still wet from the shower, a couple of hours later. He'd watched her descend the caravan steps as though climbing down a twenty-foot ladder in gale force winds, then head for the paddock where she kept that damn horse she'd rescued from the saleyard. He growled in his throat. Maybe he'd have tried harder to talk her out of buying the horse if he'd known both she and the skeleton-on-four-legs would land here at *Windsong*, only a few hours later.

Or would he? The memory of Kiah's two terrified green eyes staring up at him last night when he woke her from a bad dream to smooth her sweaty hair away from her face, then ask her name and what day it was for the third time, tugged at his chest, made him determined to find out more about this mystery woman. Why she'd arrived out of nowhere and applied for a job as a track rider and groom, when she clearly hadn't been anywhere near a horse for some time. Was she running away from domestic violence? She'd been calling out in her sleep, pleading with some rat called Richard, to stop, she was sorry, she'd never try to leave him again. Jack's fists clenched at the memory. Virtual steam billowed from his ears. He'd like to get his hands on this Richard guy — five minutes would be enough

— bale him up in a dark alley and show him what he thought of men who hurt women.

Jack flicked a quick glance over his shoulder at Kiah, her arms around that ragbag of a horse's neck, and felt a tug at his heart. He wanted to see her smile, lose her fear of whatever or whoever was taking over her dreams, and if it could be achieved by helping to turn her neglected nag into a 'silk purse', then Jack would do whatever he could to make it happen.

"G'day, mate. You Jack Sullivan?"

Jack nodded at the wiry man in dirty jeans and rumpled shirt leaning against the side of the horse transport. A week's stubble darkened his face, his hair was wild; he looked completely bushed. "That's me. Got a big chestnut gelding going by the name of Magnifico in there for me?"

"Yeah, last one to deliver, thank the bleedin' crows." The driver pushed himself off the side of the vehicle and began to wind down the ramp. "Sorry about the delay. Been a blasted nightmare getting through the floods up north. Some poor buggers left homeless, houses completely under water. Took an extra couple of days, 'cos I had to get here via the scenic route, and believe me, I wasn't there for the scenery." He made his way up the now-lowered ramp toward the lone horse secured between two dividers in the last bay. If horses could talk, this one would be letting fly with four-letter words not fit to be heard in public. Clearly cheesed off with being cooped up in the transport for so long, his ears were flat, eyes at half-mast, and as the driver unfastened the first divider, he stamped his foot and snaked his head. "All finished now though," the driver said, ignoring the horse's antics while attaching a lead rope to the halter, "so I'm off home for a shower, a shave, and a couple of ice-cold stubbies." He licked his lips and grinned down at Jack. "Might even make that a six pack."

"Go for it." Jack took possession of the cranky-looking chestnut from the driver and smoothed a calming hand down the horse's sweaty neck. Magnifico had come with good reports, but this was the first time Jack had seen him in the flesh. He usually liked to get a feel for a horse, see it run, before agreeing to train it, but when the two owners, old school friends, had bought Magnifico for Jack to train as a surprise, the day after they collected second prize in the lottery, how could he say no?

He stood the horse up and ran an eye over him. Intelligent head, good length of pastern, nice sloping shoulders, strong hindquarters. All good. But it was as he walked the horse towards the stable block that a glimmer of excitement twitched the corners of his lips. The big chestnut had a long loose walk with at least a six-inch over-track, which meant he'd have a huge gallop. Maybe he *could* win the Kangaroo Downs Cup after all. He lifted a hand at the driver who'd finished winding the ramp back up and was climbing wearily into the cabin. "Thanks, mate. Drive carefully."

Dodging a snap of teeth, Jack led the horse into the stable block and tied him to a loop of twine on the rail. "What do we call you?" he said, preparing to give the horse a good brush and rub down. After spending three days jammed into a horse transport with seven other horses, the dried sweat along his back would be making him itchy, and irritable. "Magnifico's a bit of a mouthful. What about Mags? Nifico?" He took a step back and studied the horse more closely. "You look more like a Zorro with that white blaze that looks like a mask, but think I'll stick with your full moniker. Magnifico. Suits you."

After Jack finished brushing off the dirt and sweat, he threw a light rug over the horse's back, fastened the straps, and led him into stable 28, where fresh water and a full hay net awaited him. He left the back door of the stable open so the horse could wander out into the day-yard and stretch his legs, after being cooped up for so long.

One hand on the stable door ready to let himself out, Jack looked up and blinked, did a double-take. Big Lofty was strolling past. Eyes bright, a smirk on his face, he was heading for stable 10, his stable, and the half dipper of oats waiting in his feeder. What the heck? How did Lofty get off the walker?

And then Kiah's face appeared under Lofty's neck. Her smile tentative. "The timer went off and the walker thingy stopped moving. The other horses are okay, but Lofty was digging a hole to China, so I thought I'd better bring him in. Hope that's okay?"

Jack nodded. With that smudge of dirt down one cheek and dressed in loose tracksuit bottoms and what looked like a baggy top she'd picked up at some charity shop, she didn't look much older than Taylor, or even Belle, and he knew by the application form she'd half-filled out, that she was 39. Only two years younger than him. By now, Jack thought she'd be back on her bed, recovering from her hangover and concussion, but, like everything else about this woman, she didn't do the expected.

Like yesterday morning. Jack was sure she'd quit after the first horse he'd assigned her, but no, she'd not only survived Lofty's fun and games, but also coped with Jack's next two tests — Zipper the Nipper and Jumpy Jade.

"Wow! Your new horse is gorgeous!" Kiah's voice cut through Jack's thoughts. "If that's Magnifico, he's certainly well-named. Is he in work? Ready to race?"

"No, three wins in country New South Wales and then turned out for a spell before a couple of my owners bought him for me to train." Jack wiggled his eyebrows. "Five numbers and a sup in the Lottery. We're hoping they've bought the future winner of the Kangaroo Downs Cup, and then, maybe even a race in the city."

"Well, if looks can win a race, he's home for all money."

"Talking of home, thought you'd be back in your caravan lying down by now."

"Strangely enough, Marg's fry up settled my stomach." She tipped her head to the side and her eyes met his. "Do you need a hand here? The girls said you're on your own with the horses on Sundays."

"No, I'm fine." He quirked one eyebrow at her. "*Plus*, it's your day off."

She shrugged. "At least let me help get the horses off the walker."

Jack laughed and stepped out of the stable, being careful to lock the door behind him. "No one works on their day off, Kiah."

"I don't mind."

Standing this close, Jack could smell Kiah's shampoo. The sweet tropical smell of coconut; Bianca's all-time favourite. He lost his breath for a moment, his heart thudding at the memory of his nose buried in his wife's newly washed hair, laughing, telling her she smelled like coconut ice cream. Swallowing the lump in his throat, he pushed past Lofty to get out. "I-I'll go get the next horse. And thanks, I'd appreciate help bringing them in. I have a ton of paperwork to get through this afternoon."

Striding out to the mechanical walker, Jack shoved his hands deep in his pockets to steady them. Even after eight years, certain smells, voices, sights, brought Bianca's memory back. It was like a knife twisting in his heart, and the jolt of evoking her memory hurt every time.

"Daddy! Daddy! Can I ride Goldie back into the stable?" Silvery blonde hair flying loose behind her, Angel flew out of the house, front door crashing behind her. She was down the steps in one leap and beside him before he'd unhooked the first horse. "Please. Please. Pretty please. Put me up on Goldie, Daddy. She likes me."

"They all like you." Unhooking Golden Circle, a solid chestnut mare who'd only been in work for a couple of months and was showing promise, Jack ran a hand down the horse's neck and scratched behind her ears. He bent down and hefted Angel up onto the mare's broad back. "You know the rules. Hang onto the mane and don't kick her. Pretending you're riding in a race just stirs her up."

"Hey, Kiah, look at me!" As Jack led the horse towards the stable block, Angel waved to Kiah who was coming out, a lead rope swinging in one hand.

"Hi, Angel. Looking good up there."

"I'm going to be a jockey when I grow up." Angel leant forward on the horse, knees tight, hands moving forward and back like she was riding in a race.

Jack rolled his eyes. Not if he had any say in the matter. He quickly steadied Goldie, who'd started to jog, then with one quick movement lifted his daughter off the horse and deposited her back onto the ground. "What did I say?"

"Sorry, Dad, I forgot." She gave a dramatic sigh and flicked both hands, palms up. "Can't help myself sometimes. It's my inner-jockey. She just takes over."

Jack smothered a grin. "Well, your inner-jockey can wash the dinner dishes tonight. And dry them and help Marg put them away."

"I'm sorry Dad." Like ice cream on a hot day, Angel's contrite smile made Jack's heart melt. Little minx. She did it to him every time. He bent down and hugged her to him. "You know how unpredictable racehorses can be, Poppet. That's why you have your own pony to ride."

Angel pulled away, her face lighting up like a switch had been turned on. "Do you think Kiah would like to see my pony?"

"You can ask her, but it's Kiah's day off and she's probably got her own things to do." He lifted an eyebrow at Kiah who'd been slowly unhooking the next horse, taking her time, clearly enjoying the exchange between father and daughter.

"Love to." Kiah said smiling down at Angel. "I'll just finish helping your dad put the horses away and then, I'm all yours."

Jack looked first at Angel and then Kiah. His daughter had latched onto this woman and her horse the moment they'd arrived. "You sure?"

Kiah nodded.

"Look, I can finish here." Jack mock-frowned down at his daughter. "But don't let Angel talk you into taking up too much of your time. She's tricky like that. You need to rest up for work tomorrow."

"Yay," said Angel, taking hold of Kiah's hand and pulling her away from the horse-walker in the direction of a small stable block and paddock on the other side of the house.

Kiah looked down at Angel. "What's your pony's name?"

"Biscuit. But his show name's Billabong Gold."

"Oh, I like that. Billabong Gold is a lovely name."

Jack, who'd taken the horse's lead rope from Kiah, stood and watched the pair of them walk away, Angel's small hand in Kiah's larger one. Silvery blonde head looking up at a head of wild red curls.

"I named him Biscuit 'cos that's his favourite treat. Once he walked in through our front door into the kitchen and stole a whole packet of gingerbreads from the table."

Kiah laughed. "Maybe you should have called him Gingerbread. What color is he?"

"Palomino with a white mane and tail. You'll love him."

"I love him already."

Jack forced himself to look away. He had horses to attend and paperwork to finish. That feeling of tightness in his chest brought on by watching Angel and Kiah together was purely indigestion caused by eating the pork pie he'd had for breakfast, too quickly.

SEVEN

Her heart cartwheeling like an Olympic gymnast, her throat scratchy from shouting, Kiah's grip on the race-track's white running-rail tightened. Seven horses swept around the bend in a cloud of dust and thundered into the home straight. Big Hoss, Lofty to his friends, was lying in third place and running on strongly. "Go, Lofty!"

As though he could hear Kiah shouting encouragement, the big long-striding horse, ears flat against the sides of his head, dug deeper. With a flick of his tail, he passed the long-legged grey hugging the rails, and set off after the leader.

"Go! Go! Go!"

Lofty's stride lengthened even further. With his head and neck stretched to the max, he caught the fading leader in the last few strides of the race and streaked past the winning post, a length clear of the field.

Big Hoss had won the eighth race of the day at the Wattle Park country race meeting.

"Yeeess!!" Kiah couldn't stop the inane grin from spreading across her face. Big goofy Lofty, the clown of the stables, one of the three horses she was responsible for, had won. "You little beauty!"

"Whoohoo!" Belle let out a loud whoop that could have been heard on the other side of the track. "I put my last ten dollars on Lofty's nose at 10/1. I'm rich." She grabbed Kiah in a bear-hug and danced her up and down on the spot, making her laugh. "You're celebrating at *The Creek* with us tonight."

"Me? Oh, I'm not really—"

"No excuses. He's one of yours." She lifted her chin. "It's a tradition."

Kiah let out a sigh. Damn. She couldn't very well buck tradition. After a shaky start to the job, she was now an accepted member of the team, a cog in the well-oiled racing-wheel, and loving every aspect of her new life. Especially her friends. She grinned at the younger woman's eager face. "Okay, but I can only stay for a few drinks. Still not used to these early morning starts."

Belle threw back her head and fist-pumped the air. "And the first drink's on me!"

Olivia, wearing little more than what looked like a large handkerchief and post-box red thigh-high boots, came bouncing up to them, her grin so wide it was almost tearing a hole in her face. "If *you're* paying, make mine a Sex on the Beach."

Kiah laughed. "Do you actually know what's in a Sex on the Beach?"

"Nope. But it sounds like something I'd like."

Olivia was trailed by a large, tattooed, bikie type guy, clad in tight black leather trousers and a figure-hugging *Black Devil* tee that delineated every one of his steroid-enhanced chest muscles. "This is my new friend, Buzz Devlin." She reached up, ran a hand through his long greasy locks and grinned. "Cute, hey?"

Yeah, as a shark. Kiah sent Buzz I-Crack-Rocks-On-My-Pecs Devlin a sharp nod, before exchanging a discreet oh-my-God eyeroll with Belle. Olivia had dumped her sleazy jockey friend when she'd discovered she wasn't the only member of his adoring harem, but her choice of boyfriends had spiralled drastically downhill. Seems like she'd hit rock bottom with this one.

"Anyway, big party at *The Creek* tonight," Belle continued. "Even Kiah's promised to exchange binging her usual British crime dramas and popcorn, for partying with us."

Olivia raised one thumb. "Might even, like, get her up on the stage, singing, *Who Let the Dogs Out*."

"Only if we get her drunk."

"And only if the boss is there, to like, sweep her up in his arms and carry her off to his man-cave."

Kiah's cough was loud, deliberate. "Hey, guys, I'm standing right here, you know."

Listening to Belle and Olivia bantering, teasing her, Kiah let out a sigh of contentment. If someone had told her ten weeks ago, that she'd be enjoying a day at a country race meeting with her colleagues, celebrating the success of a loveable, but goofy racehorse that she was responsible for, Kiah wouldn't have believed them. Probably accused the storyteller of being into the dishwashing liquid.

Yet so much had happened in that ten weeks. She'd bought a horse and called him Jet. She'd swapped a smart two-bedroom apartment in an elite suburb for a salmon pink refurbished 1980 caravan propped up on bricks. She'd worked harder than she'd ever worked in her life, riding and caring for a team of unpredictable racehorses. She was employed by a man with grey-blue eyes that could turn from stormy to kind in the blink of an eye — and fallen in love with his eight-year-old daughter. Thinking of Angel, Kia's heart smiled. She'd never had anything to do with children before but had connected with Angel on that first day when she'd rumbled up the driveway of *Windsong* stables looking for a job and a home for Jet, and found an ally in the boss's daughter. Now, every Sunday they'd go riding, Angel on her pony, Kiah on one of the retirees, a picnic lunch provided by the inimitable Marg packed carefully in Angel's backpack. Just the two of them; riding, enjoying each other's company, and discussing everything from how a man could walk on the moon when it was so far way, to how to treat poxy boys who called you names.

And Kiah was happier than she'd been in years.

She came out of her musing in time to spot Dillon, proudly wearing the stable colours of green with white stars, riding Lofty on a loose rein out through the now-open gateway from the track to the unsaddling area. She hurried towards them, flinging a quick, 'See you later, girls', over her shoulder. It was Kiah's job to secure her charge by attaching a lead rope to the big horse's bridle, so his jockey could dismount, weigh in, and be declared correct weight, without having to worry about his mount.

Dillon, sliding off the horse's back, couldn't supress his grin. He undid the girth and dragged his race saddle off the now prancing Lofty who was showing off, pretending a leaf fluttering past was the big bad boogieman. Like he knew he could get away with any of his party tricks today and still be treated like royalty. Wins at *Windsong* had been far and few between lately.

"Congratulations." Kiah clapped Dillon on the back, while dodging the big horse's plate-sized hooves as he tried to barge through her.

"Thanks, Kiah, but it was all Lofty's doing today. Leader flattened like a pricked balloon twenty metres from the post and Lofty galloped straight past him. Even gave him the finger by farting in his face."

"That's our Lofty."

While Dillon strode off to be weighed-in by the stewards, his saddle slung over one arm, an un-wipeable grin plastered on his face, Kiah cooled her charge down by walking him around the outer paddock; a necessary procedure to prevent tying up.

For a horse who'd given his all in a race, Lofty was still full of beans.

"Cut it out, you big goof!" Kiah stumbled forward as Lofty nudged her in the back with his dinosaur-sized head, following it up by answering a whinny from the other side of the paddock with an elephant-trumpeting neigh that blasted her eardrums. "And no, you can't pick on the grass," she told him, yanking his head up. Thwarted, the big horse nibbled on Kiah's shirt collar, before rubbing his sweaty, itchy face across the sleeve, leaving yellow saliva streaks in his wake, then finished off by sneezing black snotty sludge all down the front.

Luckily, she'd brought a change of clothes, but doubted whether her favourite shirt in the stable's colours of green and white would ever recover.

Jack was a good trainer and today's win was a direct result of his meticulous planning. Like five days ago, he'd given Kiah the job of trailering both Lofty and Goldie (Golden Circle) who'd come 2nd in an earlier race, to Wattle Park race-track for a trial and to familiarize the horses with the track they'd be racing on. An important cog in the overall training machine.

Up before the sun, she'd hooked the two-horse float to her SUV, loaded both horses, and after travelling to Wattle Park in the pre-dawn darkness, met up with Dillon and Taylor, their respective jockeys, and watched them put both horses through their paces on the track.

Result — a win and a second placing today. Kiah knew if only Jack could attract rich owners who'd buy him faster horses, he'd train city winners too. Prizemoney at small country tracks didn't go far, but today's first and second should keep the howling dingos from the back door for a little while longer.

While continuing to walk Lofty around, Kiah thought back to what the racetrack had been like at 5 a.m. the morning of the trial. Instead of the zing and movement of race day, a hazy misty fluorescence had hung around the lightbulbs illuminating the track and stabling area. To the east, as the sun poked its nose over the horizon, the sky had turned orange, pink, red, gold. She'd stood at the rails, breathing in the crisp early morning air and enjoying the amazing spectacle of galloping horses silhouetted against the backdrop of a muti-coloured sky.

Kiah had once asked Jack why horses had to be worked so early, why they couldn't be trained in the afternoon, and received a lecture for her troubles. He'd looked so earnest and cute, his eyes lighting up, his head tipped to the side, his lips well-rounded and malleable as he explained the numerous reasons why 4 a.m. was the best time of the day for both equine and human athletes to exercise. Not that she was a convert to any of them.

Still thinking of Jack's well-rounded, malleable lips and how they would feel pressed against hers, she led Lofty to the hose bay and tied him to the rail. It was as she turned on the water that Kiah sensed the man's presence directly behind her. Smelt his aftershave; woodsy with a sprig of lemon this time.

Heat pulsed in her cheeks. Her mouth went dry. She played the hose on Lofty's legs and up across his back and neck, being careful not to get any water near his ears — his pet hate — and waited for Jack to speak first. With the flush of her cheeks, could he tell she'd been thinking of him? And why couldn't she contain her stupid tell-tale blush? It's not like there was anything between them other than boss and employee. Even if her pulses did go slightly haywire whenever their hands accidently brushed or she'd caught him staring at her with an odd, almost longing, expression on his face. She was off men for life. And he was still in love with his dead wife.

"I've been looking for you, Kiah." His voice was a soft rumble that had her heart stuttering, missing beats. "The big horse looked a hundred percent out there today. You've done a top job as his strapper over the last three months, and I'm proud of you."

She forced herself to take in one deep centring breath, before turning around to face him. "Um…thanks," she muttered, then mentally kicked herself. She was so damn worried about Jack deciphering the cause of her pink cheeks, all she could come up with was a dumb, *Umm…thanks*? How old was she? Fifteen? Or was it how ice-cream lick-ably good Jack Sullivan looked dressed in a suit, a few dark hairs curling over the collar of his open-necked white shirt? She hadn't seen the man in anything other than working jeans or moleskins before today. She took in his smoothly shaven jawline — and he'd even had a haircut. Instead of brushing his shoulders, his dark hair was slicked back, a few rebellious curls breaking loose, giving him a dangerous air, and making him look younger than his forty-one years.

"It all counts, you know." Jack's eyes met hers, lingered. "My Uncle Dan used to say, 'a happy horse in the stable is a happy horse on the track'." He nodded his head at Lofty, who was currently rolling his lips back and showing his teeth. "Look how happy he is — he's smiling at us."

Kiah let out a laugh, built-up pressure releasing from her chest. "Nah," she said, shaking her head, "that's just Lofty asking if you remembered to bring him a carrot."

Okay, the girls had repeatedly warned her that Jack didn't do relationships, plus she had no intentions of ever letting her guard down with another man — not after Richard — but her boss was in a bantering mood, she was on a high after Lofty's win, and could feel herself responding to his teasing. She flicked him a conspirator's grin. "As for being happy — this big goof's only happy when he's clowning around or getting cussed."

She turned all the way around, better able to soak up his grin, enjoy the teasing, and as she did so, the hose, slippery in her fingers, bucked, causing a stream of water to hit Jack in the face, splashing onto his good suit. Momentarily frozen, she watched him slowly wipe water from his eyes with the sleeve of his jacket.

"Sorry," Kiah held her breath as she directed the hose back onto Lofty's legs. "Didn't mean that. Hose slipped."

"You sure about that?" His voice, low and rumbly, promised

retribution, while his eyes narrowed as though she was a pesky fly and he was the fly-swatter. He reached for the hose, prised it from Kiah's wet fingers and with a determined flick, sprayed water all over her.

"Hey! Not fair!" Laughing, she grabbed for the hose, missed, so reached across and turned off the tap. "Mine was an accident."

She brushed at the front of her blouse, noticing, with another tell-tale blush, that it had become semi-transparent. She tugged the damp material away from her skin, not daring to look up.

"Kiah..." Jack hesitated, as though experiencing an inner tug-of-war, processing his next words before letting them loose. "Would you like to have dinner at the house tonight? Say, 7 o'clock? And maybe stay for a few drinks after Angel goes to bed? You know, to celebrate Lofty's win."

Ready to say yes, she'd love to, that dinner with Jack and Angel, followed by a few drinks would be a perfect way to end a perfect day, Kiah suddenly remembered she'd agreed to go to *The Creek* with the girls. She kicked at the hose with one foot. Damn. Damn. Damn. "Sorry," she said. "I can't."

He straightened his shoulders and she watched his face close down. "Can't? Or won't?"

Kiah didn't like the way he said that, but turned to him, a regretful smile on her face. Maybe, like her, he was disappointed. "I promised the girls I'd go to *The Creek* with them."

"Hope that works out better than last time." Like a rabbit from a magician's hat, his smile had disappeared, replaced by a tightness that could have been anger, disappointment, or maybe even relief. Relief that she'd knocked back the offer he'd felt compelled to make as a boss/employee whose horse had just won a race? "I'll see you back at the stables then." His voice had lost all its early warmth and humour and he'd transformed from Jack back to the boss again. "And make sure you put a light rug on Lofty before loading him into the float."

"Of course." Her voice as cool as his, she narrowed her eyes at him. Now he was pissing her off. She wasn't his whipping girl. He didn't have to tell her to put a rug on Lofty when she—

"Kiah! Kiah! Come quick!"

Kiah spun around to find Belle, dancing from one foot to the other, an anxious expression on her face. "What is it?"

"Just put Lofty in the cross ties and come quick." She side-eyed Jack, gritted her teeth and seemed to dance on the spot. "You're...needed elsewhere."

"What's happened?" Jack stepped forward; all irritation forgotten in his anxiety. "Is it Goldie?"

"No, no, nothing to do with the horses. It's er..." Belle, fingers plucking at her jeans, looked ready to grab Kiah, and make a run for it. "It's...it's...um...it's girl stuff."

Jack let out a breath and rolled his eyes. "Riight," he said, drawing the word out as far as it would go. He flicked a help, I'm-out-of-my-depth glance at Kiah, picked up the scraper and shooed her off. "I'll finish Lofty, you go check on your sidekicks. I'm pretty damn sure, 'girl stuff', isn't listed anywhere on my trainer's contract."

"Thanks, boss, you're the best." Belle grabbed Kiah by the sleeve, drew her closer and whispered in her ear, "It's Olivia."

Olivia? Kiah let herself be dragged away, calling out a quick, 'yeah, thanks boss', over her shoulder and receiving an exaggerated sigh and another eye-roll in return. Her head spun as Belle towed her towards the men's toilets. The MEN'S toilets? Her stomach churned like an out-of-control cement mixer. What the heck had Olivia got herself into this time?

✶✶✶✶✶

The colourful art-work on the side of the men's toilet block showed a cartoon dog with his leg cocked high on a fire hydrant. Cute, and definitely validated the artist's attempt to brighten up the tired looking building, but Kiah was glad he hadn't decided to flaunt his humour on the side of the ladies' toilet block as well. She didn't want to imagine what the dog would be doing in that cartoon.

Belle, still twitchy, checked the immediate area in front of the toilets, then, evidently deciding there were no males in desperate need, shoved the door open.

Kiah gasped. "What are you doing? We can't go in there." She grabbed hold of Belle's sleeve, and arching back, tugged her away from the doorway.

"We have to," said Belle, swinging to face Kiah, her frown even deeper.

"Look, I'm no happier about this than you, but Olivia has locked herself in one of the stalls and won't come out."

"Why did she do that? And why the *Men's* instead of the Ladies?" This was all becoming too farcical, too 'who's on first' for Kiah. She was a responsible adult, not a curious teen looking to explore the idiosyncrasies of a man's world via finding out what the inside of the men's toilet block looked like. Damn Olivia. If she wanted to play childish games, why couldn't she play them in the ladies' facilities?

"Olivia said this was the only place he wouldn't think to look for her."

"Which he?" Kiah couldn't keep up with all Olivia's 'he's'. And then the thought of the badass dude she'd been with earlier, hit her. Goosebumps skittered up her arms and a tight knot, like a lump of stone, hardened in the pit of her stomach. She grabbed a fortifying breath, then let it out slowly. "Not that neanderthal she was hanging out with over by the rails?"

With a roll of her eyes, Bella nodded.

"What did he do to her? If he hurt her, I'll kill him."

"Actually, it's more what *she* did to *him*."

Kiah gasped. "Oh God, no. She didn't lead him on and then give him the cold shoulder and he turned nasty?"

"Worse." Belle closed her eyes as though that might help blank out her next words. "She scratched his motorbike. His Harley. Made him cry."

Kiah couldn't stop herself. A laugh tickled her chest then rose up and burst out of her throat. "And *that's* why she's hiding?"

"Well, wouldn't *you*?"

"But why the *men's* toilets?"

"Says that's the only place he won't look for her." Belle pushed against the door and strode inside. "Come on, Kiah, we have to get Olivia out of here before someone reports her. If the track stewards get wind of what she's doing, and where, she could get her stable-hand licence suspended."

Sidling into the toilet block behind Bella, Kiah blinked at the garish artificial light coming from the overhead fluorescents and reflecting off the white porcelain urinals and wash-basins. Should have brought her sunglasses. Her nose twitched at the distinctive smell of the facility. Strong, acidic, and with a dash of testosterone. She grimaced. Even the familiar pine disinfectant was more heavy-duty than in the ladies.

An elderly man, shapeless trousers belted up under his armpits, stood hunched over the wash-basin, rinsing his hands. When he saw the intruders, his mouth gaped, he went to speak, but something about the look in Bella's eyes must have told him to get out of there in a hurry — do not pass go — as instead of using the blower, he quickly dried his hands on the sides of his trousers, and, grumbling about women's rights taking over the world, fled through the open doorway.

"Olivia! Where are you?" Kiah bent to check under the closed door of stall one, but all she could see was a pair of brown scuffed trousers resting on top of a pair of brown scuffed shoes.

Definitely not Olivia.

"She's down the other end," said Belle, pointing to the last stall where the door was firmly shut.

"Olivia?" Kiah fisted her knuckles and drummed on the door. "You can come out now, we're going home."

"I'm never coming out."

"Don't be ridiculous. It's time to load the horses and we can't just drive off and leave you here." She rattled the door handle, but it wouldn't budge. Okay, she'd try another approach. "Olivia, the guy's a snake. Not worth getting upset over."

"I know," Olivia wailed. "That's why I'm, like, never coming out!" *Aaarrgh!!*

Belle, busy examining the six identical urinals lined up against the back wall, let out a snort. She screwed up her nose. "How do they do it? How do guys just stand here, next to a stranger, and…you know…without feeling the least bit embarrassed? I'd rather burst than…than…do *that* in public."

Kiah, caught off guard, couldn't supress a grin of solidarity. She chuckled at Belle's horrified expression. "Like pigs at a trough?"

"Exactly." Belle shook her head, clearly unable to fathom the inexplicable differences between the sexes. "No question about it…guys are born minus the self-conscious gene."

"*And* minus a sense of humour," growled Olivia from behind the closed door. "You'd think I'd, like, burnt Buzz's house down or murdered his dog, the way he lost his shit. Geez, it was only a scratch."

"Yeah, but Bikie Guy *does* have a point," said Belle leaving the curiosity of men's urinals and joining Kiah in their mission to extract Olivia from behind the closed door. "You should *never* touch a bikie's Harley. It's the love of his life. Nothing is more important to him than his bike, not even his mother, so—" She stopped mid-tirade when Kiah's vigorously shaking head suddenly registered and she realized they were supposed to be urging Olivia to come out of the stall. Not rent it for the next month. "Um…yes, but he'll get over it once he calms down…which he most likely has already…because a scratch on the paintwork can easily be fixed."

Olivia sniffed. "He's going to tear me apart, isn't he? Like, when he finds me."

"No, because he's not going to find you, okay?" Kiah suddenly felt tired. It had been a long day and although she was excited about Lofty's win, all she could think of now was letting a hot shower run all over her body, towelling off, and then crashing on the bed for an hour before getting dressed to go out. *The Creek* held no excitement for her but she'd promised, so she'd go, have a couple of drinks, and then drive home. "Come on, sweetie, unlock the door," she said, her voice softening. Olivia was scared. And Kiah knew exactly what that felt like. "Belle and I won't let Buzz get anywhere near you. What say, we smuggle you into the back of the float, cover you over with horse rugs, then we'll load the horses and take off back to the stables? Come on, Olivia, open the door. Please."

"But—"

"For God's sake, do as she says, Olivia." The deep voice, dripping with exasperation, came from behind the only other closed door in the facility. "I'd really like to leave this cubicle sometime today and I'm not showing my face until you've all gone."

It was the owner of the scuffed brown shoes and matching trousers inside stall one.

A heavy silence followed and the moment Olivia stepped out of the cubicle, Kiah darted forward, her fingers wrapping around the girl's arm and hanging on like a terrier with a rat. No way was she letting Olivia change her mind. Belle, smothering an embarrassed giggle, snaffled Olivia's other arm and between them they marched her toward the exit, where, as Kiah reached forward to open the door, Olivia dug her heels in and they slid to a stop.

"I'm not going out there unless one of you check first," she said, shaking her head. "What if Buzz is, like, waiting for me on the other side of that door, a sawn-off shotgun in one hand and a hunting knife in the other?"

Belle let out a hoot. "Sawn-off shotgun? What bad-ass series have you been binging on lately?"

"It's okay," said Kiah, recognising the pinched face, the rocking body, the wide-eyed stare and identifying with the emotion. She brushed gentle fingers across Olivia's cheek. "It's okay," she repeated. "I'll go first and make sure the coast is clear. Just stay put. I'll be back in a tick."

Eyes alert for one angry bikie dude, with or without weaponry, Kiah barrelled through the doorway only to slam into the back of Jack Sullivan. He was standing, arms folded, blocking entry into the toilet block.

"Jack?" Kiah's face immediately grew hot, the heat spreading down her neck. "Um…are you waiting to go in?"

"Kiah?" He swung around, his hands reaching out to hold her as she stumbled into him. "Everything okay in there?"

"Almost. But what are you doing here?"

He lifted one eyebrow and a smile creased the corners of his lips. "Well, someone had to inform the patrons that the toilets were closed due to a plumbing disaster and then direct them to the old toilet block on the other side of the track."

"You did that?" Kiah, the heat of Jack's fingers seeping into her arms, suddenly felt like hugging him. He must have seen them go into the Men's, worried they'd be disturbed, and after finishing up with Lofty, decided to guard the door. "Thanks, Jack, you're a star. Now, all we have to do is get Olivia into the back of the horse float without being seen, and Lofty and Goldie loaded, and we'll be on our way home."

"Horses are already loaded, so there's only Olivia to sort out."

"Wow! Not just a star but a whole galaxy of them."

There was no sign of Buzz Devlin, or any of his leather-clad bikie friends, so after giving Bella and Olivia the all-clear, Kiah watched them slink furtively through the doorway and take off in the direction of the horse floats. She didn't immediately follow. Instead, deciding Jack deserved an explanation, she hovered, first on one foot, then the other. "What happened with Olivia," she said, finally, "was she crashed—"

"Don't tell me." Jack held up one hand in an I-don't-want-to-know gesture. "Knowing Olivia, it would only give me heartburn and I've run out of antacids." He took a breath and moved closer, lifting a hand to smooth a lock of hair away from her face. "I'm not here because of Olivia — I'm here because of you."

"But—"

"Let me finish." He took another deep breath. "I want to apologize. I was churlish, disrespectful, and that's not acceptable behaviour. Naturally you want to celebrate with your friends at *The Creek* tonight." A smile twitched at the corners of his lips. Lips that were much closer to hers than it was safe for them to be. "Marg would call me an ass, and she'd be right. Marg's always right. Anyway, I'm way out of practice at this sort of thing — so — would you like to come for a meal tomorrow night, instead? We have a roast for Sunday's dinner with crunchy roast potatoes and…and other vegetables and…and…and then we can play Monopoly. Do you like Monopoly? My mother gave Angel a Monopoly board game last Christmas and the kid's been bugging me to play ever since." He stared down at his feet, rubbed a hand across the back of his neck. "Oh God, I'm making a right mess of this. Kiah, would you like to come for a meal tomorrow night and…and…play a game of Monopoly with us?"

Kiah laughed. "Are you asking me out on a play date, Jack?"

Jack grinned, letting out a breath of relief as though finding the right words had taken a lot out of him. "Shall we call it that to start with?"

"Sounds perfect to me." Warmth spread across Kiah's chest. She returned his grin with an even wider one of her own. "I might even bring a couple of barbie dolls along and between us we can play dressing up."

Still smiling, she hurried toward the parking area where she could see the *Windsong* horse float already hooked up to her SUV. Had Jack really asked her on a date? Or was he merely inviting her to spend time with them for Angel's sake? Whatever. He'd made her feel good about herself and she hadn't felt that way for a long, long, time.

Checking out faces in the crowd, ever-vigilant for a sign of Olivia's angry bikie dude, Kiah froze as a familiar face — dirty blonde hair, chiselled jaw, twice-broken nose — appeared amongst a group of men approaching from the opposite direction. All city slickers, all laughing, cracking jokes, as though they'd had a good day's punting and were now off to celebrate.

She shivered, a cold clammy lizard crawling across her skin, then hunched over, pretending to retie her shoelace as the group passed by. She'd seen the face of a man who could bring her new life crumbling down around her ears. The man who spat at her, when she told him what really happened the night the sainted Lieutenant Richard Stanton dropped dead of a heart attack Threatened to make her pay heavily if she ever vilified her husband's name again.

Richard's best friend. Senior Sergeant Connor Preston.

EIGHT

Two days later, after working her butt off all morning, Kiah had had enough.

Her boss wasn't cute. He wasn't dreamy. Didn't send zingy shock waves through her whenever his hand brushed against hers. In fact, Jack Sullivan was an asshole. And, if she didn't get out of the stable, away from him, right now, she'd end up quitting, or hurling a shovel full of manure at his head.

She stamped her foot in frustration. What the heck was he going off about anyway? All she was guilty of was bandaging a horse's leg too tightly — not chopping it off at the shoulder.

With a deep throated growl, Kiah flung herself out of the stable block, then boot-scooted past the wash bay where a horse tied to the rail raised its head and snorted its disapproval, past a large galvanised shed housing the stable's four horse-floats, and finally through a gateway leading into the retiree's paddock.

Since seeing, Senior Lieutenant Connor Preston at the track two days ago — so close, if she'd taken two long steps forward, she could have reached out and touched him — Kiah had been finding it hard to keep her mind on the job. In fact, her concentration was up there with the fairies; her emotions down with the mud crabs. The same question kept spinning around in her head…what was Connor doing at the Wattle Park races? He'd never been a fan of racing so was it merely a coincidence that he was there with friends, or had he traced her whereabouts through the racing industry? And if so, why? Why would he be looking for her now? He'd made his point — very forcibly — the night Richard died. What else could he do? Make sure she never revealed the truth by silencing her forever?

Overhead, the sky had turned a bruised shade of iron grey, a thick dense blanket that pressed down on her, stealing her breath as she stomped through the wet grass. Ugh…just what she needed — more rain, more boot-sucking mud, more sludge and dirt to clean off the gear and the horses after each workout.

Still simmering like a kettle coming to the boil, Kiah's thoughts returned to the incident in Zipper's stable. There'd been no need for Jack to humiliate her in front of her co-workers. He could have explained the problem with the leg bandages, not screamed and carried on like she'd committed a crime worthy of ten lashes followed by a witch-dunking ceremony.

Okay, maybe she had been a little distracted while wrapping Zipper's front legs after her morning gallop. And maybe she had bandaged one a tad tightly. But, hey, as well as evading the mare's sneaky nips, she had two more stalls to clean, another horse to gallop, gear to clean, feeds to mix, and since seeing Connor at the races, her brain had turned into a leaky sieve with a loose handle. But for Jack to say she was an idiot and a threat to the welfare of his horses. And in front of everyone. Not acceptable.

She kicked at a small round stone, sent it spiralling in the direction of two crows squabbling over some tasty treasure they'd unearthed in a pile of fresh horse manure. Letting out loud squawks of disapproval, they flew off, only to circle around twice, hover in the air, and finally land on the top rail of a nearby fence. Their hostile black eyes urging her to move on, pronto; they had a clash of ownership to establish.

Breath short sharp puffs, anger bubbled in Kiah's chest. She'd promised herself never to allow anyone to bully her ever again and was determined to give Jack a piece of her mind — a very large, fiery piece, wrapped up in barbwire — once she'd stopped shaking. After scrambling through a thorny gap in the hedge, she sprinted along the gravel path leading to the solitude of her caravan; a place she could let go, cry, scream, punch a pillow. Whatever helped.

Reaching her home on wheels, she ripped open the door, and, enjoying the sound of the wood and metal bouncing off the side of the caravan, flounced inside and slammed the door shut behind her. The slam reverberating through the air like a pistol shot. Still not finished venting, she dragged off her riding helmet, hurled it on the bed with a *whop* and sank down beside it, fists tightly wound, body rigid.

Jack Sullivan was an asshole.

After last night, when she'd gone to the house for a meal, a couple of glasses of wine and a laugh-filled game of Monopoly — where Angel somehow acquired Mayfair, Park Lane, the Electric Company and three railway stations, thereby cleaning them out — she'd been lulled into believing Jack was different. A man who treated her with respect. And when she was leaving, the way he'd gently run his knuckles across her cheek, then leaned forward and kissed her lightly on the forehead, made her want to grab him by the front of his shirt and pull those soft lips down against hers.

Running stiff fingers through her sweaty helmet hair, Kiah shook her head at the memory of how close she'd come to making a fool of herself. Who was she kidding? Men were all the same the world over and she didn't need a man in her life. Ever. She was woman, hear her roar.

A lethargic looking fly caught in a cobweb running between the bed and the cupboard caught her eye. Most likely male. Probably out on the town, enjoying himself, while his meek little wife stayed home laying eggs. Well, he wouldn't be enjoying himself much longer, not once his eight-legged host appeared on the scene, licking her lips and waving a knife and fork in his direction.

Kiah bent to pull off her boots, once again cringing at the memory of Jack bellowing at her in front of her friends. She'd seen Belle and Olivia's shocked faces as she'd run past them, and even grumpy Steve had raised his eyebrows at Jack's tirade. Frustrated, Kiah kicked the boot across the caravan floor then pounded one fist into her pillow, catching the side of her little finger on the sharp edge of the reading lamp clamped over her bed.

"Ouch!" Jumping up and down, she held her pulsing finger to her chest. That was Jack's fault too. Blasted man made her so mad she didn't know what she was doing.

Grabbing a tray of ice from the small refrigerator tucked in next to the sink, Kiah tipped ice-cubes into a wet flannel and wrapped the flannel around her hand. She couldn't afford to have a sore finger. Not when she was riding Jet for the first time tomorrow.

At the thought of her beloved horse, Kiah's heart slowed and the tight muscles in her shoulders and neck relaxed, one by one. She smiled at a photo of Jet peering out at her from a plastic frame on the chest of drawers beside her bed. She couldn't get over how much he'd changed since that fateful day at the horse sales when she knew she couldn't walk away and leave such a beautiful soul for Cockroach, the creepy horsemeat dealer, to add to his kill list. Back then, Jet's coat had been dull, dry, and brittle; now it was healthy, clean, and shiny. And since he'd been put on a special diet, planned by Greg, the vet, overseen by Jack, and implemented by her, her beautiful black horse had thrived.

She let out a loud huff and scowled at the photo. Okay, Jack had gone out of his way to help her with Jet, but…he was still an asshole.

Muttering under her breath, she yanked off her other boot before topping the kettle up for a much-needed drink of coffee. She banged the kettle on the portable stove and switched on the gas, not caring that water bounced up through the spout and made a pool on the floor. The self-worth she'd inched back over the last three months, the feeling that she wasn't useless after all, that she could do anything she set her mind to, had been blasted to smithereens by Jack's acerbic remarks that made her want to hide in the nearest feed shed and never show her face again.

A loud knock broke through her inner rant.

Immediately, Kiah's hands closed into tight fists, while her eyes, narrowed to slits, fired imaginary bullets through the garish pink wood of her caravan door.

If it was the asshole — he could knock till his knuckles turned purple.

*****

Jack finished rebandaging Zipper's front legs, tucked in the ends, and snorted out a frustrated curse. Had he been too hard on Kiah? Should he have quietly taken her aside and pointed out her mistake, explained how much damage tight bandages could do to a horse's legs?

There was never an excuse for carelessness or lack of concentration when in charge of a horse's wellbeing; especially in a racing stable where an animal's soundness, its ability to race, was in the hands of its groom.

But did he have to yell at her? In front of his staff?

The anger whooshed out of his chest leaving him slumped beside the dark bay mare, guilt a sharp pain behind his ribs. He liked Kiah. And after last night, maybe he was starting to feel something more than 'like.' She was brave, resourceful and loved the horses. Always the first to put her hand up to work extra hours or learn more of the racing industry. Jack was no fool. The first day she arrived, towing that scrawny, thin-as-a-rail rescue horse, begging him for a job, he could tell she knew nothing about working in racing stables. But he'd said yes, anyway. Then stood back and over the next three months watched her literally hit the ground — several times — get back up, straighten her shoulders, tip up her chin and prove to him and to herself that she was capable of anything she put her mind to. Even though there was an intriguing vulnerability about her, Kiah Stanton was one hell of a woman. A woman he'd come close to kissing last night, of contemplating maybe taking the next step on from friendship. Yet today, through his own thoughtless idiocy, he'd wrecked everything.

"Looks like I might have to eat dirt, Zipper," he told the mare as he dodged another nip aimed at his bare arm. "Otherwise she might pack her bags, load her horse in the float and drive out of our lives."

And he couldn't have that. Couldn't imagine the stables without Kiah's twinkling green eyes and happy smile. A smile that made him wake each morning with a new lift to his heart, a spring to his step, hope for the future. Something he thought he'd never feel again when he'd lost Bianca.

Yep. Time to eat that dirt.

Ten minutes later, Jack, a book tucked under one arm, strode up the path to Kia's caravan and knocked on the door.

There was a flurry inside followed by a loud clunk that sounded very much like a boot hitting against the inside of the caravan door. "Go away! I'm not in here!"

He sighed. What did he expect? A box of chocolates and a foot rub? "Open the door, Kiah. Please. I need to talk to you."

"I said I'm not here! Now go and hurl abuse at someone who cares!"

His lips twitched. Good, she was wild-dingo angry and, in his opinion, anger was the best way to get through any bad stuff life hurled at you. Stopped you from cracking. And he'd never forgive himself if he made her cry. With a lift of his shoulders, he banged on the door again. Harder this time. "Kiah, are you decent?" No answer. "'Cos I'm coming in."

Holding his breath, he edged the door open, and, expecting more boots to greet him, popped his head through. The first thing he saw was a set of narrowed green eyes. Cobra eyes. And they were aimed directly at him. "Kiah? Sweetie?" he said, his voice desperate. "I have something to show you."

"Don't want to see it." Kiah spun around and, stretching on tiptoe, reached into a cupboard over the sink.

One hand still on the doorknob, Jack hesitated. Was she reaching for a gun? A blowtorch? A packet of sharp knitting needles?

She dragged down a Winnie-the-Poo coffee mug.

He let out his breath. "Kiah, I…I've come to apologize for acting like a constipated Sergeant Major and bawling you out in front of your friends. That's my bad — and I'm really, really sorry."

"Yes, it was your bad." Not meeting his eyes, Kiah scowled at the half-full jar of Nescafe sitting beside the lone mug on the sink. "And no way am I offering you a coffee. You hurt me, Jack. And I've been hurt too many times in the past to forgive easily."

"I understand."

"No, you don't," she snapped, whirling around to face him, her eyes hot lasers that punctured his chest. "You know nothing about me."

"Well, then, tell me, I'm listening."

"Why should I? You're a man. You wouldn't understand." She stepped away, measured a teaspoon of coffee and one and a half sugars into her mug, her face a mask.

He could see she wasn't ready to discuss anything with him — a man who thought a poxy apology would be enough for what he'd put her through — so he held up the photo album he'd retrieved from a drawer in his office file before venturing across to her caravan. "Is it okay if I show you what can happen to a horse when its legs are bandaged too tightly?"

When she nodded, he placed the album on the bed, open at a photo of a magnificent chestnut horse with weeping pressure sores on both front legs.

Kiah moved closer to the bed and stared down at the photo, frowning. It was a full minute before she spoke and when she did there was a slight crack in her voice. "Are you saying tight bandages caused this?"

Jack nodded. "Restricts the circulation. What happens is the blood supply to the tendons in the horse's leg gets compromised when a bandage is wrapped too tightly."

She was quiet for a moment, studying the photo, head tipped slightly to the side. "I've seen a picture of this horse somewhere else." She continued to stare down at the photo before drawing in a quick breath. "Is that the horse in the painting over your front gate…the horse the stable is named after?"

"Yes. It's Windsong. The fastest horse my Uncle Dan ever trained." Regret, like a ten-pound iron ball, smashed Jack in the chest. Didn't matter how many times he looked at the photo in the album, it affected him the same way. "He was favourite for the Derby three years ago and destined to win more group races than you could poke a stick at."

Kiah's face softened as she looked up at him. "What happened?"

"A rogue groom, cousin to the connections of the second favourite in the Derby — that's what happened to him."

"What do you mean?"

"Lowlife deliberately tightened the bandages on the horse's legs over several days and consequently, Windsong didn't race in the Derby." Jack let out a sigh. "In fact, he never raced again."

He watched Kiah's eyes widen. "Did your uncle go to the police, lay charges against the groom?"

"He denied everything." Jack shrugged. "Blamed Uncle Dan. Claimed the trainer was responsible for the bandaging, not him."

"Mongrel. Did your uncle take the matter further?"

Jack's chest clenched. He shook his head. "I'm afraid mud sticks — even when it's false — so when Uncle Dan's other owners started taking their horses out of the stable, he stopped talking, lost interest in everything around him. Two weeks later his body was found in his crashed car at the bottom of a cliff." Jack closed his eyes, still seeing his uncle's mangled body on the table when he went to identify him at the morgue.

"Ohmygod!" Kiah grabbed Jack's hand and squeezed. "I'm so sorry."

"There were no signs of braking on the road — he just aimed the car at the edge of the cliff and accelerated," The lump in Jack's throat was so large it almost choked him. "When the lawyer read the will and told me Uncle Dan had left Windsong Racing Stables to me, even though my family were dead against me giving up my position in the family business to train horses, I vowed to make Windsong a place where horses were trained with care, respect and integrity."

A tear ran down Kia's cheek. "I'm sorry for being careless with the bandages, Jack. I-I didn't know. I'll do all the dirty jobs no one else wants to do to make up for it."

Jack nodded, not trusting his voice. Kiah's tears were doing strange things to his emotions. Snarling them in bunches and making it hard for him to breathe.

Jack moved closer, tugging her gently against him. All the better to breathe in her minty chewing gum smell, to feel the wild beat of her heart as it hammered against his chest and hear the soft little hiccuppy sounds that made him want to comfort her. With one finger under her chin, he tipped her head back to look up at him. "Alright, Kiah?"

"Mmm…" She reached up to run her fingers lightly across his cheek, the tip of her tongue slowly wetting her lips, her eyes never leaving his.

"Oh, God, you're killing me here, Kiah," he growled, the fabric across his groin tightening as the fingers on her other hand smoothed under his shirt, every touch on his bare skin an electric shock that sent zings of pleasure all the way from the top of his head down to his ten toes clenched inside his scuffed work boots.

"That's good," she whispered, the hint of a smile on her lips.

"Good," he repeated, his voice cracking as he leaned in, both hands resting on her shoulders. "'Cos I've wanted to do this from the very first day I saw you."

She responded, her tongue lapping, twining with his, her hungry moans causing all extraneous non-Kiah thoughts to fly from Jack's head and out the caravan window.

Heat, a blazing fire, stroked and then roared into every infinitesimal part of his body. He had to have more of her. With his lips glued to hers, he dragged her harder up against him, his grip tightening, his mind spinning as the kiss intensified.

It took him a few moments to realize she'd stiffened in his arms. Then both fists slammed into his chest, hard, shoving him away. Surprised, confused, he lost his balance and stumbled backwards, the sharp corner of the sink catching him on the right hip before he could steady himself. "Kiah…?"

"Go!" Face pale, eyes wild, she backed away from him, visibly shaking. What had just happened? It was like she wasn't in the caravan any more, like she'd gone somewhere else in her mind. "Please, Jack. Just go."

NINE

The following day, Kiah stood in the middle of the sandy lunging arena and asked her horse, Jet, to walk around her in a twenty-metre circle. The rain from yesterday had disappeared and been replaced by a surprisingly hot sun that was busy drying out puddles, while down in the paddock nearest the front gate, the young foals, bushy tails aloft like flags, were prancing and squealing and chasing each other, flecks of mud splattering from their tiny hooves as they darted around their long-suffering mothers.

She'd been dodging around Jack all morning, keeping her head down so as to not meet his eye. God, what must the poor guy be thinking? That she was a manipulator? A tease? A total kook? She'd virtually instigated that kiss, yet, when he'd responded — and oh, how he'd responded — she'd pushed him away, no, shoved him away, so hard, he'd stumbled in the close quarters of the caravan and banged his hip against the corner of the stainless-steel sink. Must have hurt, but the pain didn't appear to register, instead, he'd just stared at her — his eyes bewildered, then frustrated, and finally seemingly horrified at what he'd done. After apologizing in a gruff, slightly strained voice, he'd scooped up the photo album from the bed and hurried out, muttering something over his shoulder about making sure she didn't forget to give the new horse in stable 12, his stomach-ulcer medication.

Kiah had stood on the rickety steps of the caravan and watched Jack stride off, his neck and shoulders rigid, his fingers clamped like eagle's claws around the photo album. She'd wanted to call him back. Explain why she'd panicked and pushed him away. That she was soiled goods, too damaged by her past to ever trust her heart again. Let him know that it was nothing to do with his stolen kiss.

But she couldn't do it. Didn't have the words.

Kiah's cheeks warmed at the memory of the kiss. Of Jack's soft lips feathering against hers. Of her legs turning to stretchy toffee. Of the tingly ache down below. And when his tongue licked at her bottom lip and she'd tasted coffee, spearmint and the salt from her own tears, she'd actually reached up on her toes for a better angle at his hot mouth… and then he'd tightened his arms around her, and she'd freaked. She'd been catapulted back into painful memories of being held so tightly, so forcefully, she couldn't breathe. Of iron fingers digging into her arms leaving bruises. Of rough, ugly, forced kisses and a thick phlegmy tongue shoved dispassionately down her throat, choking her, cutting off her air, making her think she was going to die…

With difficulty, Kiah pushed the memory of the incident in the caravan aside and prepared herself to stay cool and detached in the future. Jack Sullivan was her boss, that's all. And today, she was going to ride her very own horse for the first time, enjoy the experience, and forget all about a certain man's strong jaw and his feathery-soft lips.

With one hand, Kiah tugged the front of her battered Akubra further down over her eyes. She rarely ventured outside in the sun without its protection now. Yet, when she'd first arrived at *Windsong*, a complete and utter newbie, she'd thought bush hats were only for cowboys. Didn't take long to work out how wrong she was. After a week of being exposed to the skin-damaging Australian sun, especially that hour after lunch spent pushing a wheelbarrow around the rutted paddocks collecting manure, Kiah realized if she didn't change her views on wearing a bush hat, she'd end up looking, not like a cowboy, but his battered leather saddle. And the day she'd finally bought an Akubra in a second-hand store in the main street of Shadow Creek, she'd strutted into the stable block, imagining the hat would make her blend in and become an accepted part of the team. Only to be met by dried up, taciturn old Steve, ever the pessimist. He'd quickly deflated her pleasure by informing her in that rusty voice of his that between twelve to fourteen rabbits had to die so she could wear the hat.

"T-r-o-t." Kiah's heart did a little two-step dance of love for her horse, as, on the end of the lunge lead, Jet moved from a walk into a smooth regular trot. She'd named him well. His coat was now a shiny jet black, and although still needing more weight, his muscles rippled with every stride.

Sand kicked up onto the metal sides of the lunging arena making rhythmic ding sounds as Jet trotted around, ears pricked, enjoying his time out of the stable; one ding louder than the others, giving him an excuse to shy and perform a joyful exuberant buck, followed by a high-pitched squeal. Kiah grinned and gave him the order to canter, laughing when he gave another playful buck before settling into a ground covering lope.

After twelve weeks of being worked on the walker, lunging, swimming, special feed, new shoes and veterinary care, Jet was almost ready to join Jack's racing team. They'd tracked his passport via his microchip and discovered, although he'd never actually raced, his registered racing name was Party Pooper. At four years old he was a little late starting a racing career, but to Kiah, it didn't matter whether he made it on the racetrack or not; he was her love, her best friend, and he would have a home with her for the rest of his life.

Once she'd finished lunging, she was going to put her foot in the stirrup and swing up into the saddle — be the first to ride her horse since he'd arrived at *Windsong*. Her stomach clenched in both anticipation and the thought of all those jockeys Jet had unceremoniously dumped in the dirt on the way to a barrier trial. Eight times in total. The reason he'd subsequently been ostracised by the jockeys, beaten by the owner and thrown into a dusty paddock at the back of the property, where, for the next six months, he'd existed on what he could forage — until the owner finally went bankrupt and his livestock sent off to the sale.

"Whoa…" Bringing Jet to a halt she asked him to walk across to her so she could unclip the lunge line from the halter fitted over his bridle.

As though to make it easier for her, Jet shoved his nose into her chest. She grinned. More likely looking for treats than being cooperative. "Just one," she told him, mock stern, as she dug a small piece of carrot from the front pocket of her jodhpurs and held it out on the palm of her hand. As he snuffled it up, his soft whiskery nose tickling her palm, her heart softened into one big squashy marshmallow. This horse, with the big personality and the heart of a lion, was hers. All hers. She swallowed the sudden lump in her throat and sniffed. Even after twelve weeks, two days and five hours, it was still hard to believe, after all those years without anyone or anything to care for — she was now the proud mother of a horse.

After swapping her Akubra for her riding helmet, she tugged both stirrups down, adjusted them to her length, and then led Jet across to the blue plastic crate she'd brought into the ring to make it easier to mount.

Instead of the light racing saddle she normally rode in when galloping the horses on the track, Kiah had 'borrowed' a large beautifully tooled leather Western saddle from the tack room. She'd found the saddle under a pile of discarded moth-eaten horse rugs and inside a fluffy pink saddle cover featuring a myriad of tarnished silver stars. Everything in the tack room was there for all to use, and as she'd feel much safer in a bigger saddle with a horn on the front to hang onto in an emergency, she didn't stop to ask who owned the Western saddle. Instead, she'd stuck to the communal code of — 'first in best dressed'.

"You'll look after your mum, won't you?" Kiah said, gently pushing Jet's nose away from her pocket where he'd been rummaging for more treats. She flicked a long piece of his forelock from under the browband of his bridle and smiled. He was such a handsome boy. "Don't worry," she told him. "There'll be lots of treats later. When we finish our ride."

Speaking of handsome boys, she could see Jack Sullivan striding towards the lunging arena, head thrown back, his dark hair gusting in the wind. Thor, the God of Thunder, dressed in well-fitting moleskins and scuffed R M William's riding boots. If she hadn't panicked yesterday, she'd have enjoyed this picture of masculinity heading her way. Welcomed the vision with an appreciative smile. Instead, fingers feeling fat and clumsy, Kiah fiddled with the chin strap on her riding helmet, missing the connection three times before managing to do up the buckle.

By now, Jack was close enough for her to discreetly assess the five o'clock shadow emphasizing his strong jaw and to award the work of art a point-score of ten out of ten. What now? Stare at the ground and avoid eye contact? Or pretend yesterday didn't happen?

She was so tired of all these conflicting emotions and how they were affecting her new life. Of the ugly memories that sometimes made the pain inside her chest so severe she didn't think she'd be able to draw the next breath.

Would she ever get over what Richard had done to her? She sighed. And where was her warrior princess persona when she needed it?

Sensing Jack's eyes on her, Kiah rubbed at an imaginary speck of dirt under Jet's silky mane.

"Kiah? What the hell do you think you're doing?"

Kiah's head shot up. Immediately forgetting the imaginary spot of dirt, she straightened her shoulders and glared at him; a slow simmer of anger beginning to ignite in her chest. "What does it look like?"

"It looks like you're about to do something you'll regret later. A common trait of yours." She watched him drag in a breath and let it out slowly. "This horse hasn't been ridden for almost a year. He's dangerous."

With a flick of her head, she stepped onto the crate and glared at him. "My horse. My danger."

"Don't be ridiculous. Let me ride him first, then, when I've settled him, you can hop on."

Ridiculous?

Now he'd gotten her really steamed. Given her Alta ego a razor-sharp poke in the ribs, woken her, and she was spitting fire. "Why? Because you're this fancy pansy hot cowboy who can last eight seconds on the wildest, meanest buckjumper at the rodeo — and I'm what? A helpless powder-puff female who needs a big man to protect her?"

Kiah could see Jack's eyes narrowing, his frown deepening. Had she gone too far? She hunched her shoulders, held her breath, waiting for a Richard-like explosion. However, when Jack spoke again his voice was quiet, soothing, as though talking his eight-year-old daughter, Angel, out of a sulk. "I'm not suggesting you're incapable of riding your horse, Kiah. It's just that I break in all the youngsters before they go into training, so I'm more experienced at surviving a series of bucks…and…and I'm worried you'll get hurt." He ran a hand through his curly black hair, making it stick up at the back like a cocky. "Remember, the last time Jet was ridden, he dumped his jockey in the middle of the track and galloped off, leaving the poor guy lying in a heap with a broken collarbone."

Kiah could feel her bottom lip doing one of those stubborn, teenage-like juts. "Whatever…I'm still riding Jet first." She knew she was being completely irrational, probably *did* sound like his eight-year-old daughter in a sulk. She also knew Jack wasn't like Richard, wasn't telling her what to do because he was a bully — he was only looking out for her. But after twelve years of being told what she could and couldn't do, Kiah was determined to look out for herself. She didn't need a man to do that for her. Whether she ended up in the dirt, or even in a neck-brace, it was her decision. Lifting her chin in defiance, she did the girth up one more hole and patted her horse's warm neck. "Jet will look after me. He loves me."

Jack gave a snort.

"And *I* love *him*."

"What? And that's all it takes to prevent a horse from breaking your neck?"

At Jack's words her steadfast resolve wavered a smidgen. She checked Jet's eyes, prayed that sparkle in the corner of his left eye was an expression of love and not a contemplation of naughtiness. "Er…yes."

"Your call." Jack gave her a thumbs up and leaned his elbows on the lunging-ring gate. The muscles on his arms pushed against the short sleeves of his polo as though the cotton material was restricting his masculinity. "By the way, nice saddle you've got there."

Kiah frowned. Maybe the communal code of 'first in best dressed' didn't apply to everything. "I found it buried in the corner of the tack room."

Eyes still on the finely tooled Western saddle, Jack nodded, then patted the top rail of the lunging arena. "So, is it okay if I sit here on the fence and watch you two lovebirds in action? Ring for an ambulance if necessary?" His eyes twinkled and the corners of his lips hitched in a grin. "Or would you rather do *that* yourself too? I can always hand you the phone so you can dial 0-0-0. You know…once you regain consciousness."

Kiah couldn't stop a wayward giggle from bubbling up and tickling her throat. She let out a loud laugh and looked at Jack properly for the first time since he'd shown up. God, he had beautiful eyes. Grey-blue like the sky on a clear day. How had she managed to push him away when he kissed her yesterday? Richard had a lot to answer for. "Well, okay, I guess I can let you do that."

"I'm honored." Jack bowed his head and grinned and then his face changed, became more serious. He looked at the ground, shuffled his feet before speaking. "Kiah, before we go any further, I-I need to clear the air between us." He slowly snaked in a deep breath that seemed to steady him. "I just want to say, I'm sorry for what happened yesterday."

"Which part of yesterday?"

"All of it. I'm sorry I yelled at you and I'm sorry I kissed you."

"You're sorry you kissed me?" Kiah raised both eyebrows.

"Well…"

"I'm not," she said, and so as not to look into those mesmerizing eyes that did weird tingly things to her insides, Kiah fiddled with the stirrup, letting it down one hole then putting it back up again. "And, if we're into apologies, I'm sorry too."

"No, Kiah, you have no need to—"

"I'm sorry I bandaged Zipper's legs too tightly and…and I'm sorry for what happened later. For the way I reacted to your kiss. It was all just a bit too…" She paused, tried to find the right words to explain why she'd freaked out. That when his arms tightened around her, she'd felt like her air supply had been cut off? That she wanted to scream, throw things? That her heart was hammering so fiercely against her chest she'd feared it would break free from her body? Kiah chewed on her bottom lip. How could she tell Jack that he'd caused her to have a panic attack without going into details about her life prior to arriving at *Windsong*?

Jack gave a sheepish half-smile. "All just a bit too…*soon*?"

Yes, yes, that would do nicely. She nodded.

"*My* bad," he continued. "I'd just thrust a picture of Windsong's damaged legs in front of you and then told you the sad story about my Uncle Dan. You were upset and I took advantage of your vulnerability. Hell, you had every right to toss me across the room." He ran a hand through his hair, before giving her puppy-dog eyes. "So…are we okay now?"

She screwed up her nose, pretending to think about it. "Hmm…guess so. As long as you stop trying to put me off riding Jet."

Jack settled himself more comfortably on the fence then flicked a grin in her direction. "In that case, what are you waiting for? Let's see some action." He crossed his arms, as though waiting to be entertained. "Come on, you can't ride your horse unless you climb on board."

"Yes, sir. Of course, sir. Whatever you say, sir." Kiah, glad Jack had moved on, gave a mock salute, then gathered up her reins, set her foot in the stirrup, and swung into the saddle. She could do this. She could ride her unpredictable horse. And if she did fall off, so what? The sand in the round yard looked soft. Jack Sullivan, the man she would *like* to trust, *like* to try kissing again sometime soon, sat perched on the fence, a wide grin on his face. And if she did hurt herself, he was ready and waiting to pick her up and carry her to bed.

Which may not be such a bad thing after all.

*****

Six days later, Kiah couldn't stop the grin from hijacking her face. It kept ballooning and unrolling and spreading, until her jaw ached.

She and Angel were on their usual Sunday morning ride; Angel aboard her pony, Biscuit, while Kiah rode Molly, a sweet-natured 17hh grey thoroughbred from the retirees' paddock and Kiah was in the middle of telling Angel about how amazing it had been when she'd first ridden Jet.

Instead of bucking, he'd behaved like a pony-clubber, first in the round yard, and then in the open paddock. And wow. What an experience. The ride had left Kiah on the most amazing high of her life. And she could still feel it, *six days later*. Who'd have thought riding her own horse for the first time could result in so many heady endorphins and peptides and wild uncontrollable fireworks jetting their way into her system…with not a drug, nor a glass of alcohol in sight.

"That's *so* cool." Angel's eager voice brought Kiah's wild euphoria back to earth with a jolt. Biscuit and Molly were mooching along, their riders content to let them follow a sandy track running alongside Shadow Creek, the crystal-clear, pebble-bottomed winding waterway which the small country town was named after. Their destination, a flattish piece of land on top of Wombat Hill; perfect for setting up their picnic and surveying the countryside spread out below like a timeless rural painting by Streeton.

Riding beside Kiah, a blonde plait poking out from each side of her bright pink Frozen riding helmet, Angel regarded her with the same gray-blue eyes as her dad. "And, what? Jet didn't buck? Not even once?"

"Well…" Kiah wriggled her nose at Angel who was absorbing every word of her story with wide eyes. "Only one *teeny, tiny* naughtiness. Just a couple of little pigroots that didn't even shift me in the saddle," she admitted, touching Molly lightly with her heels to keep her from dropping her head low enough to grab a tempting bite of grass. "But it wasn't Jet's fault. It was the Mumma kangaroo that's been hanging around the property. You know, the one with the cheeky little joey who keeps popping his head out of the pouch to see what's going on."

Eyes lighting up, Angel nodded. "Awww…I *looove* that joey."

"Well, as we were nearing the tractor shed, Mumma popped out from behind and then went bounding across the paddock. Naturally, Jet spun around and got a bit humpy for a minute or two." Kiah grinned, the excitement hitting her smack bang in the solar plexus again. "Other than that, nope, my big bad buckjumper was a pussycat."

Kiah bit back a chuckle. Unlike Jack, who'd got a bit snippy when she'd proven him wrong. Proven that if there's a special love between a girl and her horse — and if she's riding in a big Western saddle with a horn on the front — she's less likely to get bucked off.

"Race you to the top of the hill!" Angel let out a sudden yell, her nose crinkling, her eyes already on her destination as she leaned over Biscuit's neck and urged the pony forward. "Last one there's a three-legged goat with a smelly bum!"

Kiah laughed as she watched Angel, body lying flat against her pony's neck, heels banging against his fat sides, take off up the hill at a gallop. No doubt about it, Jack was going to have a hard time talking this kid out of becoming a jockey. She was a natural.

And of course, Kiah, taken by surprise and too busy laughing, ended up being the 'three-legged goat with a smelly bum'.

Sunday lunch, prepared and packed by the inimitable Marg, was always a surprise, a goodie-box to be opened and drooled over. Sometimes they'd find little home-made pies and pasties in Angel's backpack, or dagwood sandwiches with fillings that made their mouth water, and one Sunday they'd even unwrapped half a roast chicken, little roast potatoes and still-warm, home-made bread. However, today's lunch of pizza, juicy peaches and two plump, almost obese, home-made chocolate and coconut lamingtons, one each, proved a hit with Angel.

"Yummo. This has gotta be my favorite," Angel said, between giant-sized bites of pizza, the sauce oozing onto her chin. "Marg says Margarita pizza is her sig…signal…sinnital…"

"Signature dish?"

"Yep. That dish." Angel nodded. "But when she makes them for me, she adds pineapple and cuts the pineapple into wacky little horsey shapes and then sprinkles them across the top." Her grin widened. "And she does all that just for me."

"Marg spoils you," Kiah said, as she unsaddled Molly and let her loose in the roped off yard with Biscuit. She leaned the finely-tooled Western saddle against a tree, being careful not to scratch it, before squatting on the blanket next to Angel. The beautiful big saddle had been so comfortable when riding Jet, especially after using the barely-there racing saddles on the race horses, that she'd decided to 'borrow' the saddle for their Sunday morning rides in future, as well.

"Nah. Marg loves me." Angel tipped her head to the side and grinned. A grin that said she knew she could twist the motherly housekeeper around not only her little finger, but every finger on both hands. Maybe even her toes.

"Same thing." Kiah laughed and made a grab for the last slice of pizza before Angel could snaffle it. The kid might be small, but, boy, she was unfillable.

"Your saddle…" Angel wiped her mouth with a napkin while studying the hand-embossed leather saddle propped against the tree beside her. "I think I've seen it somewhere before."

"Do you know who it belongs to? I found it buried under some old horse rugs in the tack-room. Looked like it'd been there for years, so I cleaned it up and rode Jet in it last Monday. Beautiful saddle. Extra comfy. And that horn in the front is perfect for hanging onto in an emergency." Kiah let out a laugh. "And I figured, riding Jet for the first time, I needed all the emergency support I could find."

Angel, eyes still on the saddle, climbed to her feet and moved closer. Lost in thought, she ran a small hand over the quality leather, caressing the saddle as though it were a long-lost puppy. "Um…think I saw it at our old place, before we came here. I was only little then, so it's hard to remember."

"Where did you live before you and your dad came to live at *Windsong*?"

"With my Granny Sullivan. In Adelaide. But when Daddy and I shifted here, three years ago, Pop said Granny couldn't come and visit us. Said it was too dangerous. Something about crooked gangs and dirty horses." Her frown deepened. "And he made Granny cry."

Kiah ached to give Angel a hug. Never knowing her mother and then having her grandmother taken from her…what this little girl had endured was crazy sad. "I'm sorry, Angel. That's awful. So, what? You don't see your grandparents anymore?"

"Oh yes, once a month we go to my grandparent's house for dinner. My Uncle Michael, Aunty Jem and two *boy* cousins go too." She rolled her eyes. "Jamie and Cruz. Both icky. 'Specially Cruz. He pinches me when no-one's looking and when I punch him in the face 'cos his pinch hurt, *I'm* the one who gets in trouble." Angel, still examining the saddle, lifted the flap and peered at something underneath. She let out a cry, and as she turned to Kiah, she was dancing up and down on the spot, barely able to contain her excitement. "Look! Look at this, Kiah!"

Grabbing a lamington, after all there were only two available and knowing Angel's insatiable appetite and propensity to grab cake first and be questioned whether it was hers or not, second, Kiah leant closer to see what Angel was getting excited about.

Two letters were imprinted under the flap. B. S.

She'd noticed the two letters when she'd been cleaning the saddle earlier in the week, but thought nothing more of them at the time.

"B.S. Bianca Stanton. I-It's my mum's saddle." Angel's voice was soft, breathless, almost reverent as she ran one finger over the letters imprinted into the leather. "I knew I'd seen the saddle before. I remember when I was little watching Daddy oil it every Sunday afternoon. Sometimes he let me rub the leather with a special soft cloth. He told me my mum had bought this saddle, just before I was born, but she never got to use it." Angel let out a soft sigh. 'Cos my mummy died having me."

The bottom fell out of Kiah's heart. She opened her mouth to speak, but no sound came out. No wonder Jack had been staring at the saddle on Monday when she'd put it on Jet to ride him for the first time. It was his dead wife's saddle. And he hadn't said a word. "Oh, Angel, sweetheart, I'm so sorry. I didn't know the saddle belonged to your mum. I should have asked, but everyone just takes whatever they need from the tack room, and-and I thought it was okay. Sweetheart, I-I don't know what to say."

"It's okay, Kiah." Angel patted Kiah on the arm, her smile a little wobbly. "I didn't know my mummy, but I know she'd be happy for you to use her saddle. Daddy said she was not just beautiful on the outside, but an angel on the inside. That's how I got my name."

Kiah felt a sting of tears behind her eyes. She sniffed, forced her lips into a smile. This little girl was not only wise for her years, she'd also inherited her mother's beautiful soul. "Thank you, Angel. It will be an honor for me to ride in your mum's saddle and I'll clean it every Sunday afternoon, just like your dad used to." She bit back another teary lip wobble before going on. "You can help me, if you like"

Kiah nodded. "I'd like that."

"It'll be the cleanest and best cared for saddle in the whole tack room. I promise."

"Okay," said Angel. "Now, I'm still hungry. Any pizza left?"

Kiah leant forward and tickled her. "Not unless you hid a slice in your pocket."

The two horses lifted their heads from the grass to watch them roll around the ground, laughing and tickling each other. 13hh Biscuit and 17hh Molly, like Danny and Arnie in the movie, *Twins*, were standing shoulder-to-leg inside the roped off enclosure Kiah had constructed the day after their very first Sunday ride. Knowing the horses would be a lot happier loose, eating grass, than tied to a tree, she'd spent two hours with rope and wire, constructing a permanent yard for them.

Once the last peach had been eaten and the pizza and lamington crumbs siphoned up, Kiah and Angel returned the loose wrapping paper to Angel's lunch box, before saddling their mounts for the return journey.

The sun warmed their backs and warbling magpies conversed from behind the gum leaves high in the Eucalyptus trees as they wandered back alongside the creek. Kiah, happy to listen to the sound of the running water and enjoy the distinctive strong waft of eucalyptus, couldn't stop thinking about Bianca's saddle. She was tossing up between asking Jack's permission to continue using the saddle, to return it to its dusty grave in the tack room, or merely pretend she knew nothing about the original owner, when Angel broke the silence. "Kiah?" she said, fiddling with a piece of Biscuit's mane. "Do all boys smell a bit funny?"

"Depends what you mean by 'a bit funny'."

"You know, like stinky socks and…and the inside of a school backpack on a hot day when you've brought sardine sandwiches for lunch."

Kiah bit back a laugh. "Ooh, that smelly, hey?" She could definitely relate to the smell of sardine sandwiches by lunch time, having endured the same totally inedible lunch herself, way back in primary school. "Why don't you just tell Marg you don't like sardine sandwiches?"

"Oh, no, Marg wouldn't make me eat…no, no, that's not what I meant." Angel frowned at the ground, clearly searching for the right words to express herself. "I'm just saying, that's what boys smell like." She looked up, the little frown lines between her eyes deepening. "Do they smell better when they get older?"

"Definitely." Kiah grinned. "You wait until they find out about underarm spray and cologne. Even a nice scented soap or shampoo." She leant across and tugged on one of Angel's plaits, her grin widening. "Give the little stinkers another six or seven years and their smelly boy stage will be over." And then of course Jack's worries would *really* begin. Her grin widened even further at the thought of Jack's lustrous black hair getting greyer with every nice smelling boy Angel brought home.

"Race you to the turn off." Angel, evidently content with that explanation, grinned up at Kiah before leaning forward and booting Biscuit into a gallop.

"You're on!"

Kiah let Angel get fifty yards ahead before she urged Molly into a gallop, but even with a head start, Biscuit's little legs couldn't compete with Molly on the homeward trek. The old thoroughbred knew that before she rejoined the other retirees in the shady paddock near the house, there was a tasty molasses flavored meal of chaff, oats, and bran waiting for her in the spare stable next to Biscuit.

When they reached the final stretch, the grass verge beside the road leading back to *Windsong*, Kiah insisted the horses slow down, walk the rest of the way on a long rein so they'd be cooled down by the time they arrived home. There was a bit of jogging involved, but mostly Molly and Biscuit were content to stride out at the walk, ears forward, in anticipation of food.

Like every Sunday, once they'd hosed their horses down, scraped and toweled them dry, chatting and laughing the whole time, Angel skipped back to the house while Kiah stayed in the stable block a little longer, making sure to clean any sweat or dirt off Bianca's precious saddle, before zipping it back into its faded pink saddle cover which she'd washed during the week. As well as being filthy, it had smelt of mice and their droppings. She was still debating with herself whether to bring up the subject with Jack re continuing to use the saddle or not as she wandered along the graveled path to her caravan. Would seeing Kiah ride in his dead wife's saddle cause Jack more pain? Or would it help him to move on?

Her caravan, hidden from prying eyes by a straggly hedge, shaded by an enormous weeping willow tree, the branches so low, on windy nights they caressed the roof of the caravan, Kiah had come to love living there. At first, she'd been appalled that the accommodation mentioned in Jack's advert turned out to be an old but modernized caravan, but over the weeks, and now months, she'd come to love her own little piece of paradise, tucked away from the noise and hustle of life in a racing stable.

Kiah smiled to herself, remembering Angel's funny and sometimes insightful questions on their weekly rides. She should write a book for kids.

Listening to, and answering Angel's many questions, had given her enough material to write a 300-page tome.

Humming to herself, while anticipating a hot shower, a change of clothes and finishing the latest e-book on her Kindle, an hilarious cozy mystery by her favorite author, Kiah smiled at the thought of Angel, in six years' time, when boys stopped smelling of week-old socks and creek yabbies, and more of pimple cream and their father's underarm spray. Hand outstretched, ready to open the caravan door, she stumbled to a halt.

Her heart stuttered, her eyes bugged, couldn't believe what they were seeing, and her throat closed over in white hot fear. Blood was splattered across her pretty pink caravan door. And affixed to the middle with a bent rusty nail was a large grey gutted rabbit, its lifeless eyes staring at her in flat reproach.

She skidded backwards, almost tripping over her feet in her haste to get away, her hand covering her mouth to prevent the silent scream from escaping. Who would do such a thing? Who had a mind so sick they'd kill a rabbit and hang it on her door?

Her legs gave way and she crumpled to her knees. She could hear someone keening, moaning, making soft whimpering sounds. And then realized the sounds were coming from her and forced herself to stop. She couldn't let fear dictate her life any more. Those days were behind her.

Heart still thumping in her ears, she pushed to her feet, and with legs weaker than a day-old lamb, lurched forward. There was a shocking menace in this grizzly message. Menace that sent cold chills piercing her chest with sharp fingers of ice that stabbed and twisted and robbed her of breath. Was this the work of the man she'd seen at the Wattle Park race-track last week? Richard's best friend, the granite-faced Senior Sergeant Connor Preston? The man who'd threatened her the day Richard died?

If so, why? What else was he trying to tell her?

And why now?

TEN

"What in the blue blazes…?"

Kiah spun around so quickly her legs threatened to give way under her. Breath hooked in her throat, she let out a gasp of relief. "Jack? You gave me a scare…"

"Are you alright?"

She steadied herself by leaning against the side of the caravan, making sure no part of her body brushed up against the door. *Was she alright*? What, with a bucket of blood covering her front door, plus a chilling message that screamed: 'this could be you if you open your mouth'?

"Yes, yes, I'm fine," she said, attempting to hold back the bubble of hysterical laughter threatening to hijack her throat. "I get dead animals nailed to my front door every second day."

"Kiah…" Jack closed the gap between them, his arms immediately folding around her, drawing her body up against his. Kiah closed her eyes and breathed in his every-day Jack smell — horses, hay and sunshine. His solid chest, covered by a soft woolen sweater that fit like a glove, pressed against her cheek, so warm, so solid and safe. His arms wrapped tightly around her weren't making her gasp for air like the day in the caravan; instead, she welcomed their comfort and snuggled closer. If only she could stay like this forever. Never leave the safety of Jack's arms. Never have to look in that poor mutilated rabbit's dead eyes again.

"Bloody hell…" Jack's chest pulsated as he spoke. The vibration from his words scraping her cheek. "Who did this? And how the blazes did they get in without me seeing them? I've been in and out of the stables all morning."

Exactly Kiah's thoughts. Along with how glad she was that her horse, Jet, was installed in the stable block with the other racers now. If he'd still been in the paddock behind the caravan, would it have been *his* mutilated body she'd found, instead of a rabbit's? "Well," she said, looking up from Jack's chest and pushing that thought away before it consumed her. "Whoever it was, didn't wander down the driveway, gutted rabbit in one hand, and a bucket of blood in the other."

He lifted one eyebrow; the corners of his mouth set in a straight line as he met her gaze. "The only way anyone could get in without me seeing them is from Old Man Jones's property."

"Along his boundary road?"

"Yeah. Then across our back paddock to your caravan." She felt Jack shake his head. Heard him curse under his breath. "This is my fault," he said. "I should have had cameras installed on your caravan the day you arrived. Damn it. Didn't realize how isolated you are back here."

"I've enjoyed the privacy — until now." She looked up, spearing him with her eyes. "And it's *not* your fault. *You* didn't do this."

Jack let out a frustrated breath as he gently pulled away from her and stepped back. She wanted to haul him against her again, beg him to stay. Instead, she sent him a weak smile when he squeezed the top of her arm then walked over to the caravan to study the furry corpse.

Kiah shivered, the chill slamming into her with the loss of Jack's comforting body-warmth. She watched him examine the gutted animal from all angles, being careful not to touch the evidence. Probably thought the culprit might have left fingerprints for the police to match. Unfortunately, Kiah knew, if Connor was the culprit, he'd have worn gloves. There'd be no fingerprints. No trace of his DNA left behind. Policemen learned all the bad guys' tricks during their investigations. The corrupt ones utilizing them for their own personal benefit.

"I have no idea what the gutted rabbit's all about. Nor the blood." Jack flicked a glance at her. "You?"

Kiah shook her head.

"Right, let's get you into the house. You look cold as a frog and whiter than Casper's ghost. Reckon you could do with a strong coffee." A tight smile creased his lips. "Or maybe a brandy."

Kiah shivered again. She flicked a glance in the direction of the rabbit pinned like a butterfly specimen to her blood splattered door. "What about Bugs?"

"He's not going anywhere." Jack took one of Kiah's cold hands in his, massaged it between his larger rougher hands to warm it up, then swapped over and rubbed the other one. It was so personal and comforting Kiah struggled not to cry. "Come on, let's get that drink and talk about this. See if you can think of anyone who has a grudge against you." He linked his hand with hers. "Without a freaking rabbit staring us in the eye."

Holding hands, Jack's strong fingers entwined in hers, they made their way along the graveled path away from the caravan. The straggly hedge on one side, the overgrown geranium bushes, their bright red flowers highlighted against the dull greenery, on the other. For a moment she allowed herself to forget the nightmare pinned on her caravan door, forget the fear of Connor's threats, and enjoy the little jolts of lightning that were currently zinging between Jack's hand and hers. She took a shaky breath and let it out slowly. Was Jack feeling them too? Or was he was merely being kind, typically Jack? And then she decided that was enough, for now. This feeling between them. She'd step back, take a deep breath, and let Jack's strength and kindness soothe her rattled nerves.

But it didn't last long…

"Do we *have* to get the police involved?" Kiah sat on the chair Marg had pushed forward for her the moment they'd walked into the kitchen. A cup of hot sweet tea in her hand, Kiah stared up at Jack, willing him to agree. How could she answer police questions that might lead to her past?

"But Kiah —" began Jack, his hair on end from frustrated finger raking.

"It's not like they can actually *do* anything," she said. "All rabbits look alike — especially when they're dead — so there's no way to trace the evidence. Look, it was probably some local kids on a dare. The back of my caravan looks out onto where the lads often go rabbit shooting. One kid's likely got all cocky, dared the other to nail the dead rabbit onto my caravan door and they've both gone off laughing like loons."

"And the blood?"

"More likely raspberry cordial."

"Raspberry cordial doesn't smell like blood," said Jack, not looking convinced, "and the thing is, I can't just let this go, Kiah. What if it's not kids? What if there's a madman out there and not only you, but Angel, Marg, or my horses are in danger too."

"I was the one targeted, so there's little chance of any danger to anyone else," Kiah said, jutting out her bottom lip. "The rabbit was nailed to my door so I think it's up to me whether to bring the police in, or not."

"You don't really mean that."

Marg slid a second hot cup of tea in front of Kiah and let out a loud *hrrmph*. "Can I put my two bobs' worth in?" she said, her no-nonsense voice dripping with frustration. "Or are you two hotheads going to continue sniping at each other and getting nowhere fast?"

When neither Jack nor Kiah answered, Marg frowned. "Look, why don't you go for a nice long walk along the creek, talk your problems out like two rational human beings, while I get rid of the poor rabbit and give the caravan door a scrub?"

Kiah jumped up so quickly her chair scraped against the wooden floor, almost toppled over. "Good idea." She linked arms with Jack and dragged him toward the kitchen door. "Leave the blood though, Marg, I'll clean it up when we get back. But if you could give Bugs a decent burial, I'll owe you one."

Jack pulled away from Kiah and shook his head. His expression incredulous as he stared at her. "But that would destroy any evidence and—"

"Exactly." Marg regarded Kiah with a questioning eye-lift. "And that's what you *really* want. Isn't it, Kiah?"

Kiah blinked at the housekeeper's words. She looked at Jack who was visibly upset. His hair standing on end. A deep frown creasing his forehead. Of course, he was worried about his family. Jack Sullivan was a protector. A man who'd stand up against anyone who'd threaten his loved ones or his precious horses.

Kiah suddenly felt incredibly small. Selfish. An insignificant worm stuck to the bottom of these wonderful people's shoes. Here she was asking them to ignore the threat of danger, pretend it wasn't happening. Just to protect herself. No. This wasn't all about her. It never was. She wasn't that scared little mouse who'd cringe and shake whenever Richard nailed her with one of his arctic stares or bullying threats. Not now. She'd left that insipid creature behind the moment she'd driven away from the funeral and swung the wheel of his precious Range Rover out onto the open road. "You're right," she said, her eyes meeting Marg's, silently asking forgiveness. "Don't touch a thing. Leave the evidence for the police."

The sound of scattered gravel and a vehicle coming to a stop outside the house, shortly followed by the slamming of car doors, brought the conversation to a sudden halt. Kiah frowned at Jack, then scooted across to the kitchen window. She tugged the corner of the pale blue brocade curtain to one side and checked the scene outside. Two uniformed policemen were heading up the steps toward the house. "What? How did they…?" She sent a frown over her shoulder at Jack, then shook her head. "You've already rung the police."

"Walking toward your caravan I saw what was on the door and rang the police before I joined you."

"But you didn't say…you made me…"

There was a hollow knock on the front door and before Kiah could find the words to finish telling him exactly what he made her think, Jack left the kitchen and let the two policemen inside.

"Come on, sweetie, it's for the best," said Marg coming up behind Kiah and resting a hand on her shoulder. A hand that felt incredibly comforting. She was so lucky to have found *Windsong* and its people. They were like family. "No need to tell the police anything other than the fact that you've been away all morning and you came home to find some drunk deadbeat had tampered with your front door and you have no idea who it could be. Okay?"

Kiah smiled at Marg. The motherly housekeeper was right. Kiah didn't have to mention Connor, or that she was the late Chief of Police's daughter-in-law. In fact, she didn't have to bring up her past at all. And who knows — maybe it really was kids on a dare. She let out a sigh. Yeah, and maybe pigs could fly.

Marg squeezed her hand. "Just leave it to the police. Okay?"

Fifteen minutes later, after the two constables had asked a few desultory questions, given the rabbit a cautionary poke, and then taken the poor creature's photo (possibly for their Instagram account), Kiah was back in the kitchen standing by the window. She watched the police car rumble back down the drive, spit a spray of gravel near the brood mare paddock causing the foals to squeal and kick up their heels, and then, after passing through the gateway, turn left onto the road.

"Cops didn't seem to think there was much hope of finding out who strung the rabbit up." Jack strode back inside the house, removing his now muddy boots before entering the kitchen. "Said, there were no distinct footprints on the gravel around the caravan and without security cameras they had nothing to go on. They'll ask around, talk to our neighbors, see if anyone spotted a trespasser, but have little hope of finding the culprit. Thought it was probably kids."

Kiah lifted one eyebrow at him in an *I told you so* motion, adding a smirk for good measure.

"Okay, okay, but I don't like it. Not knowing, that is. First thing in the morning I'll arrange to have cameras installed over the door of your caravan." He shrugged, the corners of his mouth lifting. "Anyway, what's your beef with the police? Escaped convict? Or are you hiding the Hope Diamond in your underwear?"

Kiah snorted. "In my underwear? You...I'll have you know—"

"As I suggested earlier, why don't you two go for a nice long walk in the fresh air. Get things sorted in a calm and orderly manner," said Marg, transferring the used coffee cups from the wooden table to the dishwasher. "I'm glad Angel went to her friend's house for a play date. Seeing you two fighting would not be good for her emotional stability." She rolled her eyes and growled. "Fair dinkum, the air between you two hotheads at the moment is combustible. I'm expecting fireworks to ignite at any moment. Go for a walk, talk it out, and by the time you get back, I'll have a batch of my special lemon scones ready for you to try out." Her eyes sparkled with mischief. "Nothing beats a scone piled high with jam and cream to settle an argument."

"Good idea." Jack flicked his hand at the doorway. "Kiah?" he said indicating for her to go through first while he put his boots back on. "There's something I've been meaning to show you. I guess now's as good a time as any."

Kiah's anger fizzled and died. Naturally Marg and Jack would be wondering why she was averse to talking to the police. She closed her eyes, felt the tightness between her shoulder blades hitch another notch. Was she putting everyone in danger by staying at *Windsong*? Would she ever escape her past? She opened her eyes to see Jack looking down at her, his eyebrows quirked in concern. Maybe it was time to reveal a little of her past; accept help. After all, if she couldn't trust Jack, then it was definitely time to climb back in her Range Rover and move on.

Find herself a new beginning somewhere else.

She looked up at Jack, his eyes warm and reassuring as he stood waiting for her to precede him through the doorway, and realized with sudden clarity, that she couldn't leave Angel, Marg and her other new friends. She'd miss them. And more importantly, that her feelings for Jack Sullivan were starting to edge into something more than *like*.

*****

Jack loved the sound of the creek as it scurried and swirled under the rustic wooden bridge. It was always busy, always moving, as though in a hurry to get where it was going, but determined to enjoy every step of the journey. He leaned over the side of the bridge and pointed to the tiny fish, silver flicks, darting between the rocks below.

"This place is magical." Kiah, close beside him, leaned over the rail, her eyes wide, the sweet coconut smell of her shampoo blanketing his senses. "It's like something out of a fairytale. You almost expect to see a big ugly frog transmute into a handsome Prince, then emerge from the creek bed, shake the water from his gold-embossed cloak, and ride off with the beautiful Princess."

"Wrong time of day," said Jack, breaking the spell with a cheeky grin. "Any Prince worthy of his crown. would choose *sunset* to ride off to his local pub. A screaming princess strapped to the roof rack of his mud-encrusted Holden."

"Philistine." Kiah punched him lightly on the arm. "How many fairy tales have *you* read?"

"Well…"

Kiah let out a hiss and gritted her teeth. "Oh, God, I'm sorry, Jack. You've probably read all the stories to Angel. Can likely recite the words of the evil Queen when she gazes into her mirror."

"Mirror, mirror, on the wall, who is the fairest of them all?"

"Huh! Everyone knows that one." Kiah mock-frowned. "How about something a bit harder. Who said these famous words: 'It's no use going back to yesterday because I was a different person then.'"

"That's easy. Alice, in Alice in Wonderland."

Kiah's face was one big grin. "Okay, okay, I admit, you know your fairy tales."

"Hey, I can even tell you the names of the seven dwarfs," Jack said, enjoying the dimple that had appeared in her chin. Only a slight crease that he hadn't noticed before but it was doing strange things to the beat of his heart. "There's Happy and Grumpy and Doc and—"

"Enough!" Kiah punched him on the arm again. Harder. Grinned when he flinched. "You win." She stared down at the water for a moment before looking back up at him with those intense green eyes that seemed to be capable of delving into his innermost thoughts. "Must have been difficult bringing up a child on your own."

Difficult? Jack suddenly found it hard to breathe. For the first three months after Bianca died, he barely registered that he *had* a child. If it wasn't for his mother taking over, caring for Angel, he didn't know what would have happened. Probably Social Services would have stepped in. Taken his baby from him. But all he'd been able to think about during those early months was Bianca. That he'd never see her again. Never hear her bubbly laugh. Never feel her warm loving body wrapped around his at night while they slept. His soulmate was gone. Forever.

It had taken a huge scare when Angel was three months old to bring him out of his coma-like existence. Angel, his baby girl, had been rushed to hospital with whooping cough, in a terrible state, and he'd suddenly seen his daughter for what felt like the very first time. *His daughter.* Bianca's parting gift to him. From the moment Angel was discharged from hospital two weeks later, with medications, future appointments and a new sweet smile she'd found just for him, his daughter had become the most precious person in his life. His reason to get up in the mornings — and the middle of the nights when she had colic, teething, or just to stand beside her cot and look down at her. He took over her feeding, her dressing, her bathing and even her bedtime stories. There was nothing Jack wouldn't do for his daughter. He'd vowed there and then that she would always be number one.

Jack blinked at Kiah's upturned face. Realized from her expression that she'd been reading him, almost listening to his thoughts. Or maybe she was just waiting for an answer. He nodded. "No harder than it is for single mums, I guess. And Angel and I were living with my parents for the first five years. Unfortunately, Bianca's parents live in Cornwall, England, and I've only met them twice. Once for our wedding. And when they came over for Bianca's funeral." He cleared his throat. "Anyway, there was always help nearby and my mother was amazing with Angel."

Kiah gave a tentative grin, as though to break the tension. "But you were the nominated teller of bedtime stories?"

"Yes. And it's still ongoing." He smiled down at her, relieved to be brought back to the present. "We've progressed from fairytales, through to Disney, and lately Angel's had me reading pony books to her." He shook her head, still smiling. "I keep telling her she can read her own books, doesn't need her dear old dad. But she insists. Says my voice sends her to sleep."

A larger red-gold fish swam from under the bridge down the stream, its scales reflecting little gold sparks in the sun. The water churned as the fish pushed against the ripples. Jack felt Kiah move beside him. Move from one foot to the other. And then she spoke. "Jack…"

"Hmm…when someone starts a sentence with my name and then stops, it's usually something I don't want to hear." He turned to her with a smile, lifting one eyebrow to show he was joking.

"About that western saddle…" She stared down at the creek, studying the water like she could find the words she wanted to say written on the rocks. "Angel told me the saddle belonged to her mother." She lifted her eyes to meet his, a vulnerable query behind them. "Why didn't you say it was your wife's saddle? That you hated me using it? That you wanted to dump me in the manure pit for being so crass as to take the saddle from the tack room without asking who it belonged to?"

Jack grabbed a breath, let it out slowly. He'd been wondering about that himself. If anyone else dared touch Bianca's saddle he'd have had their guts for garters. Seeing it on Kiah's horse, looking so at home, so 'right', as if that's where Bianca would want it to be — he'd let himself enjoy watching Kiah ride Jet in the saddle, watch her hang onto the front horn when Jet spooked at the kangaroo, knowing that if she'd been in one of the racing saddles she'd have likely been bucked off. Maybe even hurt.

"Thought it was time it got used," he said. "Plus, the saddle suits you."

Kiah blushed. "It's a beautiful saddle and I'll take good care of it."

Jack took her hand in his. "Come on, there's more to show you." He led her off the bridge and down a dirt path that led to a heavily bushed area that had become overgrown over the years. A place he'd come to as a child when staying with his Uncle Dan.

"In here," he said, pulling Kiah behind him as he pushed aside a bush to reveal a closed-off shady area, set up with two tyre swings attached to branches of a large Oak tree. Swings his uncle had set up for him and his younger brother, Michael, all those years ago. And even now, when he'd had an exceptionally bad day, he'd come here, alone with his thoughts, sit on the swing and let the peace and tranquility filter through to his brain and body; make him whole again.

"It's lovely," said Kiah, running over to the swing and wriggling her bottom into the first tyre. "Like your own personal island — without the sharks or the crocodiles watching your every move."

"I don't come here much now," he admitted following her across the grass to the swings. "Just knowing I can if I need to is enough."

He'd spent a lot of time here after Bianca died. Almost joined her one really bleak day until the face of his baby girl swam into his mind and he ended up blind drunk down at the local pub instead.

"Come on, Jack," Kiah said, her grin widening. "Bet I can get this tyre to swing higher than yours."

"You're on."

Five minutes later, both laughing and exhausted from trying to outdo each other, Kiah slowed down her swinging and he could see her getting ready to talk to him. To maybe open up at last. He spoke first. "You don't have to tell me anything about your past, Kiah," he said. "I know you're a good person and that's all that matters to me."

"Thank you Jack, that means a lot." She started swinging gently. "I-I'm sorry for pushing you away when you kissed me the other day, but…I have…issues. Panic attacks they're called. I-I freak if I'm held too closely. I can't breathe and I lash out."

"But why?"

"My husband was a violent man, a control freak. He'd hold me so tightly I couldn't breathe and he'd hurt me more if I tried to get away from him."

"Why didn't you go to the police, have him charged for domestic violence?"

"Because he *was* the police, Jack." Kiah paused, letting these disturbing words hang in the air for a moment. "Senior Police Lieutenant Richard James Stanton. Son of the late and highly decorated Chief of Police. To others, Richard was a legend, a big cheese, a man of honor. Who would believe that this paradigm of justice would beat his wife, lock her in the bathroom and leave her there all day?"

Jack's stomach curdled. A deep primaeval black rage invaded his senses. If Richard Stanton was standing in front of him right now, Jack didn't know if he'd be able to control his fury. His fists curled tighter, knuckles going white, at the thought.

When he spoke, his voice was soft, almost a whisper. "Why didn't you leave him, Kiah?"

"It's never as easy as that, Jack. Men are stronger than women. It's a fact. And men like Richard use that strength to threaten, hurt, and intimidate." She stared at him; her face a mask, as though not showing her feelings was the only way she could hold herself together. "I knew, without a doubt, if I left him, my husband would find me, and kill me."

"But…you did. Eventually. You're here with us now." Jack attempted a smile but found his lips wouldn't cooperate. "And good for you." A sudden image of the mutilated rabbit on Kiah's blood-soaked door flashed across his mind like a macabre painting on the wall of an art gallery. "The gutted rabbit? The blood? Do you think it's the work of your husband?" His stomach lurched. "Kiah, we need to inform the police. Tell them—"

"My husband had nothing to do with the rabbit, Jack." Kiah took a breath and he watched a tic near her left eye twitch. "Richard dropped dead of a heart attack two weeks before I arrived at *Windsong*."

Jack whooshed out a breath. When she'd filled out her job application, she'd written *Mrs.* Stanton, but he thought she was either divorced or separated. But dead? He let out a breath he didn't know he'd been holding. "So, is that why—".

"I-I'd rather not talk about it anymore, Jack." She looked up at him, her vulnerability tearing a hole in his heart. What had that monster put her through? Bullied and hurt by a man who was sworn to protect her.

Jack pushed himself off the tyre and stood up. Time to lighten the mood. "Come on, let's take off our boots, roll up our jeans, and go for a paddle in the creek."

He watched her turn a grateful smile into a mock pout. "But what about the fish? And-and those bitey little crabby things?"

"Shadow Creek fish are exceptionally shy and we don't have crabs, just tadpoles," he told her, eyes fixed on her pouty bottom lip that was crying out to be kissed. "They're a bit slimy to the touch, but definitely have no claws. And if it makes it easier for you to deal with them, imagine the tadpoles changing into frogs and then into handsome Princes."

"Hmm…that might work."

She reached for him; her small hand disappearing inside his large one as he struggled to pull her to her feet. Somehow, while swinging, her bottom had become wedged inside the rubber tyre. He let out a snort of laughter. "Are you going to help yourself a bit here or are you just going to sit there, grinning, and let me get a hernia?"

She wriggled her nose at him, half-laughing, as she pushed against the tyre with her free hand. "I'm trying! I'm trying!"

"Wriggle harder. Otherwise, you'll be wearing that tyre home and I'll be cutting it off with my electric saw."

"Aarggh!" The tyre spat Kiah out of its confines like a willful cork from a wine bottle, hurling her bodily into Jack with the force of an atomic missile.

Unbalanced, taken by surprise, Jack staggered backwards, his boots flaying for purchase on the slippery grass. Desperate to protect Kiah, he pulled her to him, wrapping his arms around her, holding her close to his body as he went down.

He hit the ground with a bone-jarring thud; every breath of air knocked out of him. And if the pain in the middle of his back was anything to go by, he'd landed on a rock and he'd sport a nice big purple bruise by morning.

But what did he care? Currently lying stretched out on top of him, all five foot two inches of warm womanly body pressed into his…was Kiah. He could feel the softness of her breasts, her gravelly nipples teasing him, rubbing against him when she moved. "You, okay?" he wheezed when he finally found enough air to speak. "Did I hurt you?"

Her eyes were on his mouth, her voice breathy. "No, no, I'm fine. What about you?" She touched his face, one finger tracing the small scar he'd acquired the day he'd bought his first motor bike at eighteen and thought he was the next Giacomo Agostini. He'd ended up in a ditch, a sharp stone embedded in his chin, and needed five stitches at the local hospital.

"Suits you," she said. "Makes you look interesting." She ran her tongue across her bottom lip sending lightning jolts of heat to his groin. "In my opinion, flawless people haven't really lived."

"Glad you like it," he croaked, swallowing the lump in his throat. He could feel her heart-beat, racing, banging against his chest, her fingers splaying hesitantly in his hair, see the tip of her tongue protruding from that sensuous mouth.

She was so beautiful. Rich auburn red hair a contrast to her pale skin, green cat's eyes focusing on his, full lips so close he could feel her hot breath grazing his cheek.

He lifted his head, his lips aching to touch hers. "Kiah, is it okay if I kiss you?"

She let out a breath. "Please."

"You sure?" Her lips, a hairsbreadth away from his, were tempting him, teasing him, but he didn't want to set off another panic attack, like in the caravan.

"Jack…" Her voice came out husky, frustrated. "I said, *please*."

That's all he needed. He trailed feather light kisses along the length of her neck, found the little crease in her chin, touched her lips, increased the pressure, and when she opened her mouth to let him in, he slid his tongue gently inside, basking in the heat, her little moans, robbing him of breath.

Suddenly she pulled away, and it was like the sun had gone out, leaving him cold, disorientated; as though he'd lost part of himself.

"Jack," she whispered, her breath a coarse rasp as she blinked down at him. "I like you. I *really* like you. But…I need to take things slowly." She rolled off him and sat up, sending him a tentative grin. "Look, my feral hormones might be running around high-fiving each other and yelling, 'Go! Go! Go!', but I'm scared to jump head-first into another relationship. Too much has happened to me in the past and I can't trust myself not to hurt you. So…" Those intense green eyes gazed into his, pleading with him to understand. "I need to take this — whatever *this* is — slowly. Okay?"

Jack sat up and swiveled around to face her. He leaned forward so he could skate his fingers down the planes of her face, over her cheekbone, feather-soft across her lips. "As much as I'd like to rouse your feral hormones to fever pitch *slowly* suits me perfectly." He imagined Bianca, felt her smiling down at him, cheering him on, as though telling him it was time. Time to let go.

But did he want to?

He leaned forward and gently tucked Kiah's hair behind her ears. "If slow was a person," he told her, attempting to convey the sincerity of his message through touch, "then his name would be Jack Sullivan."

A smile transformed her face into bright sunshine, highlighting the beauty and serenity of Jack's special hideaway, his boyhood sanctuary. An unspoken pact had been formed between them. At the same time, something heavy had lifted from his heart.

He watched Kiah scramble upright and brush dry grass from the seat of her jeans. She grabbed both his hands, and, letting out an infectious laugh that echoed through the tree tops, tugged Jack to his feet. "In that case, Mr. Sullivan," she said, "let's go find ourselves some tadpoles."

ELEVEN

Kiah had never before experienced such exhilarating speed. Turning into the home straight, she leaned flat along Magnifico's outstretched neck; felt herself become as one with the horse. Eyes half-closed, the strong wind, rushing and whooshing in her ears, whipped at her face, while the rhythmic thud of galloping hooves beneath her became an aphrodisiac, a spur to go faster.

One last effort, she thought, touching her heels to his sides and urging him on. Immediately he exploded like a thunder clap beneath her; the bunching, the straining of muscles as he responded, making her cry out with abandon.

Whoohoo!

This must be what it felt like to fly.

It was two weeks since the rabbit scare, and with the police no closer to finding the culprit, Kiah had spent several restless nights tossing and turning, alert for strange noises and with her phone switched on beside the bed in case her tormentor returned.

Since then, two questions kept bugging her. Wouldn't go away. Was it Connor who'd left her the grizzly message? And if so, why now?

On a brighter note, it was also two weeks since she and Jack had kissed under the tyre swings and come to an understanding. So far, he'd kept his promise of taking things slowly. A quick kiss behind a stable door, a smouldering eyelift from afar. But she had to admit, Jack Sullivan really, really knew how to kiss and there was a growing attraction building between them.

Today, she'd used her charms to convince Jack to let her ride Magnifico in trackwork. The horse's usual rider, Dillon, had been booked by another trainer to ride at a small country race meeting a hundred miles away. And after experiencing the horse's amazing speed, Kiah knew Magnifico was well on his way to being spot on for the Kangaroo Downs Cup in two months' time

Still on a high, she gradually slowed the big chestnut down to a long, loose-limbed trot. She slapped him on the neck, laughing when he tossed his head and pranced, showing off. How amazing it would be to ride a horse like this in an actual race? To become a jockey? She let out a sigh. All those years wasted, dodging fists, walking on egg-shells, trying to be the perfect wife; while on the other side of the door lay a world of colour and excitement.

Richard had not only crushed her spirit — he'd stolen twelve years of her life.

"Kiah, you are *so* dead." Olivia, trotting up beside her on a lightly-framed grey gelding, broke into her thoughts. The teenager shook her head, a worried frown stamped across her forehead. "Jack's instructions were to, like, give him a *pipe opener*, not to ride like you're on the favourite in the 3.40 at Randwick."

At the same moment, Belle, expression equally as worried as Olivia's, came cantering up, easing back to a trot when she came alongside. "What happened? Did Magnifico bolt with you?"

"Bolt? No, no, I just got a bit carried away." Kiah eased the big chestnut back to a walk, ready to do two laps on a long rein to cool him off before returning to the stable block.

"Well, you'd better hope *Jack* doesn't get carried away when he starts yelling at you."

Belle's words brought Kiah back to reality with a bump as she recalled Jack's instructions on how to ride Magnifico in trackwork — 'let him stretch out, give him a little pipe-opener, but keep him under control at all times. Whatever you do, don't push him.'

She'd let her excitement at feeling all that power under her get in the way of common sense.

"You are *so* dead," Olivia repeated, her voice the timbre of a funeral director regarding a new client.

After two laps at the walk, Kiah trailed Belle and Olivia toward the gateway opening out from the track and onto the path leading to the stable block. As usual, Jack was sitting on an ancient fold-up camp chair beside the gateway, his iPad balanced precariously on his lap. As well as timing each horse, he'd note down the slightest stumble, shortening of stride or unusual behaviour and follow this up with a hands-on assessment once the horse had cooled down.

"Is his face red?" whispered Belle, now glued to Kiah's right side. "Does he look like he's going to blow?"

"Hard to tell. He's, like, staring down at his iPad. Maybe we'll get past without him seeing us," said Olivia from her other side.

They were almost through the gateway when Jack spoke. "Ah, Kiah," he said, his eyes still on his iPad.

"Um…yes, boss."

"Auditioning for stable jockey?"

"Um…no, boss."

He looked up, eyebrows hitched in a query, head tilted slightly to one side. And was that a quirky twitch to his lips? "That was some pipe-opener…" As he spoke, his voice smooth, almost caressing, Kiah couldn't take her eyes off those twitching lips. She wanted to leap off her horse and kiss the living daylights out of them.

"Um…er…sorry about that." She struggled to get the words out. "I got a bit carried—"

"Make sure Magnifico's cooled off completely before you return him to his stable," he said, dismissing her to watch Goldie gallop on the track. As he averted his head, Kiah could see him fighting a grin. Damn. He knew he'd been turning her on. "And don't stand there gawking," he growled without taking his eyes off Goldie. "Get those horses cooled off, hosed down and settled into their stables. Time's money."

Kiah slowly let out the breath she'd been holding, stuffed her libido back in its box and covered it with several ice packs. "Yes, boss. You've got it, boss."

"I don't believe this," said Belle as they walked along the path, reins hanging loose on their horses' necks. "Jack didn't boil you in oil *or* rip out your liver."

"That was totally and incomprehensively weird," agreed Olivia. "Like, I was expecting at least a beheading."

"I know," said Kiah smothered a grin at Olivia's words. "Do you think maybe he's on a health kick and read somewhere that yelling isn't good for the heart? Or maybe the doctor prescribed a packet of Be-calm pills?"

Olivia snorted. "Be-calm pills? More like he fancies you." She slid a thoughtful glance across at Kiah and frowned. "Are you sure you and the boss aren't, like, an item?"

Kiah stared down at her horse's mane and gave a smothered laugh. "An item? Where did you pick up that archaic term? Find it in an actual hard cover dictionary at the library?"

It was an implied understanding between Jack and Kiah that their new relationship wasn't to be made known to her co-workers. Their relationship — or whatever it was — was so new, so fragile, she didn't know if it would even last the full month. "Maybe he has other things on his mind. You know, like how to find rich owners to fill his stable with city class horses so he can actually make a profit and pay his bills."

"Whatever it is," said Belle with a grin, "let's not knock it."

But Olivia wouldn't let it go. "Maybe it's, like, someone he's met outside the stable that's put him in such a good mood?"

Belle rubbed her mouth, in thought. "What about that busty blonde who was here the other day? Even the birds in the trees could see she was into him."

Kiah frowned. "What busty blonde?"

"The rep from Big Horse vitamins." Olivia slid one finger into her mouth and imitated vomiting. "*So* not his type. Poor Jack spent the entire conversation, like, dodging the woman's hands. She was all over him like sauce on a pie."

A frisson on annoyance whipped through Kiah as she pictured the busty blonde from Big Horse vitamins flirting with Jack; hands *accidently* brushing against him, fingers running through his hair. Gritting her teeth together, she glared down at a harmless black crow perched on the arm of a wheelbarrow parked in front of the manure pit. The bird was meticulously cleaning his feathers but cocked his head to the side to watch them as they passed by. Kiah whooshed out a breath and frowned. Not the crow's fault. Damn. If she was like this when she and Jack were going 'slow' what would she be like if they took it up a notch?

After attending to Magnifico and making sure he was comfortable in his stable with a warm rug and a small feed of oats, Kiah snaffled her grooming bag from the tack room and hurried along to Jet's stable. If she was quick, she'd have time to fit an extra grooming session in, work on his ratty mane, before she had to saddle up Lofty and ride him in trackwork.

Jet greeted her with his usual shrill, body-shaking, *that's my-mum*, whinny. Her eyes stung and she wiped a finger under her nose as an all-encompassing warmth engulfed her. After existing for so long in an environment as sterile and loveless as a war zone, Kiah still hadn't quite got accustomed to having another living being looking at her with such total adoration. Even if that living being *did* have four legs and a tail. Jet snuffled his nose in her pockets hunting for treats as she clipped a lead to his halter and tied him to the ring beside his feed bin. "Got to watch your diet now you're in training," she told him while sneaking half a carrot from her grooming bag where she'd hidden it under the polishing rag. She held the treat out on the flat of her hand, smiling as his whiskers tickled her palm. God, she loved watching this horse eat carrots. His eyes seemed to soften, go all misty while he ate, the orange saliva oozing out like foam over his lips.

With Jet in full training, the plan was for Taylor, the stable's female jockey, to ride him in track-work to prepare him for racing. Jack figured, if they didn't want a repeat of Jet's naughty habit of bucking his jockey off on the way to the barriers on race day, this was the way to go. Less chance of the horse acting up if he knew his jockey.

But Kiah was still his groom. No way would she ever give up the care of her horse to another person.

After lightly spraying Jet's mane and tail with *Fastgro*, a new product she'd bought from the Shadow Creek fodder store that promised to not only make the mane — 'grow like Sampson's hair', but also to ensure it was, 'silky soft and shiny', Kiah set to work with the brush. His tail was looking good, but his mane was still what you'd call, 'a bit ratty'. However, with one hundred and eighty-nine, five-star reviews for this product on the *Fastgro* website, she had high hopes of success.

Lost in the dream of Jet's mane becoming long and beautiful along with his tail, she didn't realize Jack was in the stable until a trail of soft kisses landed on the soft skin at the back of her neck. Quickly followed by a gentle nip on her left earlobe.

"Please don't ride like that again," he said softly in the ear he was busy nipping. "You almost gave me a heart attack."

Without turning around, she said, "Only if you promise not to sneak up on me. Next time I might mistake you for a pervert and clobber you with a body brush."

"That might be fun."

"Shouldn't you be out there yelling at some unfortunate rider?" she said, leaning back against his well-muscled body as he drew her closer, his arms around her, his mouth now in her hair.

"Don't feel like yelling today," he said into her hair. "Feel more like kissing."

He turned her around slowly, his lips finding hers and all thought of ratty manes and fast-galloping horses trickled out of her brain like stuffing from a hole in a cushion. Jack Sullivan's kisses were special. Soft, sweet kisses that robbed her of breath and made her legs go wobbly. Hard, all-encompassing kisses that went straight to her lady bits.

"Come with me and Angel to my parents' house next Sunday," he said, slowly lifting his lips from hers and tucking a lock of hair behind her ears. "I want you to meet my family."

"Meet your family?" She pulled back and stared at him. "What happened to going 'slow'? What happened to 'if slow was a person his name would be Jack Sullivan?'"

He lifted one side of his mouth in a half-grin. "Too soon?"

"Jack, it's only been two weeks."

He bent forward and took the tip of her ear into his mouth, sucked gently, making her moan. "Maybe next time?"

"Not a chance." She laughed as he took her face in both hands, the warmth and gentleness of his hands at odds with their size. Since she'd told him of her panic attacks, of the reason why she had an aversion to being held tightly, Jack had treated her with such care. It made her like him even more. "We should at least perfect our kissing techniques before we talk about meeting your family."

"Good point," he said, his lips closing on hers oh-so softly, so tenderly, she almost melted into a splodge of gooey toffee at his feet.

A movement on the other side of the stable door had Jack quickly slipping out of her arms and bending down. He lifted one of Jet's legs, bent it at the knee and pretended to examine the shoe.

"Hi guys." It was Taylor, saddle over one arm, bridle and helmet swinging from her other hand. "Am I interrupting something here?"

"No, no, come on in, Taylor. Get Jet ready for his workout," said Jack, not missing a beat. "I want you to up his workload today. Let him swing along at the gallop for the full three furlongs." He stood up, dropped the horse's hoof back into the sawdust and nodded at Kiah. "You were right. I'll speak to the farrier tomorrow morning about changing these shoes for a slightly heavier set."

And with a sideways wink at Kiah, he strolled out of the stable, leaving her hot, red-faced, and facing a highly-suspicious Taylor whose eyebrows were still up around her hairline.

*****

Jack Sullivan was perplexed. Whenever he got anywhere near Kiah, all he wanted to do was kiss the daylights out of her and then take her to bed. Not for a mindless fling — but to spend the night adoring her. Gentling her. Getting her to trust him. Prove to her that he was nothing like her asshole of a husband and it was safe to take their relationship to the next step.

But the thing that perplexed him the most, was…why? What was it about this woman that made him go all gooey inside, yet want to don his shiny knight's armor, pick up a sword, and defend her against the world? He hadn't been interested in another woman since Bianca. Okay, he wasn't a monk. He'd had a handful of one-night-stands, mainly brought on by imbibing too much booze. But he hadn't thought of another woman, not the way he thought about Kiah, since the day his wife died.

He let out a frustrated huff and closed his eyes. This 'going slow' plan they'd agreed on was fine in theory, but could he keep it up? He knew if he pushed her, even a little, she'd retreat. And then he'd lose her. And he didn't want that. So, it was up to him to prove that a relationship with him could be gentle and fun and loving. Which came back full circle to…he had to 'go slow'.

But it was hard. Every time he kissed her, he wanted to take it further. To feel the silkiness of her skin rubbing against his. Hear her moans of desire as he tantalized every part of her with his lips and tongue.

He sighed. Blew out a cooling breath. Easy pardner. He had to remember that 'going slow' suited him, too. What if Kiah decided to take it further but he couldn't move on from Bianca's memory? Then Kiah would get hurt. And hadn't she been hurt enough already? No — he had to back off. Stick to their agreement.

And maybe indulge in more cold showers.

His mind on the soft skin on Kiah's neck, that special spot behind her ear, Jack transferred the plates and cups and cutlery from the kitchen table to the dishwasher, added a tablet, and switched on the machine. Then stepped back and pictured himself kissing behind Kiah's ear. Scraping his teeth lightly across the soft skin, setting it on fire with his tongue…

"For goodness sake, Mr. S …. what are you doing? Those dishes were clean. I've just finished setting the table and you've gone and put everything in the dishwasher."

Dragging his mind away from the tantalizing softness of Kiah's neck and into the everyday world of the kitchen, Jack blinked at his now scowling housekeeper. "Sorry, Marg. I'll get more dishes out of the cupboard and set the table again."

Marg lifted one hand in the stop-right-now sign. "No. More. Helping. You'll send me shillyshallying up the wall like a spider overdosed with Mortein spray. Go outside. Shovel manure. Run around the track." She shook her head, the loose hairs poking out of her bun standing up, pressing her point. "Or better still, go talk to Kiah. Ask her out for a drink. The pair of you are mooning around the place like love-sick teenagers and think no-one's noticing. Your dinner will be in the oven and you can heat it up when you get back."

"But—"

"Angel's not due home from her friend's house for another hour. I'll see she eats her vegetables and does her homework." Marg made shooing movements with both hands. "Now, go! Get out of here. Or do I have to get the broom and chase you out?"

Jack strode down to the stable block, a smile on his face. He'd only seen Kiah an hour ago when he left Belle and her to finish feeding the horses, while he did some book-work in his home office. Yet, he couldn't wait to see her again. Geez, he had it bad.

He found Kiah in the feed room. She was bending over, slotting a freshly-scrubbed white feed bucket in between bucket number 26 and 28, all lined up in order, ready for the morning feeds. Hair escaping from her pony tail, a smudge of what looked like either dirt or horse saliva on her left cheek and shirt hanging from the back of her jeans, she had never looked more beautiful. He ached to kiss that smudge on her cheek and slowly edge his way down to her lips.

"Jack?"

He hitched a breath. Oh, God, were his thoughts reflected on his face? He pushed them away. Think 'slow'. Think snails on the garden path. "Um…hi, Kiah. Wondered if you'd like to go for a drink? At The Creek?"

Kiah straightened and he could see she was struggling to keep from grinning. "Are you asking me out on a date, *boss*?"

"Maybe. And it's after-hours, so I'm not your boss."

"Well, *Jack*, what is it? It's either a date or it's not."

"Okay, okay, if that's what you want to call it. It's a date."

Jack's breath caught in his throat as Kiah tipped her head to the side and that tiny dimple popped into her chin. He bit his bottom lip and thought of cold showers, frosty mornings, and surfing in the middle of winter. When that didn't work, he swiped a stable broom from the rack and began sweeping the aisleway. "I'll finish off out here. You've got twenty minutes to shower and change."

Her grin widened. "It's true! You're asking me out on a *real* date!"

Half way along the aisleway he stopped, called out over his shoulder. "I'll pick you up at six thirty-five. And don't keep me waiting."

He could hear Kiah laughing as she trotted off. This was so embarrassing. The woman could read him like a book. She knew he wanted to kiss her senseless and that he was finding their 'go slow' pact a lot harder than he'd imagined. Was she finding it hard too? Was she looking to up the pace? Or was it all on his side and he was acting like a horny teenager instead of a mature adult?

He bent to scoop bits of loose hay onto the shovel and grinned. Felt a spring in his step. They were going out for a drink. Could he really count that as a date? Probably not. But it was a start. They could talk. Get to know each other better. Move their relationship up a couple of notches. Kiah had been through hell with that son of a bitch who'd married her, then treated her like a punching bag. Jack would never raise his hand to a woman. Despised men who used their superior strength to intimidate and bully those weaker than themselves. All Jack wanted to do now was comfort Kiah, respect her, show her that he was nothing like Richard.

And find out where this new, fragile relationship led.

The Creek was only quarter-full when they arrived. No workers from *Windsong*, but as Shadow Creek was a small community, Jack had at least a nodding acquaintance with most people in the town. They found a quiet table away from the bar. In the corner, where they could hear themselves talk without shouting,

Dressed in clean jeans, boots, and a warm fuzzy jumper that matched the color of her eyes, Kiah looked cute, but a little awkward. Maybe the fact that Taylor's fiancé, Greg, was behind the bar and the smug grin on his face when they walked into the pub, together, meant that everyone at *Windsong* would know by morning. After ordering a beer for himself and a lemon-lime-and-bitters for Kiah, Jack deposited the drinks on the table and dragged out a chair opposite her. He wanted Kiah to relax, get to know him better, but he also needed to see her face and catch her expressions. Make sure she was comfortable with him.

"As far as dating goes, I'm terribly out of practice," he said, stretching his long legs out in front of him and leaning back in his chair.

"Ditto. So, what do we do now?" Her lips twitched and those green eyes danced below long thick eyelashes. "Ask each other to divulge their favorite color?" She paused and that wicked grin appeared again. "In case you're interested, mine's green."

"Funny that," he drawled. "So's mine."

She laughed. "I don't believe you. Come on, let it all out. I won't tell anyone. What's your favorite color, Jack?"

He shook his head at her, enjoying their banter. "Hate to be a spoilsport here, but to be honest, I don't have one. Not a lot of men worry about the color of the shirt they're wearing, as long as it shows off their muscles."

"Sounds about right." She took a sip of her drink and his gaze strayed to her lips as she licked at their wetness. "What about movies?" She had one eyebrow tipped up. Teasing him. "Do men have favorite movies? Or is it just anything with guns and shoot outs and fast car chases?"

"Hey, don't forget the dames. Always gotta have a dame with a rough smoker's voice, short skirt, and legs that go up to her armpits."

She gave a mock tut. "How old did you say you were, Jack? Fifteen?"

He leaned forward on his elbows and stared her in the eye. "Old enough to have forgotten how much fun it is to take a beautiful woman out on a date."

"And I'm old enough to know when a guy's hitting on me."

He grinned. "And is it working?"

She took another sip of her drink, eyes never leaving his as with an upward twist to the corners of her mouth, she deliberately changed the subject. "What did you do before you took over your uncle's racing stables five years ago? Were you always a horse trainer?"

"No, but I helped out most weekends, learned a lot from my uncle, which made it easier to take over *Windsong* when he died. Before that, I was a yes-man, working day and night for my father's business, Sullivan Electronics." As much as he tried, Jack couldn't keep the submerged anger from his voice. The day he told his father he didn't want to be the next in line to run the business still played on his mind. His father, a cold hard man who always put work before family, had virtually disowned him after that memorable day. Jack quaffed half a glass of beer before shoving his thoughts to the back of his mind. This wasn't the place to unearth toxic family matters. "What about you? Where did you work before showing up at the stables with a bedraggled horse in tow?"

She hesitated. "I worked three days a week at the police station as Richard's secretary. Only on the days he was in attendance and could keep an eye on me. Never when he was away from the station." Her shoulders stiffened and she looked down at her drink. "Which was better than spending the day cleaning non-existent dirt off windows and scrubbing a kitchen floor that was already clean."

Jack watched Kiah's hand shake as she picked up her glass and emptied it in three gulps. Time to leave the painful stuff and get back to their previous lighthearted banter. "Hey, you finished there? Ready for another lemon lime and bitters, or would you like to try something with a little more zing?"

She lifted her head and seemed to shake herself before sending him a teasing smile. "What do you suggest?"

"I hear Olivia swears by Sex on the Beach, but never having tried it myself, I can't recommend it."

She winked at him. Actually winked. "Sounds a bit too sandy for me," she said. "I'll have a white wine thanks. Sounds more comfortable."

The next hour and a half flew past. Keeping conversation light while playing half a dozen games of darts, learning more about each other and drinking slowly, Jack wanted the night to last forever. But 4 a.m. starts, meant early nights, for both of them.

The drive back to Windsong took no time at all and when he pulled up on the path in front of Kiah's caravan, she leaned across, kissed him lightly on the cheek and opened the car door. "Thanks, Jack. I enjoyed myself tonight. As far as dates go…I'll give it a 4 out of 5. If you're looking for an extra star — maybe add dinner."

"I'll remember that next time."

Her smile indicated she'd be happy for there to be a 'next time'.

"Wait. I'll walk you to your door." Jack climbed out of the car, moving quickly around the bonnet to catch up to her.

Kiah's dimple flashed. "You're going to walk me to my door?"

"Hey, they don't call me Gentleman Jack for nothing." He gave a mock bow with an exaggerated arm flourish.

"Oh, very Count Dracula."

Jack laughed then bared his teeth and made a show of hovering over her neck before quoting the Count in a scary voice. "First, a little refreshment to reward my exertions."

Kiah pushed him away and let out a giggle as she shook her head. "You *are* talking about coffee, I hope?"

By now they'd reached the steps leading to Kiah's front door. The motion detector light Jack had installed flashed on. Jack smiled down into Kiah's eyes; all play-acting forgotten. When she returned his smile, he brushed a stray tendril of rich red hair from her face, the softness of her cheek silky against his fingers. "I had fun tonight," he said, his voice soft. "Even if you did cheat at darts."

Kiah grinned and the night light enhanced the twinkle in her eyes. "I did not cheat. It's you. You need glasses. That last dart landed inside the bullseye."

"Definitely over the line." He gently tipped up her chin, his eyes never leaving hers. The soft fruity scent of her perfume wrapped around him, taking his breath away.

"Jack…" There was a longing in her eyes, together with uncertainty. She ran her tongue over her lips, let out a small mewing sound like a skittish kitten.

He lowered his lips to hers, drawing her closer until he could feel the hesitancy of her body, the hammering of her heart against his chest. He waited. No way would he break her trust. Kiah was like a bird with a broken wing. A beautiful bird that had been continually ripped by a predator's vicious talons. He stroked her hair, all the while gently moving his mouth against hers, until he could feel her gradually melting into him. All soft curves and sensuality. Her mouth opened. Her fingers brushed the nape of his neck before moving lower, exploring the sharp planes of his back. Warm, soft, exploring. Oh God. He took the kiss deeper as zings of want hit his groin making him move against her. She moaned into his mouth, her tongue dancing with his.

Before he took her there, on the steps of her caravan, under the motion light, he pulled away, his breath labored. "Don't suppose there's any chance of coming in for that coffee?"

Even to his ears, his voice sounded more like the croaking of a frog than Count Dracula inviting himself in for a feed.

Lips slightly apart, breath fluttering, Kiah opened her eyes, took a breath and literally shook herself. "Coffee?" Changing emotions flicked across her face. She chewed on her bottom lip while her eyes, pools of light, seemed to be darting around, unable to look at him. "Um-maybe…"

Looking at her white face, emotions rolling off her in waves, Jack sucked in a deep breath and let it out slowly. Kiah had been forced to have sex — *raped* — continuously for the last twelve years? If he didn't keep to their agreement, let Kiah guide the way, he could lose this desirable but vulnerable woman. Suddenly he knew he didn't want to lose her. He wanted to hold her, caress her silky skin, rock her in his arms, let her know he was prepared to wait for as long as it took.

She climbed the steps, used the key to open the door before turning and coming back down. She looked up at him, raw vulnerability in her eyes. "Jack, I—"

Before she could finish, he placed a soft finger against her lips. "Shh, shh, shh…."

"But, Jack—"

"Coffee's *not* a good idea. Tends to keep me awake and I have an extra early start tomorrow." He leaned forward and placed a soft kiss on her forehead. "We had a cracker of a time tonight, didn't we? And I promise to add dinner, next time. Okay?"

As Jack walked back to his car, he hitched at the tightness in his pants, forced his southward flowing blood back up into his brain. It looked like he'd be having another cold shower the moment he walked into the house…

But he couldn't take the smile off his face.

TWELVE

Kiah was dreaming of Jack.

A lovely dream, in which Jack was a strong handsome Prince, dressed in a red velvet, long, flowing cape, edged in gold. He wore leg-moulding hose and black knee-high boots. Magical boots. Thistledown soft, with long pointy toes.

Against the night sky, a myriad of stars turned the scene into a fairy paradise, where elves sprang from tree to tree, playing chasing games. Where Tinkerbelle's cousins, carrying night-lights, flew overhead, chattering and laughing amongst themselves.

And Jack, astride a powerful white stallion with eyes like rubies, was the sexiest jewel in the crown.

"Come with me, Kiah." His voice was a soft caress as he leaned down from his prancing steed, his hand reaching out to her.

She gazed into his hypnotic blue-grey eyes and her heart soared. Angels sang. Twittering fairies scattered gold dust through her hair. And when Jack's strong fingers wrapped around hers and he swung her up into his saddle, told her he loved her, there was nowhere else on Earth she would rather be.

With Jack behind her, body pressed hard against hers, every movement of the galloping stallion sent shivering waves of desire spiralling southward. Rock. Rock. Rock. Jack's hot mouth sucked and bit at her neck. She squirmed as she rode the smooth grain of the saddle. He took one hand off the reins to cup her breast. Oh, so gently. And when he found the nipple, circling, rolling, pinching the nub between his fingers, she moaned, wanting more.

"My Royal bed awaits us!" Holding her to him, he spurred his stallion into a faster gallop as they rode off into the sunset together. The sound of his horse's hooves drumming…drumming…drumming…

"Kiah! Wake up!"

Not wanting to be jerked from the hottest dream of her entire life, Kiah rolled over and dragged a pillow over her head.

The banging became louder, more insistent. "Kiah! Open up!"

Kiah growled as she reluctantly broke through the last shreds of her dream and sat up, the drumming of hooves still in her ears. She stared at the caravan door. The sound of horses' hooves appeared to be coming from outside. Still blinking sleep from her eyes, she reached up and switched on the light over her bed. "That you, Jack?"

"Yes! Open the door!" His heavy pounding and the panic in his voice sent her out of bed, pulling on rubber boots and a coat over her pyjamas, before she was fully awake.

"What's going on?" She opened the door to find Jack, not in his royal cape but in a faded checked flannel shirt that looked like it was ready for the rag bag and a pair of old track-pants a couple sizes too large. His hair was mussed, and a worried frown dug deep into his forehead.

"I need your help. Someone let all our paddock horses out."

"Of course."

He thrust a halter at her then ran a hand through his hair, mussing it further. The sensual movement made heat rush into her cheeks. Jack didn't need a long flowing red velvet cloak to make him look sexy. He'd look sexy in a chaff bag. "You'll need a torch."

"Okay. But who—?

"No time to talk…a couple of the retirees escaped onto the bitumen road before I could close the front gate. I'm off to catch them."

That's when she noticed Jack was holding onto the handles of a dilapidated bicycle that was as far removed from a Disneyesque white stallion as you could get. She lifted one eyebrow. "On a bike?"

"Easier than a car. I can lead one horse each side. Can't do that from a car." He swung his leg over the bike and lifted a hand to her. "Right. I'm off — only needs a speeding car and a horse to suddenly pop up out of the blackness and there could be an horrific accident."

She suddenly wanted to drag him off the bike and hold him, keep him warm and safe and out of harm's way. "Jack, be careful."

"I'm always careful," he said, one side of his mouth lifting in a grin. "Now, go help Marg. Last I saw she was chasing a foal out of her vegetable garden and she wasn't happy."

After grabbing a torch from the top drawer by the sink, Kiah pocketed a small bag of chopped carrots she'd prepared for Jet earlier. Anything to help catch the loose horses. Then, standing on the top of the caravan steps, she swept the beam of her torch over the chaos below.

By the light of the moon, brushing the surrounding darkness with its soft lunar glow, she could see horses and shadows milling on the driveway and spilling out onto the lawn in front of the house. The air was alive with noise and movement. Dust. Hoofbeats. Foals calling out to their mothers, their shrill baby voices cutting through the night air like scythes through wheat.

Who would be so low as to let their horses out? Surely this wasn't Connor's doing? What did he know about horses? And then a thought struck her, chilling her to the bone. Connor had been assigned to the Mounted Police earlier in his career. She remembered him boasting to Richard how he'd barged through the protesters with his horse, knocking one of them over because they didn't move out of the way quickly enough. Was this her fault? If any of the paddock horses were injured, or worse, would it be because she'd brought her troubles to *Windsong*?

Her torch light picked up the shape of Jack astride his old bicycle. He was pedalling towards the front gate, the headlight between his handlebars illuminating spooked horses spinning and taking off at his approach. A shiver brought goosebumps to her arms. One wrong move and both he or a horse could be injured.

As she descended the steps, two dark shapes lumbered out of the darkness, one human the other equine, startling her. "This little blighter dug up all my herbs and ate the heads off my prized azaleas." It was Marg, leading a prancing, totally unrepentant foal that was currently squealing and shying at imaginary boogeymen. Marg's hair, normally in a bun off her face now hung loose around her shoulders making her look years younger. She wore a pink chenille dressing gown tied with a sash around her ample middle, gumboots poking out beneath the hem.

"Marg? You, okay?"

"Yes, but I can't say the same for whoever let these blasted horses out. When I find the culprit, I'm gonna fire a shot of saltpetre up his backside and then hogtie him and reach for the branding iron."

"Hey, I'll hold him down while you stoke the fire."

Kiah walked beside Marg, her torch light swinging from side to side to assess the situation. "Let's start with the brood mares," she suggested, peering through the darkness at the moving shapes. "With any luck the foals will follow their mums back into the paddock and once they're settled, the retirees should be easy to catch."

"Right." Marg lifted a thumb in agreement and then strode off, the azalea-loving foal gambolling like a battery-charged pogo stick beside her.

At the left of her caravan, Kiah's torch picked out what looked like a pregnant mare with her current foal pressed close to her side. The mare was busy pulling out chunks of grass and thistles that grew each side of the path leading to the back paddock where Jet had first lived. With a chunk of carrot on her outstretched hand, Kiah approached slowly, cooing softy. The mare looked up; eyes wary in the torchlight. She went to spin and gallop away, but the smell of carrot proved too tempting. While the mare snuffled the treat off her hand, Kiah slipped the halter over the horse's head and fastened it. Two down, about another eighteen horses to go.

It was as Kiah turned away after closing the paddock gate on the last broodmare and her foal, that she caught sight of a small moving light coming from inside the stable block. That couldn't be right. She closed her eyes and when she opened them again the light was gone. Did she imagine it? Or perhaps the light was from Marg's torch. Maybe she'd spotted one of the horses straying down in front of the stables. Kiah shone her torch around, looking for Marg, found her over by the house, honing in on one of the retirees, who'd evidently decided grass growing outside his paddock was tastier than the grass inside.

There it was again. Just a pinprick of light that went on for a few seconds inside the stable block, then went out again.

Like the stab and twist of a sharp knife, a sudden sick feeling sliced across Kiah's stomach. Jet was in there. Her heart stuttered, stopped, then hammered against her chest. What if the intruder was Connor? She already suspected him of being behind the gutted rabbit on her door. What if his reason for letting the horses out was to distract them so he could get to Jet?

She flicked her torch light in the direction of the front gate. No sign of Jack. No time to get Marg's attention. And no time to grab her mobile from the caravan to ring the police.

She had to move fast.

Running toward the stable block, the sick feeling in her stomach intensified. How long had the intruder been in with the horses? What damage had he already done? If it was Connor, surely he wouldn't risk his career to get back at her by causing criminal damage, by hurting Jet? It didn't make sense.

The light had gone out by the time Kiah reached the stables. She paused, tried to slow her heartbeats and quieten her breathing so whoever was inside didn't hear what sounded to her like clashing cymbals and a bevy of bongo drums banging away inside her chest.

Slipping through the doorway, she turned off her torch and stood still, so as to acclimatise herself to the dark and wait for her eyes to adjust. She could hear the horses moving restlessly, as though things were not right. As though they were anxious. Big Lofty was banging on his feed bin down near the end of the block. A loud thud came from Magnifico's stable. The grey horse in stable two snorted as she passed. Goldie from stable three pawed at the ground. And a soft welcoming whinny from stable 4 made her heart smile in relief. She let out a deep sigh.

Whoever was in here wasn't after Jet.

But there was still an intruder in the stables. And he was up to no good.

Hardly daring to breathe, Kiah felt her way along the aisleway, checking on each horse. She spotted the stable office door slightly ajar. That wasn't right. Jack was a stickler for routine and he always locked the door of his office before going up to the house at night. Had the intruder broken in there? Was he or she still inside? Kiah sidled up to the office door and holding her breath, poked her head around the edge. What a mess! Okay, Jack wasn't the tidiest person she'd known, but he wouldn't leave the room in such a state. By the light of the desktop computer, which had been switched on, she could see papers and books scattered across the desk and over the floor. An upturned rubbish bin littered the carpet. File drawers had been pulled out and files scattered with abandon. Whoever was in the stables had been in there searching for something. But what? And why?

And where were they now?

Wanting to know more, Kiah tiptoed across the room, intent on discovering what the intruder had been looking for on the computer. She stared at the screen. A floor plan of the stable block, including the name of each horse with a stable number beside it, stared back at her.

Not good.

It seemed whoever had broken in had a specific plan. She edged her way out of the doorway, stifling a scream when the stable's feral cat, Piglet, suddenly sprang from the rafters and landed at her feet. She dodged back out of sight. Afraid to breath. Oh God, now she was shaking. She definitely wasn't cut out for this Nancy Drew malarky. Nerves ready to split, she waited while a torchlight swept the aisleway, halting on the now bristling Piglet, who let out an angry yowl and leaped onto the nearest stable door, disappearing inside.

Kiah waited until the light retreated before easing herself out from the office and edging forward again. It was worse than she'd first thought. The light had come from the stable opposite Lofty. The stable where their star racehorse was currently housed. The horse that was going to win the Kangaroo Downs Cup and put *Windsong* back on the map.

Magnifico.

She recalled the athletic chestnut's speed, the power of his muscles beneath her when she rode him in trackwork, and the sheer breath-taking surge when she'd asked for more. No way could she let anyone hurt this magnificent creature. He gave his all to his humans. Thinking of him terrified, hurt, by some black-hearted villain, had her hunting around for a weapon. Jack was out of reach. Marg was still chasing retirees. It was time to dig up her Xena the warrior princess persona.

She heard a thud and a muffled curse followed by another panicked squeal from Magnifico. Time to act. Her hand closed around the handle of a shovel; the only thing close to a weapon she could find. Where were Xena's spears and slingshots when you needed them? Maybe if she could sneak up behind the intruder and bang him over the head with the shovel it would give her time to tie him up and ring the police. That's if she could stop her hands from shaking long enough to use the shovel.

As she reached the last stable, the torch light came on again inside. There was a thickset man skulking around in there, his back to her. He held a pitchfork in one hand, a torch and syringe in the other. Magnifico, the whites of his eyes wild and terrified in the light from the torch was backing away from him, shaking his head, snorting, the muscles on his neck bulging and lathered with sweat.

"Stand still ya mongrel, or I'll punch ya lights out...."

Kiah let out a loud gasp. She recognized that voice. Knew who it was before he swung around, the sharp points of his pitchfork now aimed at her.

"Well, well, well, if it isn't Miss Goody Two-shoes." The voice was rough, laced with menace. The smile conveying as much warmth as a hungry crocodile eyeing off its dinner. "Didya enjoy the present I left on ya caravan door?"

A bead of sweat trickled down Kiah's forehead and her hands shook as they fisted around the handle of her shovel. A weapon that suddenly felt as useful as a feather duster. "What are *you* doing here, Cockroach?"

The man in stable 28, intent on injuring their runner in the Kangaroo Downs Cup, was the cruel horsemeat dealer from the saleyard.

For a moment her heart slowed and all she could think of was: *Thank God it's not Connor. Neither the dead rabbit nor this break-in had anything to do with her. She hadn't jeopardized everyone's safety by coming to Windsong.* And then a switch went off in Kiah's brain as the danger she was in hit her with the force of a ten-ton truck.

Could she take this man on? Would a shovel be enough to stop him? As Jack pointed out at the sale yard, Kiah was at least eight stone lighter than Cockroach. She swallowed the dry ball of fear in her throat, felt the rough edges scratching against the tender skin of her gullet as the lump went down.

If ever she was going to switch into warrior princess mode…now would be a good time. Heart leaping and cavorting like it was perched on an ant's nest, she sucked in a breath, forced herself to return the man's sub-zero stare, and took a step forward.

Magnifico was depending on her.

*****

Jack squinted into the weak pool of light emanating from his bike's headlight onto the bitumen road in front of him. He readjusted his grip on both lead ropes and the handlebars. Thankfully his two escapees were old stagers, Pixie and Nugget, both in their late teens and inherited as retirees from his late Uncle Dan's racing stable. He'd found them grazing on the side of the road, unfazed by their late-night adventure. Pixie had lifted her head and whinnied a welcome, while old Nugget continued to tug at the abundance of thistles lining the fence, barely registering when Jack slipped a halter over his head.

Now they were content to trot along, one each side of his bike, seemingly happy to continue their adventure. Neither giving any more trouble than an ear flick at a barking dog protecting its property, or a guarded stare at shadowy bushes on the sides of the road.

As Jack approached *Windsong*, he could see an agitated, Marg, in the dim light thrown by his bicycle's headlights. She was holding the gate wide open for him, but there was something about the way she was waving for him to hurry, that made his heart beat faster and an icicle lodge in his chest.

What now? Surely there hadn't been another catastrophe in the short time he'd been gone.

"Quick, Jack! Kiah's in trouble." Marg's voice, harsh with worry, blasted him the moment he got within hearing distance.

"Kiah? What do you mean? Where is she?" Fear sent Jack's brain spinning and his muscles into spasm. He dropped his bike in the middle of the driveway, spooking Pixie who snorted and pulled back on the lead. Instinctively, he reached up with a gentle hand to calm her.

"Kiah's in trouble." Marg repeated, her voice seeming to scratch its way from her throat. "She went into the stable block about five-ten minutes ago, and hasn't come out."

Jack frowned. "So...?"

"There's an intruder in there."

"What? With the horses?"

"Yes. I saw a torch light bobbing around inside and then I noticed Kiah running towards the stable block. I called out to her. Told her to wait for you to get back. But she either didn't hear me — or didn't want to."

"She went in?"

Marg, her breath irregular as though she'd just completed a marathon, nodded.

Shards of jagged ice churned in Jack's chest. He'd been a blind fool. More naïve than a six-week-old kitten. Letting the paddock horses out had been nothing more than a distraction enabling the perpetrator to sneak in and do God-knows-what to his race horses. Why couldn't he have seen it earlier? Now, because of his gullibility, he'd let a madman loose in the stable block. And Kiah, *his* Kiah, was in there with him. Forcing himself to keep calm, Jack turned to Marg. "Have you rung the police?"

She drew in a ragged breath and nodded. "They're on their way."

"Good." Not that he was going to wait for the police to arrive. How could he? With Kiah in danger? Fear, a writhing snake in his stomach, Jack closed his eyes and inhaled a long calming breath. "Now, Marg," he said, opening his eyes and taking control of his senses. "I want you to take these two horses and let them loose in their paddock, okay? And then go back to the house, check on Angel and wait for the police. I'll go find Kiah."

"Okay. And Jack, get her out of there." Looking every one of her sixty-two years, Marg shook her head, her eyes suspiciously damp. "A slip of a girl like that taking on an intruder. What was she thinking?"

"Don't worry, I'll find her." He squeezed Marg's hand, ice cold and shaky, before passing both lead ropes across to her. "And I promise you, if whoever's in there has hurt Kiah, scared her, or even so much as breathed heavy on her — he's history."

Not waiting for Marg's response, Jack snatched his bike up off the ground and set off towards the stable block, pedalling so fast, the rusty bike creaked and wobbled in protest. All the while, his brain anxiously bubbling and spewing like a pressure cooker on high. Surely Kiah wouldn't confront the intruder? Wouldn't try anything heroic? And then, he bit down on his bottom lip and pedalled even faster. Of course, she would. Jet was inside the stable block. And Kiah would put her life on the line to protect her horse.

As he drew closer, he could see a torchlight moving around in one of the stables at the other end of the block. Not Jet's stable, but Magnifico's. Someone was attempting to harm Jack's top performer — but who? And why? Who'd want him to lose his chance of both winning the Cup and getting the stables out of debt?

And then another thought almost took his legs from under him. Did this have anything to do with the corrupt owner and groom who'd caused the stable's fall from grace and his uncle's suicide five years ago? Was there still bad feeling there?

On reaching the stable block, Jack threw himself off the bike, letting it lay where it fell, and slipped inside the open doorway. No sign of Kiah, but the horses were restless; some pacing, some stamping their feet, a couple pawing at the ground. Goldie, from stable 4, let out an anxious whinny when she saw him. Maybe trying to warn him of the interloper.

Desperate to get Kiah away from danger before he tackled whoever was out to harm his horses, Jack peered along the aisleway, but could see no sign of her. Then, faintly, from the other end of the block, her heard her voice. And it was coming from inside Magnifico's stable.

That's where he'd seen the torchlight. Was he too late?

Fear had him wanting to rush up the aisleway and throw himself at the intruder, shove his fist down the man's throat and yank out his tonsils, cook them up for next door's sheep dogs. But he couldn't. It might put Kiah in more danger.

In an attempt to slow his heart rate down, all the better to think more clearly, Jack hooked a deep breath and let it out slowly. If he approached Magnifico's stable from the inside, even quietly, the horses up that end of the block would see him, give his presence away.

Best to approach the problem from the outside.

When Jack first took over *Windsong*, he had outside yards attached to each stable, figuring horses could walk in and out during the day whenever they pleased and it would keep them happy. He'd also had Dutch doors installed between the yard and the stable, which meant they could be safely locked in at night.

And that's how he planned to get into Magnifico's stable without being seen.

On reaching the end yard, Jack slammed the bike brakes on too quickly, stumbled, lost his balance, and only by reaching out with both hands, saved himself from burying his nose in the dirt.

Calm. Keep calm. Take a breath. Let it out slowly...

The moment his breathing was under control, Jack ducked under the metal yard rail, his eyes straining to see in the dark. If he used his torch it might give him away, alert the villain currently threatening, not only his best horse, but Kiah — the only woman since Bianca who could set his heart pounding, put a smile on his face, and make him think that maybe, just maybe, he didn't have to spend the rest of his life alone.

And then, almost as though the Universe was on his side, the moon peeped coquettishly out from behind the clouds before flouncing all the way out, lighting the surroundings with its divine luminosity. Before the man up there could change his mind and zap the moon back under a cloud, Jack ran across the deep sand to the Dutch doors and knelt down. He pressed his ear hard against the varnished wood, and listened.

Two muffled voices could be heard on the other side...one definitely Kiah's...and also what sounded like the scramble of a frightened horse.

Jack's breath caught in his throat.

If he didn't get Kiah out of there right now, she was in danger both from the intruder *and* a panicked Magnifico.

Quietly sliding the bolt across, Jack opened the bottom door a crack, just enough to see through, get the lie of the land. Plan his attack.

His gaze immediately fell on Kiah, her wild, sleep-tousled hair, gleaming a fiery red in the hard light of the torch. Jack had never seen her look so afraid, yet so strong. So dishevelled, yet so beautiful. Her face pale, she stood her ground, back straight, a determined lift to her chin.

And he'd never loved her more.

Jack's gaze switched to the intruder. The man was looming over her, threatening her with a pitchfork. Immediately, his breath hitched in his throat. A red mist descended. Anger bubbled in his chest. All Jack wanted to do was smash his fist into the man's face until it turned to pulp — but one wrong move, and Kiah could be history.

Calm. Keep calm. Take a breath. Let it out slowly…

Although Jack could only see the man's back, he looked familiar. Dirty overalls, unkempt hair, even the shape of him.

"Why are you doing this?" Kiah's voice, high-pitched and squeaky, as though she'd used up all her saliva, had Jack digging his nails into the palms of his hands to stop from crashing through the door too soon.

"'Cos ya blowhard of a boyfriend needs to be taught a lesson — that's why."

Jack went statue-still, an icy cold rage hijacking his senses

Cockroach?

What the hell?

"But why?" Kiah, her eyes seemingly glued to the pitchfork raised above the man's head, shook her head. "What did Jack ever do to you?"

"He ruined me, that's what. Some mongrel on the committee heard about the video he took at Chesterton saleyard. And then, two weeks ago, the bastards came around in force, inspected me property, and then shut me down."

"But that's not Jack's fault."

His laugh held not a shred of humor. "No? Well, maybe it's *your* fault then…" He thrust the pitchfork at Kiah, his arm muscles bunching as he lunged.

"Or yours." Kiah dodged to the side and Jack's heart did two twists and a belly flop as the pitchfork grazed her cheek. "Maybe if you weren't so cruel to horses, the committee wouldn't have to—"

"Shut it, bitch!" Cockroach lunged again, this time catching Kiah on the arm, making her cry out. "I'm gonna mess you up so bad, Jack Sullivan won't ever look at ya again."

It was time...

Like a tormented tiger breaking free of its cage, Jack smashed the door wide open and roared into the stable, fists up and bunched at the ready. "You're wrong there, Cockroach! The only one getting messed up is you!"

"Whaat?" As Cockroach spun around to face his attacker, pitchfork raised, two things happened simultaneously. Kiah swung her shovel and connected with the back of his head, while Magnifico, mouth open, ears flat, charged from the corner of the stable and took a large chunk out of the man's backside as he went down.

Jack blinked, regarded the prostate figure sprawled like a wet noodle at his feet and grinned. 'Now *that*," he drawled, raising one eyebrow at Kiah, "is what *I* call Karma."

THIRTEEN

Perched on the tailgate of the ambulance, a blanket huddled around her shoulders, Kiah wasn't sure whether to laugh or cry. She'd just come from being interrogated by a perky female detective who'd treated her like a superhero from the next Marvel movie; commenting on the trajectory and swing of Kiah's shovel as it arced towards Cockroach's head, while inviting her to join their local softball team.

The thin reedy light trickling through the open doorway of the stable block cut through the early morning darkness. It sent distorted shadows dancing across the path in front of her, while the blue and red flashing lights on the roof of the ambulance played a colourful game of tag across everything they touched.

Shivering, she tugged the blanket closer. All she really wanted to do was climb into bed and drag the quilt over her head. Blank out the memory of Cockroach's cruel black eyes when he'd lunged at her with the pitchfork. Murderous eyes that had hauled her reluctantly back to that last terrifying hour with Richard, in the cold bathroom of their luxury 2-bedroom apartment.

The cheerful words of a lanky paramedic, wearing a boyish dimple and an infectious grin, broke into her thoughts. "Okay, my lovely, I'll give you two choices." Like a boy scout, he lifted two fingers in the air. "One…" He folded down his pointer finger. "You can drive to the hospital, sit yourself down on a hard plastic waiting-room chair for three or four hours and finally get stitched up by some grumpy overworked doctor who's already been on shift for ten or more hours…OR…" He folded down his middle finger. "I can seal the wound with three or four butterfly clips. Right now. No waiting." He wiggled his eyebrows at her. "And I'll even throw in a lollypop."

Luckily, the graze on Kiah's cheek was superficial and only needed a swab and a band aid, but the cut on her arm was deeper. At the thought of those lethal sharp spikes and the deadly intentions of the man aiming them at her, the shivers started up again. She hitched her blanket up further and forced the images away. "Umm…butterfly clips."

"Good choice."

A battered SUV of indeterminate colour and four mud-encrusted tyres, came sliding to a rattling stop between the ambulance and the doorway of the stable block. Greg, the vet, tumbled out. With a knitted beanie pulled low over his messy bed-hair and an ancient Drizabone hiding the top half of his pyjamas, the poor guy was probably in dreamland when his phone rung. But this was an emergency. Had Cockroach managed to inject Magnifico? If so, what was in the syringe? Greg needed to do an immediate blood test on the horse to find out. He'd also need to check for injuries and give him a mild sedative to calm him down. Poor Magnifico. A horse that gave his all on the track, a beautiful animal that radiated charisma and power. After this experience, would he ever trust a human again?

Greg raised one hand in a wave. "You okay, Kiah?"

She lifted a thumb in the air, indicating she was fine, then watched Greg collect his veterinary bag from the back of the vehicle and hurry into the stable block.

"All done." The paramedic treating Kiah's wound patted her on the shoulder. "And if I say so myself, it's a work of art."

She glanced down at the neat row of butterfly clips white against the light tan of her arm, and realized he'd finished and she hadn't noticed. She smiled up at him. "It's beautiful. Pity you couldn't hang your work in the local art gallery."

"Thank you. Now…" His grin was catchy, like a popular song. "Orange, pineapple or raspberry?"

Kiah laughed. This guy was better than a tonic. "Thanks, but I might give the lollypop a miss this time."

Two paramedics in green scrubs, one each end of a gurney, eased their way through the open doorway of the stable block and headed toward the ambulance, a burly policeman following two lengths behind.

Kiah's laugh died in her throat.

Cockroach...

Stumbling to her feet, she could hear the obnoxious horsemeat dealer yelling abuse at the paramedics, demanding more painkillers, swearing revenge. She wanted to move away so he didn't see her lurking beside the ambulance, but her legs, spongy beneath her, refused to cooperate. Her brain kept telling her legs to run, to get far away from the oncoming madman and his abusive tirade, but it was like her shoes were glued to the ground. Her heart banged against her chest. Her breath rasped in her throat. And as she reached out to steady herself against the open door of the ambulance, her clammy hands slid on the metal and she almost fell.

A deep voice, as comforting as a warm hug, came from behind her. "Hey, Kiah, let's get you back to your caravan. You look like you could do with a hot drink and a warm bed."

"Jack?" Kiah fell into his waiting arms, her vision blurred with tears. She melted against him, snuggling closer, taking strength from his easy comfort.

How had he known she needed him?

"All taken care of here. Greg's looking after Magnifico, and this burly policeman said he'd accompanying Cockroach to the hospital and stay with him until it's time to whisk him off to jail."

"There ya are! Ya bloody mongrels! I'll git ya for this!"

Cockroach....

Kiah's gut swirled and if she'd eaten in the last five hours, she'd have lost the lot. But she couldn't allow Cockroach to frighten her. He was the offender. Not her. He was the one who'd have killed her, no qualms, if Jack hadn't appeared on the scene and distracted him. He was the one who'd invaded the stable block with one plan in mind — to hurt a beautiful horse who'd never done him any harm. That is...until tonight. She stifled a grin at the image of Magnifico's lethal lunge...teeth bared.

Drawing on her warrior princess persona, Kiah stepped out of Jack's arms and took a step toward the gurney now being loaded into the ambulance. "No, Mr. Cochran," she said, her voice steel. "You *won't* 'git' me. And you *won't* 'git' any more horses. In fact, you'll be locked up where you can't 'git' *anyone*, for a very long time."

And with that, she took Jack's hand in hers and headed for the stable block. She wasn't ready to go back to her caravan yet. She didn't feel one bit sleepy. "Let's check on Magnifico. Ask Greg what his verdict is."

Jack's fingers tightened around hers, the zing between them sending tingles all the way up her arm. "When I saw Cockroach standing over you with that pitchfork, Kiah, I swear, my heart did a nosedive and splattered all over the ground."

"It did?"

"It did. But you were brilliant."

"And so were you."

A grin curving the corners of his mouth, Jack raised both eyebrows at her. "Remember when you first took the guy on at the saleyard and I told you he had at least eight stone on you?" His fingers tightened on her hand. "You didn't take any notice of me then, and you didn't tonight."

"Yeah, but—"

"I'm proud of you, Kiah. You stood up to that brute like-like…"

"Buffy the Vampire Slayer?"

Jack's laugh broke through the stillness of the night and warmed her heart like a hug. Strange, she'd never likened a man's laugh to a hug before. When Richard laughed, it was more like a punch in the stomach, a portent to drowning in a sea of abuse.

"Hey, guys." Greg, his coat undone, revealing colourful action figures sprinkled across his bright yellow pyjamas, looked up from examining a small spike on Magnifico's shoulder. "Just a scratch. Good job this guy's agile and managed to keep out of reach."

Jack leaned over the stable door. "And the syringe?"

"Can't identify the contents until I get back to my surgery." He ran a hand down the horse's neck, before turning to close his vet bag. "The syringe is still three-quarter full, so let's hope your intruder didn't get close enough to inject any of it into the horse's system."

"Thanks for coming so quickly, Greg."

"You're lucky I was in bed, dreaming of Kylie Minogue, and not out in a freezing paddock in the middle of nowhere, bringing a reluctant calf into the world."

Jack chuckled. "Dreaming of Kylie Minogue? What would your beautiful wife have to say about that?"

"Hey, just because I'm happily married, doesn't mean I can't visualize. And anyway, Suzie tells me she dreams of Chris Hemsworth." He grinned and flicked his eyebrows up and down. "Keeps our sex life interesting."

Kiah's dream, the one she'd been enjoying before this nightmare started, flashed into her head. Of her and Prince Jack, together, on a white stallion, galloping through a magical forest on the way to his bedchamber. Of how, with every stride of the stallion, his body ground against hers, causing her to lose her breath, as well as her senses, while his scorching fingers caressed her cool skin.

Oh God! A deep heaviness settled between her legs and prickles of need had her swallowing a lump in her throat. She licked her dry lips at the thought of what would have happened in Prince Jack's bedchamber, if only she hadn't been woken up before they'd arrived at their destination.

Another black mark against Cockroach.

"Right, I've given this lad a sedative to calm him down. Best to leave him now, let him recover from the trauma he's been through and hope it hasn't destroyed his trust in us humans." Greg opened the stable door and closed it behind him. "If I had my way, mongrels like the guy who terrorized this poor horse, would be tarred and feathered and banned from being anywhere near another animal, for life."

After accompanying Greg back to his car and saying goodnight, Kiah suddenly didn't want to be alone. She knew once she returned to her caravan, tried to sleep, nightmares would take over. Not only of Cockroach, but the usual terrifying ones of Richard, where she'd wake up screaming. She glanced at Jack, close beside her, and suddenly felt the urge to run her fingers through his hair, feel the warmth of his skin, outline his lips with a wet digit. "Don't know about you," she said, keeping her voice neutral, "but I could do with that hot drink you mentioned before. How about I put the kettle on in your office, while we tidy it up?"

"Are you kidding? Tidying up can wait until tomorrow. I'll just block off the office door for now and then you're coming up to the house with me. I'll make you a coffee — and I might even find a bottle of something stronger, to top it up."

"Sounds good to me."

With the door of the office jemmied, the broken wood raw and splintering against the bright yellow paint, all Jack could do was prop a wheelbarrow against it to keep it closed.

"Bloody Cockroach," he growled shaking his head at the damage. "Who'd have thought he was behind all this? Even the dead rabbit."

Kiah leaned against Goldie's stable door and frowned. That was something she was finding hard to get her head around. "So, what's his story?" she said, turning to rub a hand over Goldie's soft nose when she felt the horse nudge her between the shoulder blades. "Why does Cockroach hate you so much?"

Jack let out a sigh and shrugged as though the story was old news. "Even back in school, Barry Cochran found life difficult. His mum left when he was ten, his dad drank and beat him up, and he turned to crime, to gain attention, I suppose. As for hating me? In his eyes I was the lucky one whose parents had money, I was captain of the footy team, and found schoolwork easy. I was the lucky rich kid who'd go to university and have a bright future, while he lived off what he could bully and steal from others. I guess losing his business because of my video was a step too far and he cracked."

"Is that why your dad's angry with you now? You know, because you're training race horses instead of paying him back for the money he spent putting you through university?"

Jack sighed. "I've paid him back, plenty. I worked for him from the time I graduated until three years ago. Now it's *my* turn to live *my* life *my* way." Jack's voice sounded like every word held a razor blade that scraped against his throat as he spoke. Finally, he shook his head as though to clear it of bad juju and held out his hand. "Come on, Kiah." His fingers closed around hers. "I have a new Nespresso coffee-making machine that's calling our names."

As they approached the house, Kiah could see Marg, dressing-gown belted loosely around her nightdress, waiting for them under the veranda light. She wrapped her arms around Kiah and hugged her so tightly, Kiah found herself gasping for breath. "You should have waited for me," she admonished. "I'd have come with you." Marg sniffed then pulled away to check Kiah out properly, her gaze taking in the bandages, the smudges under her eyes, the hay in her hair. "Your face…your arm…what did that monster do to you?"

"I'm fine. Really, I am. They're just scratches." Kiah flicked her head in Jack's direction. "All thanks to Rocky Balboa here. He appeared out of nowhere, you know, like a genie from a bottle, fists raised, ready to pummel the enemy into submission. Gave me the perfect chance to use my shovel as a baseball bat."

"Is Angel, okay?" asked Jack, eyes full of concern.

Marg nodded. "A forty-four-gun salute wouldn't wake that one."

"Thanks, Marg." Jack squeezed the housekeeper's shoulder. "What would I do without you?"

"You'd manage." Marg, head high, led the way into the kitchen where two mugs, a jug of milk, a bowl of sugar, and a heaped plate of homemade choc chip biscuits were on the table. The new Nescafe coffee machine chugging merrily away in the background.

"I wouldn't," said Jack. "And you know it."

"Don't go getting all soppy on me." Hands on hips, Marg shook her head. "But I tell you what, now I've seen you're both in one piece and I don't need to visit you in hospital, I'm off to bed." She ran a shaky hand through her greying hair and let out a huff. "I'm getting way too old for late night adventures. I need my beauty sleep."

With that, she kissed Kiah on the cheek, hugged Jack, and still shaking her head and muttering to herself, pushed through the back door and out to her granny flat in the garden.

"You'll never get too old for adventures, Marg," Kiah called out to her.

After pouring two mugs of coffee and adding a smidgen of whisky to both, Jack led the way into the loungeroom, his coffee in one hand and the plate of biscuits in the other. "Let's get comfortable in here. You look dead on your feet."

"Thanks for the compliment." Kiah laughed as she followed Jack. She placed her coffee mug on the edge of the coffee table and with legs as bendy as soft liquorice sticks, she dropped bonelessly down beside him on the squishy sofa. Something had changed inside her tonight. Something big.

Something that made her feel stronger. More alive. As though she was close to being whole again.

She sat in silence for a few minutes, leaning back, listening to the noises outside the window. The cheep of a night bird. The distant rumble of a passing car. The soft whinny of a horse in one of the paddocks, calling to its mate. But when Jack, who was pressed up against her on the sofa, reached across for the sugar, his fingers skimming her hand in the process, she suddenly became acutely aware of his touch, the texture of his skin, and what it was doing to her emotions. Heart quickening, she drew in a deep breath along with his distinct bouquet of plain soap and far-from-plain man which sent shivers of desire rocketing into sensitive corners of her anatomy. Corners that had never known such hunger before.

When he spoke, his voice was a soft rumble in her ear. "I was scared I was going to lose you tonight, Kiah."

She reached out to cup his face. A face that was growing more familiar, more dear to her every day. Strong jawline, full lips, blue grey eyes currently full of concern. "Thanks for being there for me tonight, Jack. If you hadn't jumped out and distracted Cockroach, I-I don't know how this would have ended. I-I—"

"Hey, you'd have slammed him with the shovel whether I'd been there or not." He touched her cheek, his thumb brushing lazy circles across her skin, until every nerve ending roared to attention. "Standing up to Cockroach tonight, you looked so beautiful. So brave." His hand drifted from her cheek down to her lips, tracing their outline with the dedication of an artist. "So strong. So amazing. So—"

Kiah leaned forward and stopped him; her lips flirting with his. It was time to show Jack how much he meant to her; how much he'd helped her become whole again, how far she'd fallen for him.

The kiss, chaste at first, gradually took on a life of its own as Jack tugged gently at her bottom lip with his teeth, urging her to open to him. She swallowed the warmth of his breath, tasting him, revelling in the brush of his tongue against hers, until an all-encompassing heat filled her, making her squirm against him. Wanting more, she moaned deep into his mouth, angling her head to the side to give him better access. Oh my God, kissing Richard had never made her feel like this. Like being on a rollercoaster and never wanting to get off.

And she couldn't get enough of it.

"Jack…" Almost panting, she tugged at the waistband of his trackpants, freeing his shirt so she could run her hands underneath, over his tight skin, the solid delineation of his muscles.

But that wasn't enough. She needed skin to skin.

"Jack…I really, *really,* want to go to bed with you."

Mouth buried in that sensitive spot under her right ear, Jack lifted his head. Pulling back, he stared Kiah in the eyes. "Are you sure?"

Kiah hesitated. Her throat constricted as the sounds of Richard's animal-like grunts played in her mind, the painful unnatural things he'd forced her to do, the sickening stench of his sweat, as he raped her. Could she do this? Could she trust Jack? Give herself to him? Make love to him? And then she looked at Jack. *Really* looked at him. At the kindness in his eyes, the sweetness of his concern and how her heart melted with love whenever he hugged her, letting her bury her head in his chest for comfort. How he made her feel strong.

She reached up and traced the line of his jaw, her eyes never leaving his. "Let's just say, if we don't take this further, right now, I'll combust into a squillion pieces, and you'll have a lot of explaining to do in the morning when Marg finds me scattered all over the lounge room floor."

He laughed, and kissed her again, his stubble, rough and real, scraping against her cheek. Then, gradually unwinding from the sofa, he stretched out a hand to help her to her feet. "In that case, my dear," he said, his voice like thick honey. "My bedchamber awaits you."

Kiah's smile started in her toes, skittered into her heart and finally settled on her lips. Had Jack been having the same dream as her?

FOURTEEN

Kiah rolled over in bed, yawned, and like a contented cat with a tummy full of cream, kinked her back and languidly stretched both arms high in the air. She felt comfortably lethargic, her limbs heavy, but tingling.

Almost purring, she slowly opened one eye…to find Jesus staring down at her. An eerie, unearthly glow back-lighting his sad, ethereal countenance.

What the heck?

One hand dragging the sheet over her nakedness, she jerked upright and blinked at the framed photo on the wall in front of her. It was hung between an oil painting of a magnificent chestnut horse, similar to the equine gracing the sign over the front gate, and a black and white etching of a racetrack scene, set over a hundred years ago.

Of course. She was in Jack's bed. And daylight streaming through the chink in the curtains, meant he was gone and she was alone.

When she and Jack had staggered into the room, both eager to ditch their clothes as quickly as possible, it had been dark, she'd been thinking of other things — or maybe not thinking at all — and the night light squatting on the cabinet beside his bed had been switched on low. After all, they weren't there for an inventory of his bedroom, but for Jack to show her how beautiful sex between two people who really cared about each other could be. And he'd certainly excelled at that. They'd made long, languid, exquisite love, several times, until she'd finally fallen asleep with Jack's naked body spooning cosily against hers.

With a sweeping glance, Kiah checked out the rest of the room. Not overtly masculine. Nor feminine. Instead, a built-in bookcase, overflowing with well-read books and racing magazines, ran along one wall, while along the other was a pearly white built-in wardrobe; one door slightly ajar showing a man's clothing hanging on the rail. A matching, built-in dressing table flowed on from the wardrobe, the oval-shaped mirror reflecting Kiah's wild bed hair and large curious eyes. From her perch on the bed, Kiah could see a sprinkling of toiletries, a wooden-backed brush and a framed photo of a beautiful woman wearing a colourful gypsy skirt and blouse, her long silvery hair billowing in the breeze, her face wreathed in a bubbly, endearing smile, that reminded Kiah of Angel.

Bianca…Jack's first love. With another scrutiny of the woman in the photo, Kiah chewed on her bottom lip. Such a beautiful woman. Was Jack completely over her? Was he ready for another relationship? Or was he so in love with his dead wife he'd never find love again?

And then she thought of the way he'd made love to her only hours before and sighed. A sigh that broke through her insecurities and promised hope for the future. It was Kiah who'd been in Jack's bedroom, naked in his bed. It was Kiah he'd made love to, all the while checking she was okay, that she wasn't spooked. He'd been so gentle, so tender, so inventive with his lips and tongue, she'd erupted under him — her first unfaked orgasm in twelve years.

And then her second. *And* her third

Heavy brocade curtains hung at the window, a bright chunk of light indicating it was way past 4.30 am. Leaping out of bed so quickly the pillows toppled to the floor, she dragged her phone from the side table and powered it on. Holy catnip! It was 7.30.

She was three hours late for work.

Springing out of bed, Kiah grabbed her clothes from the floor and headed for the ensuite bathroom. Even if she had to put the same clothes back on, she'd enjoy a shower first before doing the walk of shame back to her caravan. Thinking again of what happened in Jack's bed last night, she realized there was no shame. No regrets. In fact, she couldn't wait to get Jack in bed again. Orgasms were now her favourite thing.

Still grinning, she quickly showered, using Jack's plain soap to wash the sex off her body, her grin widening at the thought of all the nooks and crannies that needed washing. My God, what had she been missing out on all these years?

It was almost 7.45am by the time Kiah followed the mouth-watering smell of bacon and eggs and freshly brewed coffee to the large but homely kitchen at the front of the house. Inside, she found Angel, dressed in a navy and gold school uniform. She was spooning breakfast cereal into her mouth, while directing a barbie doll to lead a troop of battered green plastic soldiers across the kitchen table. Marg, looking none the worse for her late night adventure, hovered over the stove, busily producing the appetising smells that filled the house.

Kiah hesitated at the door. Suddenly unsure. A little embarrassed. What would they think of her spending the night? She cleared her throat. "Um…good morning."

"'Bout time you woke up, sleepyhead," said Marg, without turning away from the stove. "How do you like your bacon? Lightly done or crispy?"

Kiah ran a hand through her damp hair and smiled. "Um…crispy, thanks."

"Eggs?"

"Uh…over easy."

"Hi, Kiah." Angel wiped milk from her lips with the back of her hand before beaming up at her. After examining the photo on Jack's dressing-table, Kiah could definitely recognize the little girl's mother in her smile. "Wanna see my new soldier? He's a general."

Marg flipped the bacon over in the pan and tutted. "Kiah will think you're a tomboy, playing with soldiers."

Angel let out a long, exaggerated sigh and shook her head. "Kiah's cool, Marg. She knows all about Combat Barbie. Even made a sword for her out of an old brooch she found in the retiree's paddock. It was Kiah who showed me how to bomb the enemy with chocolate Maltesers."

Marg's lips twitched as she slotted an eye-roll in Kiah's direction. "Chocolate Maltesers?"

Angel proceeded to give a demonstration of loading a single Malteser into a sparkly pink plastic cannon and firing it into the midst of the oncoming army. When half the soldiers toppled over, Angel gave Kiah a fist pump. Then, after retrieving the ammunition, she popped the chocolate in her mouth, devouring it in three crunchy bites.

Kiah nodded. "Direct hit!"

Angel dug a larger plastic soldier from her pocket and held the toy up for Kiah to inspect. "I've called this one General Horatio Fitzgarbage."

Kiah took the General from Angel and studied him carefully before placing him at the head of the opposing red soldiers. "Love the moustache," she told Angel. "Makes him look very important."

The cheeky grin Angel sent Kiah once again reminded her of the little girl's mother. "But not important enough to beat Barbie's army."

Seemed like this war had been won before it had even started.

Marg slid a full plate of bacon, eggs, and a fat potato cake onto the table, the aroma of the food making Kia's mouth drool. "Get this into you while it's hot, Kiah. And Angel, leave your toys and get a move on. The school bus is due at the front gate in ten minutes and it won't hang around waiting for you."

"But—"

"No buts. If you miss the bus, I haven't got time to drive you to school this morning. And neither has your dad." She handed Angel her backpack and a lunch box and shooed her off.

"Bye Kiah." Angel's long squeezy hug surprised Kiah. The sweet smell of baby powder, breakfast cereal, and little girl making her wonder what it would be like to be someone's mother. Someone whose unconditional love brightened your life and made you want to be the best version of self you could be.

Once Angel had disappeared out the front door, to start the trek down the driveway, Kiah picked up her knife and fork and started in on her breakfast.

"By the way, before I forget," said Marg, rinsing off Angel's dishes under the tap over the sink, "the Master said it was okay for you sleep in, but he wants you at trackside by 9.15am sharp. Says Jet's having his first hard hit-out and he needs you there to time the gallop."

Kiah laughed. "The Master?"

Marg's eyes twinkled as she placed a large mug of coffee next to the heaped breakfast plate. "Well, he was looking very masterly and chirpy this morning. Seems like something agreed with him overnight."

Kiah, heat racing up her neck and into both cheeks, buried her nose in the coffee mug, her mind replaying the delicious things that had agreed with Jack overnight and reflecting on the fact that the 'something' had definitely agreed with her too.

After eating every morsel in front of her and even cleaning the plate by swiping a slice of toast across to soak up the remaining egg, Kiah rinsed off her dishes and set them in the dishwasher before hugging Marg, then taking off for her caravan.

So…Jet was having his first hard hit-out. And Jack wanted her to be there, beside him. She didn't know whether to dress up for the occasion, or wear her normal work wear. After deliberating for all of one minute, she laughed at herself. This was a racing stable. She was going to time her horse's gallop, and then take over, as usual, by hosing him down and getting him comfortably settled after his run. Feed him his usual carrots, groom him, pick out his feet, and let him drool all over her while she hugged him. Not something you did wearing a pretty dress and fancy shoes. And after all, she'd been wearing rubber boots and a coat pulled on over the top of her pyjamas last night and yet Jack had still made love to her.

Before she could drift off again into reliving how Jack had made love to her and how he'd made her feel when his lips kissed and sucked at every part her, she changed into jeans, tee shirt and riding boots. Then, humming to herself, she set off across the paddocks toward the training track.

"Hi sleepyhead." Jack, perched on his usual canvas folding chair, looked up and grinned.

She dropped onto a second canvas folding chair beside him. "You should have woken me up."

"You looked so cute, lying there, making little snuffly sounds in your sleep, I didn't have the heart." He leaned over and kissed her.

She smiled into his kiss and if they hadn't been in full view of the riders on the track, all eyes in their direction, she'd have taken the kiss further. Reluctantly, she pulled back, letting out a sigh as she settled more comfortably on the canvas chair. "Marg said Jet was doing a time trial."

"Yep, and he's almost ready to go." He handed her a stopwatch. "When

Taylor's finished warming him up, you can time him, while I watch his action."

Taylor, aboard Jet, trotted towards them, ready to receive her final instructions from Jack. "Hi Kiah, heard all about your experience last night."

Kiah could feel the blush warming her cheeks. How did everyone know what had happened between her and Jack last night?

"Thank goodness you saved Magnifico," Taylor continued, pulling up in front of them and loosening Jet's reins.

Of course. Cockroach. Last night. In the stable. Kiah chewed on her bottom lip as she stood and reached up to rub Jet's forehead, telling him what a handsome boy he was and to have fun in his gallop.

"Okay, Taylor," Jack interrupted. "I want to see what Jet's got under his bonnet today. Kiah will have the clock on him, so run Jet against Goldie over 1000 metres. Okay? He's been showing enough in his workouts, so push him on, see what he can do, but remember, this is a training track not the bowling green smooth turf of a city race track, so be careful."

"Gotcha, boss."

Kiah watched Jet move away, dancing, itching to get going and she felt her heart quicken. It was all very well owning a racehorse — until it was time to race and the nerves took over. And that time was getting closer.

"He's ready." Jack assured her in a voice that said he had every confidence in the horse. He squeezed her knee and flicked his head in the direction of Jet. "You could have something special there."

"Whether he wins a race or not, Jet will always be special to me."

By now, Goldie and Jet were cantering together on the other side of the track. Chestnut and black, side by side. As they passed the starting post, Kiah pressed the button on top of the stop watch and the two horses surged forward into a gallop.

Goldie had already won several country races so this was a good test for the younger and untried Jet, but right from the start the black horse kicked two lengths in front and that's where he stayed throughout the gallop.

"Time's 03:38:2," Kiah said looking down at the numbers on the stop watch.

Jack's eyes lit up as he leant across to check the numbers for himself.

"Taylor wasn't asking for more than was safe, yet he beat Goldie and ran as good a time as Magnifico did in his first hit out."

"So…you're happy?"

"Happy?" He grinned. "On a registered race track, that's a good time, so to run it on our paddock track is fantastic."

Chest tight, Kiah blinked back a tear as she watched her beautiful black rescue horse slow down into a 'look at me' toe-pointing dressage-trot and then a walk as Taylor prepared to cool him off.

"Let's celebrate by going for a picnic." Jack took Kiah's hand in his and squeezed softly.

"Could we?"

"I still have a few more horses to assess, so after you've settled Jet back in his stable and told him how utterly amazing he is by feeding him carrots, why don't you go catch up on a couple of hours shuteye before we go."

"But—"

"Go on, you didn't get much sleep last night. What say I pick you up from your caravan at around one o'clock and we'll take a picnic basket to our special spot along the river. Beside the tyre swings? Okay?"

A feeling of joy, like she'd never known before, had Kiah turning a sniff into a shaky grin. Jack Sullivan had feelings for her, Jet had just proved himself on their trial track and she and Jack were going for a picnic. Could this day get any better? "Want me to bring anything?"

"Yes…" Jack's eyebrows performed a little up and down dance. "You."

By the time Kiah returned to her caravan after attending to Jet, she was floating on such a high, she thought she'd never get any sleep, yet, within ten minutes of stripping off her boots and sweater, she'd drifted into a deep, dreamless sleep.

∗∗∗∗∗

At exactly one o'clock, Jack roared up to Kia's caravan on his Harley Davison. Gravel churned under the tyres as he came to an abrupt halt, set one foot on the ground, and blew the horn.

It was only a half hour walk to their special spot on the river bank, so he wasn't sure why he'd opted to dig into the back corner of the large industrial shed behind the tractor, remove the canvas, and dust down his Harley. Although he hadn't ridden the motor bike for a couple of years, he'd regularly, every three months, taken the machine out of the shed, washed it down, polished it, checked it out, and then stashed it back in the corner and covered it over again.

"Wow. That's one hot mother." Kiah strolled towards him dressed in jeans, long leather boots and some flowery-looking top. "I know as much about motorbikes as I know about the stock market. Diddly squat. But this beautiful big beast looks a lot like one of those sexy bikes that bikies ride. A Harley." She sent him a cheeky wink. "And all that's missing is your leather jacket and gang symbol."

"Didn't want to scare you."

Kiah laughed. "Hard to scare me when you have a prettily embroidered picnic basket balanced on the front of the beast. Love the little hearts and flowers decorating the lid."

Jack rolled his eyes. They owned several picnic baskets, but of course, Marg had to pack their lunch in the basket adorned with love hearts. He passed Kiah a fluorescent pink helmet to wear. "This should fit. Belonged to Bianca. Angel has an identical helmet which she wears whenever we take the bike out for a run."

Kiah fitted the helmet on her head and while buckling the chin strap, lifted an eyebrow at his declaration. "And when was the last time you took your daughter out on the back of your Harley, Jack, 'cos I've been here six months and didn't even know you *owned* a motorbike."

Shoulders slumped, Jack looked down, fiddling with the handle of the picnic basket. "Yeah, yeah, I know, too long." It was almost like he was talking to himself when he continued. "It's easy to get so involved with work you forget to take time out for pleasure." He caught her eye and reaching out, cupped her chin in his hand, his thumb caressing her cheek, the skin so soft under his touch. "But that's going to change. From now on, I'm going to make sure I take more time out for Angel…and for you."

Kiah's voice was soft, her eyes not leaving his. "Sounds like a good plan."

"Ready? If so, hop on the back and wrap your arms around me." He flicked both his eyebrows and grinned as he felt the tremors of her landing on the soft leather pillion seat behind him, wriggling until she was comfortable. "That's the best part."

Tightening her arms around him, Kiah laughed and the warm air that skated over the back of his neck took his breath away. "Is this how you do it?" she said, wriggling even closer.

He growled. "You'll pay for that."

"Promises. Promises."

Jack kicked off and steered the bike onto the driveway, heading for the front gate. The wind in his face, a smile on his lips and Kiah's arms hugging him like maybe she was enjoying this as much as him. He hadn't felt this light-hearted in years.

It only took five minutes to reach the river, but Jack was still glad he'd brought the Harley out of storage for the trip. It felt so good to be astride the bike again, he couldn't remember why he'd abandoned it at the back of the shed. Too many memories, he supposed.

While he propped the bike against a tree, Kiah spread a blanket on the ground under the shade of the largest eucalyptus tree then opened the basket to peer inside. "Whatever's in here smells delicious," she said lifting her nose in the air like a dog.

"Fresh ham and roast chicken and a loaf of pumpkin bread that I watched Marg take out of the oven moments before packing it in the basket. I added a bottle of wine and two plastic cups," he said, a tightness gathering in his groin as he watched her bosom rise and fall each time she lifted paper plates and cutlery from the basket. What was it about this woman that made him want to kiss every curve, every tantalising crevice of her body? He dropped into the nearest tyre swing and began to push himself back and forward to keep his mind off the image of them making love, right there on the blanket, in the middle of the finely sliced ham and chicken.

"Come and swing with me," he said, in an attempt to distract himself from his carnal thoughts. "If we exercise before eating, we'll fit more of Marg's picnic in."

Kiah looked up from extracting knives and forks from the picnic basket and flicked a mock scowl in his direction. "You only want to laugh at me when I get stuck in that tyre again. Admit it."

"Well, it *was* funny." He couldn't stop the grin from spreading across his face. "And, of course, I rather enjoyed my reward for freeing you from the big bad tyre." *Even if she did pull away as soon as the kiss deepened.* "Come on, Kiah, whoever can swing the highest wins a wish."

Kiah's lips twitched. "A wish?"

"Yep. The winner gets a wish granted."

"Any wish?"

"Well, any wish that can be granted right here, right now, beside the river."

Kiah looked Jack in the eye and frowned. A cute little I-know-what-you're-after frown that made him want to scoop her up and swing with her on his lap. "Maybe later. The smell of that freshly cooked bread is making me hungry. What do you want on your sandwich? Ham or chicken?"

"I'll have one of each, thanks."

"Okay, you pour the wine, then cut the peaches into quarters, ready to add cream for dessert." Kiah reached into the basket for the brown paper bag of peaches, before eying him over her nose. "And let me warn you, Jack Sullivan. Later, when I win the swing contest, you'll be down and dirty at my feet, doing fifty push ups."

Jack stopped swinging and headed for the picnic basket. "Sooo, the lady's wish is to drool over my muscles?"

"Maybe the lady wants to see you collapse into the dirt, nose first, after the first ten."

Jack arched one brow and gave a pretend growl before pulling off the lid of the wine bottle and preparing to pour the contents into two glasses. "It's a bet. You can swing your hardest, Stanton, cos you've got as much hope of seeing me doing push ups as you have of winning the lottery."

With the massive trunk behind him, Jack relaxed and watched Kiah pull out a container of butter, thick, yellow and creamy, sourced from a nearby dairy farm. She made up two fat sandwiches, cut them in quarters and placed them on a paper plate, before sliding the plate across to him. "Thanks." He took a bite of the chicken sandwich before leaning forward, a grin itching to make its way on his face. "What would you *really* wish for, Kiah? Right here? Right now?"

Kiah took a sip of her wine, her eyes on the clear water meandering peacefully along the river bed twenty feet away. She seemed to be inside her head, somewhere else.

"Kiah?"

That cute little frown that creased the skin between her eyes appeared as she let out a sigh, then tipped her head to the side and looked across at him. "Thought we were going to compete before we made our wishes."

"Sitting here in the sun in the company of a beautiful woman, with a glass of wine and good food, I'm beginning to lose my competitiveness." He gazed up at the sky, the lazy clouds, the two cheeky crows arguing over who knows what as they perched on a branch above his head. "Come on, what's your wish?"

Kiah smiled a shy smile and a flush of red spread across both cheeks. "Well," she said giving a small lift of one shoulder. "I wouldn't mind one of your special hugs."

"Is that all?"

She looked down at the red and white plaid of the blanket. "I didn't realize hugs could be so - so reassuring, until you hugged me. A Jack hug is special. You don't just hug with your arms, you hug with your whole body, your heart, your breath, your very soul." She looked up and their eyes met. "I've spent twelve long years without a hug, just being grabbed like a possession. And-and then you came along and I couldn't believe how warm and safe and comforted you made me feel when you hugged me."

Jack's breath caught in his throat as he listened to this beautiful damaged woman speak. How much harm had her monster of a husband done to her? He placed his sandwich back on the paper plate, stood up and held out one hand. "That's a wish I'd be happy to grant," he said, gently pulling her to her feet. And when she steadied herself, gazed up at him with those soulful green eyes, he stepped forward and took her in his arms. Gently. Carefully. Like a wounded bird. His heart went out to her as she nestled against his body, the beat of her heart gradually slowing from rapid to regular. Suddenly, all he wanted to do was protect her. Show her how much he cared. How much he was falling in love with her. With this brave, beautiful woman in his arms. He rested his chin on her head, enjoying the way her body was absorbed by his. "Any time you need a hug, Kiah. I'm here for you. Any time. Okay?"

She nodded and reluctantly pulled away, but he hung on, keeping one arm wrapped around her as he sat back down and rested against the tree, bringing her down with him, encouraging her to sit between his legs, lean back against him and use his chest for a pillow.

He gently massaged her shoulders, wanting her to relax. "Do you think you'll ever be ready to tell me about your last day with Richard? What happened? How he died?"

It took her a full minute to react. Finally, her fingers closed over his. "In a way," she whispered, squeezing his hand. "I-I think I killed him."

Jack's heart stuttered, but he returned the pressure, encouraging her to go on. "I'm not here to judge you, Kiah."

She sighed and he could feel the movement like a cry for help as it pierced his heart. "Richard had cracked my ribs the day before," she began in a monotone, as though cracking her ribs was a regular occurrence. "Some silly thing I did…can't even remember what it was…I was always doing something he didn't approve of." She cleared her throat. "Anyway, even though he'd repeatedly told me he'd find me and kill me if I ever left him, that day, I'd decided I had to take the chance. I'd rather die than stay any longer. So, there I was in the bedroom, getting ready to call an Uber, my two packed suitcases standing waiting by the front door, when the bedroom door flew open and there stood Richard. He'd come home early. Never did find out why."

Kiah plucked at the leg of her jeans and Jack felt her shudder against him. Maybe bringing up these memories wasn't such a good idea. Maybe she wasn't ready. He ran his fingers through her hair, gently massaging her scalp to soothe her while rocking her up against him. He could imagine her fear when she saw her husband at the bedroom door. Or could he? This big man, a bully, always ready with his fists? Jack swallowed the lump in his throat before whispering in her ear. "If this is upsetting you, Kiah, maybe you're not ready to talk yet."

She turned her head to look at him, her eyes damp. "It'll never be a good time, Jack. May as well be now."

Jack shifted a little to let her get more comfortable between his legs. "Up to you, sweetheart. But remember, I'm here for you."

"I know, Jack." He watched her suck in a deep breath to steady herself, before continuing. "Anyway, Richard must have seen the suitcases downstairs because he was furious. Screaming at me. Threatening to kill me. He grabbed me by the hair and dragged me into the bathroom, handcuffed me to the towel rail. I was crying, pleading with him not to hurt me. But he wouldn't listen. He just kept yelling, punching walls, punching me, and then I couldn't believe my eyes. He pulled out his taser, the stun gun that police only use on aggressive criminals who resist arrest, aimed it at me, and-and pulled the trigger."

"Jesus!" Jack went cold. That bastard had deliberately hit her with 50,000 volts of electricity. He wrapped his arms around Kiah's shoulders, drawing her closer. Wanting to soothe her, cuddle her, let her know all men weren't like Richard.

"All I remember is the excruciating pain as the force of the taser blasted into me. I was on the ground, my arms, still attached to the rail, stretched to the limit. I was twitching and hurting and-and I couldn't help it…I-I wet myself." She paused, dragged in a steadying breath before continuing. "But through it all, I could see every expression on Richard's face. It turned from crazed fury, to sick amusement, to a sudden look of surprise and then, just before I passed out, I saw him clutch at his heart and topple forward.

"When I woke up, Richard was lying on the floor. He wasn't moving." She gave an almost imperceptible shrug. "Maybe he was already dead. I don't know. I couldn't reach him. And that's when his mother came running into the bathroom. She was screaming at me for killing her son. For leaving him. For being the worst wife in the world. She left me dangling there, still handcuffed to the rail, until just before the ambulance arrived. She told me she'd see me dead too if I breathed a word to anyone about the handcuffs or the taser which she'd removed from Richard's hand. Then she shoved me out of the house and told me to make myself scarce, while she rang Richard's best friend, Senior Sergeant Connor, to take over the investigation."

Fiery tingles prickled behind Jack's eyes as he tried to picture Kiah, in pain, handcuffed to the towel rail, her dead husband sprawled on the floor beside her. Then accused by her mother-in-law of killing him. Threatened and violated by the people who should have been there for her. How did anyone recover from so much betrayal?

Jack's hands which were already massaging her shoulders crept further around to hold her, to comfort her, to assuage the memory from her mind. She leaned back and dropped her head against his fast-beating heart.

"Kiah," he croaked, his chest tight as he brushed a soft kiss on the top of her head. "You had nothing to do with Richard's death. The man was a monster. A walking time bomb of temper and rage. He caused his own death."

He closed his eyes. If only he could click on all the horrors this woman had endured and delete them from her memory. Forever.

When Kiah turned towards him, now on her knees, face level with his, her eyes, greener than the sea, were hesitant, probing, seeking comfort. He reached out, gently cupped her cheek, and kissed her. Then, easing her back onto the blanket, he slowly undressed her and let his mouth adore her and his body comfort her in the only way he knew how.

FIFTEEN

It was two weeks later. Two weeks of spending most of the day and every night with Jack. Kiah would either sneak into Jack's bed as soon as Angel was asleep, or him into hers. In deference to Angel, they mostly ended up performing awkward, body-hugging gymnastics on the caravan's not-built-for-two, single bed. A skill they quickly learned to conquer. Even if, on one occasion, they'd rolled off the bed and finished consummating their love-making on the caravan's hard wooden floor.

The blast of a car horn, loud and impatient, broke into Kiah's thoughts of their lovemaking — in either bed. She was now sitting in the passenger seat of Jack's car, on the way to meet his parents. Both hands were fisted on her lap, while the muscles between her shoulder blades were tighter than reins on a bolting horse.

Its tyres screaming a defiant squeal, a taxi loaded with footy fans, cut them off, swerved, straightened and took off again. Kiah drew in a sharp breath and grabbed for the dashboard as Jack slammed his foot on the brake and cursed. One thing for sure, she hadn't missed the noise and bustle of city traffic over the last seven months. Fuel-guzzling SUVs, endless cars of different makes and colours, lane-dodging taxies and large lumbering buses. Peering through the car window she compared the scene to Shadow Creek, where even on market day, driving down the town's main street was a breeze. She could check out the shops, wave to friends, and always find an empty parking space, if not directly in front, at least a couple doors up from her destination.

The complete opposite to city-driving.

"Ridley-ridley-ree, there's something I can see, and it starts with… P." Angel's voice from the seat behind her, brought Kiah's mind, once again, back to the present. It was Sunday and they were on their way to take part in a family lunch at Jack's parents' house.

Through the car window, Kiah half-heartedly studied the passing P's as they turned off King William St. and headed in the direction of North Adelaide and Jack's parents' house. A sigh escaped through gritted teeth. How had she let Jack, and more especially Angel, talk her into what would more than likely turn into a Sullivan Family Inquisition? With her as the unwilling hostage trapped by the conventional shackles of civility, while each and every member of Jack's family took turns at hurling questions at her, like darts at a dart board. Instead, she could be home right now, relaxing, reading a book, or washing Jet's tail with that new shampoo she'd bought at the saddler's last week.

"Kiah, you're not guessing. It's something starting with P."

Kiah forced herself to blot out the imaginary picture of her tied to a chair with Jack's family lined up ready to throw darts at her and concentrate on playing Ridley-Ree with Angel. "Um…is it pedestrians?"

"Nope."

"People?

"Nope."

"Paper shop?"

"No, silly, that's a Newsagent."

"Sorry…um…I know. Is it that girl's parka? See, the girl waiting for the bus?"

"Nope. Give up?"

Smiling at the unabashed note of triumph in Angel's voice, Kiah shrugged. "Okay, sweetie. You've got me. What P are you seeing that I'm not?"

Angel turned and pointed to the car travelling behind them. "Police car."

Kiah's heart lurched. Why was a police car tailing them? Were they chasing her to fire more question about Richard's death? For a moment Kiah forgot to breathe as she remembered the expression on Richard's face the moment it changed from cruel delight to surprise at the sudden sharp pains in his chest.

An icy finger scuttled down her spine and she shivered.

"You. okay?" Jack flicked a concerned glance her way and frowned. "Is Angel bugging you?"

Kiah forced herself to breathe. In. Out. In. Out. What was the matter with her? They were in the middle of city traffic; families visiting their relatives, enjoying Sunday shopping, or out on a Sunday drive. The police car hovering in the rear-view mirror was merely on its way to a crime scene, or heading back to the station. If this was how she reacted whenever she left the shelter of Windsong and Shadow Creek, was she really ready to move on with her life yet?

Before answering, Kiah straightened her shoulders, swallowing her irrational panic. "No, of course Angel's not bothering me," she said and turned to grin at the hyped-up occupant of the back seat. "Didn't think to look behind me for a P. You're good at this, kid."

"I know," said Angel without an ounce of vanity. "Marg said it's because I'm per- *persistent.*"

Kiah lifted her eyebrows at Jack. "You've raised a very bright child there, Sullivan."

When he continued to flick looks between her and the traffic, as though he was still concerned, she shrugged. "Okay, okay, I *might* be a teeny bit nervous about meeting your folks." She brushed imaginary lint off her dress, ran her tongue over her bottom lip. "Tell me the truth…did they know I even existed before you told them I was coming with you and Angel today?"

"Well…"

"Yes," Angel piped in. "I've told Gran all about you."

"You have?" Jack's voice sounded like he was talking through a mouthful of popcorn.

"'Cos Kiah's my bestest friend."

"Right. And what sort of things have you told Gran about your… bestest friend?"

"Well…" Angel tipped her head to the side in thought. "I told her Kiah and I go riding most Sundays." She drew her bottom lip up between her teeth and thought some more. "Oh, yeah, and this morning, before we left, I texted Gran and told her that Kiah sometimes has a sleep over, you know, just like I do when I stay overnight at my friend, Savannah's house."

Kiah's stomach tightened and the cereal she'd eaten for breakfast swirled. The missiles thrown at the dartboard during her coming inquisition had just acquired barbs. Oh my God, she wanted to stop the car, get out and catch the nearest bus back to Shadow Creek.

Jack's smothered chuckles beside her had her digging him in the ribs with her elbow. "Not funny," she growled.

He blew out a breath through pursed lips but didn't say another word. What could he say? Instead, his hand found hers and squeezed before returning to the job of steering through heavy traffic. A smile still tugging at the corners of his lips.

"Gran said she can't wait to meet you."

"She did?" The words came out like a croak.

"You'll be okay," Jack assured her. "My mother will love you."

"And your father? And your brother? And his wife? And your nephews? They won't?"

"Of course, they will. You're beautiful. You're kind. You're literature. Why wouldn't they love you?"

By now they were turning into a wide, tree-lined street in the North of the city. The mild honey-sweet smell of the Jacarandas tickled Kiah's nose as she drew in their scent through her half open window. New modern houses and apartments were interspersed between century-old, beautifully-preserved, sprawling mansions, the most charming of these belonging to the Sullivans.

The moment Jack's car pulled to a halt behind the largest and flashiest four-wheel drive Kiah had ever set eyes on, Angel was out of the car and running toward a fashionably-dressed woman in her early sixties. Hair held immaculately in place, blue-gray eyes, similar to Jack's, shining with as much love as her wide, welcoming smile. "Darling, it's so good to see…"

"Granny! Granny! Come and meet my bestest friend, Kiah!"

Before Kiah had time to fully extract herself from the car, brush herself down and stand up straight, the woman, still beaming, enfolded her in a hug. A real hug. Not a fashionable, barely-there imitation of a hug. Kiah felt herself relaxing into the embrace and smiling. So that's where Jack learned how to give great hugs.

"What a treat it is to meet you, Kiah. I've heard so much about you, from this one." The woman grinned down at her grand-daughter.

"Um…as I discovered on the drive here."

The woman let out a full-on laugh as she tousled her grand-daughter's hair. "All good, I assure you." She lifted her head to peer up at Jack. "Heard nothing from this one, though. Not a peep."

Jack bent and kissed his mother on the cheek. "Now, Mum, I'm warning you,…no firing twenty questions at Kiah, okay?"

His mother laughed and punched him lightly on the arm. "If you'd ring occasionally and talk to us, we wouldn't need to ask questions." She smiled at Kiah and linked arms, while steering her toward the open front door. "Come inside, my dear. We're all dying to meet you. According to Angel, as well as being her *bestest* friend, you live in a magical gypsy caravan."

"Magical gypsy caravan?" Kiah let out a laugh. "I live in a bilious pink, rather primitive, 1980's caravan on your son's property, Mrs. Sullivan."

"Grace, please. Only doctors and people I don't like, call me Mrs. Sullivan. I have a feeling you and I are going to be *bestest* friends."

Kiah, one arm linked through Jack's mother's, the other through Angel's, barely had time to prepare herself for the inevitable meeting with the rest of the family, before they were through the heavy panelled front door and she was confronted by an older, sterner version of Jack. Similar facial features but with more wrinkles, same colour hair with grey sprinkled through, same colour eyes but lacking his son's ever-present humour and kindness. Jack's father.

"Ah, so this is Kiah." He nodded and held out one hand, his eyes clearly telling her it would take much more than her new strappy black shoes and billowy pink top to impress him.

"Mr. Sullivan." She shook his hand, quickly deciding it was colder and less welcoming than a Queensland Cane toad in a room full of baby slugs.

"How long have you known my son?"

"Almost seven months now."

"And yet we haven't heard of you until today?"

Jack, who'd followed behind with the basket full of food Marg had sent with them, growled deep in his throat. "Dad. That's enough."

Mr. Sullivan slowly turned to his son. "Ah, and here's the impoverished horse trainer, taking time out from his busy schedule of raking up manure to visit us. There's still an executive position waiting for you in the firm, Jack, but it won't be there forever."

"Dad, do you have to bring this up *every* time I visit? I'm happy where I am, doing what I love. We have a promising racing team at the moment, one horse with a chance of winning the Kangaroo Downs Cup next month, and after that, possibly races in the city." Jack slung an arm around Kiah's shoulders. "So, if you're not going to be civil, we'll head off home again. We can always stop at McDonald's for lunch."

"Joseph...you promised."

The growl from his wife had Joe Sullivan drawing in a deep breath and letting it out slowly. Finally, lips set in a thin line, he held up one hand in the universal 'okay' position. "Alright, Grace. But I'm only stating what's best for my eldest son, and he knows it. Now, I have several important phone calls to make, so, if you need me, I'll be in the study."

Kiah watched the man stride off down a long passageway, deep rich aubergine carpet deadening his footsteps, head high, back stiff. Joseph Sullivan was a man who was accustomed to getting his own way, who took orders from no-one — his only soft spot — his wife.

Before Jack could carry out his threat to exchange luncheon locations and settle for a Big Mac, thick shake and fries, Grace shooed Kiah and Jack through the patio doors and towards an outdoor table loaded with food.

"Any tips for Saturday's races, Bro?" A younger version of Jack, dressed in a Hugo Boss polo and designer jeans — clearly the owner of the flashy SUV — looked up from flipping steaks on the barbecue as they approached.

"My tip, Mike? Don't bet. Gambling's for fools." Jack's hand found Kiah's and he pulled her to him, his arm snaking around her waist to bring her even closer. "Kiah, I'd like you to meet my baby brother, Michael, who thinks, because I train racehorses, I'll know the winner of the fifth race at Sandown next Saturday."

"Hi, Michael."

At that moment, Angel, who'd remained inside with her grandmother, called out from the patio doorway. "Dad, Granny wants you to carry the drinks out."

"Okay, sweetheart." Jack lifted a finger in Angel's direction, before turning back to squeeze Kiah's hand. "Won't be a jiff."

Kiah returned the squeeze. "I'm not going anywhere."

The moment Jack disappeared inside the house, Michael placed the spatula on the side of the barbecue, wiped his fingers on a small towel, and held out his hand. A soft manicured hand that had seen little manual work. His voice was sing-song when he spoke. "Well, hello, Kiah."

While shaking hands, Kiah smiled up into a pair of cynical blue eyes that were obviously sizing her up. "Jack's told me quite a lot about you, Michael."

"And yet he's told us nothing about you." He rubbed two fingers across his chin, eyes assessing her in a way that made Kiah want to stomp on the toe of his immaculate R M William boots. "And, of course, the twenty-million-dollar question is…where has my brother been hiding you?"

Suddenly, a Big Mac and fries sounded much more inviting than standing in the backyard of a beautiful mansion beside a table overflowing with rich food, suspicious eyes scrutinizing her every move.

"Bag it, Michael." A smart, stylishly dressed woman a couple of years younger than Kiah, scraped her chair back from the table, stood up, and moved toward her. "Please, don't judge him too harshly, Kiah. The only excuse I can give is that he's been standing in front of the barbecue too long and the heat has sweated away his manners." The smile the woman directed at Kiah was genuine. One hundred percent real. "I'm Melanie," she went on, her smile reflected in her eyes. "Wife to the moron wielding the spatula. What he *meant* to say was, we're all thrilled to meet you and the reason we're surprised is that you're the first woman Jack has brought home for lunch in the last eight years."

Kiah blinked. Now that was a revelation. No wonder the family were acting as though she was a mystery parcel in Santa's goodie bag.

The younger woman leaned forward, her smooth cheek pressing lightly against Kia's as she hugged her. "Lovely to meet you, Kiah. Now, come sit next to me so we can catch up." She flicked a chair out next to her and waited for Kiah to sit down before continuing. "Angel told Grace that you own one of the race horses at Windsong. I've been trying to talk Michael into buying a horse for us and getting Jack to train it, but I think he's a little afraid of what Daddy might say."

A flush spread across Michael's cheeks as he turned back to the barbecue. "You know that's not true, Mel. Jack needs to give up his childish dream of training racehorses. Employing him to train a horse for us would just be encouraging him."

Mel rolled her eyes. "It's not a dream, Mike — it's a reality. He *is* training racehorses."

"Well, he needs to give it up and do as Father says…take his rightful place at Sullivan Electronics. Only way he'll ever transform his unhealthy bank account from red to black."

Jack, muscles bulging beneath his figure-hugging white tee, lifted an eyebrow at his brother as he came up behind him with a crate of drinks. "What? And be unhappy because I can't breathe sitting at a desk with a phone plugged into my ear all day, forced to wear a suit and tie? No thanks, bro. Now, where do you want these?"

Michael spun around. "Can't you give it another try, Jack? You don't know what it's like working with Father since you left. He's like a bear with a sore head."

"I've been gone for five years, bro, so if he hasn't accepted that I'm not coming back, by now, that's tough. Now, the drinks?"

"In the outside fridge, of course. If you came to lunch more often, you wouldn't have to ask."

Kiah watched the two brothers stare at each other. There was a lot of friction in their relationship and she was happy to see Angel push through the patio doors and come racing out across the lawn, two boys, one younger, one older, chasing her.

From beside her, Melanie let out a laugh. "Oh! Oh! Here comes triple-trouble. That's the end of any peace and quiet out here."

Kiah, still watching the body language between the two brothers, sighed inwardly. *What peace and quiet?*

Jack transferred the drinks from the crate to the outside refrigerator and joined Kiah at the table. "Hi Mel," he said bending to kiss his brother's wife on the cheek before dragging out a chair and settling down next to Kiah. "Looks like Angel's out to give your boys a hard time. As usual."

"Don't worry, they give as good as they get." Melanie frowned at the three children now rolling on the lawn, laughing and squealing. "Anthony, David, stop acting like a couple of wild beasts and come over here. I want you to meet Jack's friend, Kiah."

Angel was the first to dance across the grass towards them, the boys following more reluctantly. "Kiah's *my* friend," she said and snaked a small chubby arm around Kiah's neck, as though defying anyone to disagree.

A tidal wave of love for the little girl now leaning against her welled up and spread across Kiah's chest, causing her eyes to prickle and her breath to catch in her throat. She tugged Kiah closer and hugged her, kissed the top of her head.

A smile passed between Kiah and Jack as Angel, happy to have proven her point, snaffled a chocolate frog from a boat-shaped bowl on the table, grinned at Kiah, and danced off to help her grandmother, who was attempting to carry three plates of little Weiner sausages out through the open patio doors.

By now both boys were lined up in front of Kiah, waiting for introductions.

The smaller of the two, his eyes on the bowl of chocolate frogs, was clearly debating whether he could get away with the trick his cousin had pulled, while the other stood with both arms folded across his chest.

"Kiah, I'd like you to meet our boys." Melanie lifted both eyebrows at the boy with his arms folded. "The one trying to hide the grass stain on his new sweater is our eldest son, Anthony," she said. "And the one who lost a front tooth when he fell off his bicycle, is David. Thinks because he's cute he can charm his way out of a paper bag, but no, David, you can't have a chocolate frog. Not until after you've eaten lunch."

Jack's mother, assisted by Angel, deposited the three plates on the table and tousled her nearest grandson, David's hair. "Go ask your dad how long before the meat's cooked, darling. We're all ready to get started."

Immediately, Jack scraped his chair back and stood up. "It's okay, Mum, I'll go grab the meat and bring it over." He touched Kiah on the shoulder and when she looked up, he leaned down and kissed her on the forehead. "You're in for a real treat," he said, eyes twinkling. "Our mother won't tell us where she buys her meat, says it's a military secret, but you're about to sample the best steak in Australia. Melts in your mouth and tastes fit for a God."

Laughing, Kiah watched Jack swagger over to the barbecue, select several large plates and stack them full of steaks of various sizes, some well-done, some medium rare; the smell making her mouth water in anticipation.

Once Jack had transferred the meat to the table, Grace clapped her hands together. "Right. Tuck in everyone. But make sure you leave room for dessert because I made cheesecakes."

"Chocolate?" asked David, eyes wide.

"Of course."

Angel clapped her hands. "And vanilla?"

"Naturally."

"What about my favourite? Cinnamon?" said Jack with a cockeyed grin that had Kiah wanting to lean across and kiss those enticingly cheeky lips.

"When have I ever made cheesecakes without including *your* favourite?" Grace, who'd pulled a chair up on the other side of her eldest son, flicked his arm with one finger.

The next twenty minutes was taken up with eating and talking. While Mel chatted away on one side of Kiah, Jack made sure his hand was always there ready to squeeze hers if he thought she was becoming uncomfortable. There was still tension between Michael and Jack, but by the time they'd finished their first steak, the brothers had started reminiscing and laughing about some friend's party they'd been to as children, where the steak was so tough the family dog broke a tooth attempting to eat it.

Jack's mother, Grace, was an accomplished hostess. Offering Kiah food, keeping her in the conversation without asking too many questions and showing concern when Jack related their chilling experience with Cockroach.

At the name, Barry Cochran, Grace frowned. "Wasn't that the boy in your class at Adelaide High who sabotaged your bike? Yes, I remember now…you ended up with a broken collarbone when the steering collapsed and you fell off on the road?"

Jack put his knife down beside his plate and reached for a large bottle of tomato sauce in the middle of the table. "Yep. That's Cockroach."

"No wonder the man's still a thug." Grace, eyes narrowing, jutted her bottom lip like a bulldog. "The school only suspended him for like, a week. I remember storming into the principal's office, demanding a *real* punishment. Said if he didn't take it seriously, I'd be talking to the police."

"And did he?" Kiah could imagine this mother hen, in full protective mode, demanding retribution for her son's injury.

"If I remember rightly, he ended up with an extra week's suspension, which was still far too little, but Jack talked me out of taking it any further. Said the boy's father was a mean drunk and he'd beat the boy if the police got involved."

Jack, chewing on a bite of steak, almost choked on a laugh that sounded more like a groan. "And what does my friend, Cockroach, do in return? Gets caught trying to dope my best horse."

"Kiah, would you like to try the prawns?" Grace sent Kiah a grin from across the table. "According to the fishmonger at the open market this morning, they were swimming in the sea yesterday, and on our dinner table today."

"Thanks, Grace, but I'm not into sea food. Plus, I'm still tackling this side of beef you guys call a steak."

Michael let out a laugh as he opened another bottle of wine ready to replenish his glass. "Grazing happily in his paddock yesterday, on our table today, hey?"

Melanie pulled a face of horror as she stared down at her plate. "Damn you,

Michael, I was enjoying that steak. Now you've put me right off." With a throaty huff she banged her knife and fork down on the table and glared at him. "No wonder so many people are reverting to vegetarianism. I've a good mind to—"

"What's this? Feed time at the zoo?" A strident voice, loud and commanding, overrode Melanie's sudden declaration of vegetarianism. As one, all eyes turned to the man standing ram-rod straight, in front of the patio doors. The caerulean blue tie against a stark white shirt complementing the crisp navy of his tailor-made suit. The patriarch of the family, Joseph Sullivan. He continued to survey the diners through steely eyes. "So busy stuffing your faces, no-one thought to let me know lunch had been served."

"Joseph?" Grace, a frown creasing her forehead, slowly got to her feet and shook her head at him. "You said you were busy making phone calls, so I saved you a platter. It's inside ready to be heated up. Now, stop acting like a bear with a sore head and come and sit here at the head of the table while I get your food ready."

"No, no, it's okay, Grace," he patted her on the shoulder and led her back to her seat. "You've done enough work today." He scowled at the other members of his family. "Just thought one of you lot might have checked on me, let me know lunch was ready."

The three young children stared open mouthed at their grandfather, while Michael, in his hurry to stand up, knocked his chair over. "Sorry, Father," he said, righting the chair. "Mum said you were busy, so I thought you wouldn't want to be disturbed. How about I barbecue a couple of fresh steaks for you."

"Thank you, Michael."

Beside her, Kiah felt Jack's body stiffen, and the irrational thought that if he'd been a cat his hair would be standing on end, flicked bizarrely through her brain. Jack continued to stare at his father, muscles tense as though preparing to spring to his feet. "Don't," she whispered and poked him, hard. As much as she thought Mr. Sullivan was acting like a jerk, no way did she want to be in the middle of a Sullivan family row. She wrapped her hand around Jack's arm and squeezed, kept squeezing until he took his eyes off his father and looked across at her. She gave a subtle shake of her head and breathed a sigh of relief when he slowly let his muscles relax and leaned back in his chair. Then, after sending her a *not-so-subtle* wink, Jack smiled at his father. "The table's still loaded with food, Dad, so get stuck in." He pointed to a solitary mini-cheesecake looking lonely in the middle of a pale blue porcelain plate. "But if you want that last cinnamon cheesecake, you'd better grab it now and hide it, 'cos that baby has my name written on it."

Joseph Sullivan tilted his head to the side and stared at Jack for a full twenty seconds without speaking, then, the corner of his lips curved upwards, and, still keeping eye-contact with his son, he leaned forward over the table, snaffled the desert from the plate and popped it in his mouth.

The ache in Kiah's chest tightened as she watched the interplay between the two men. It was plain to see that Jack's father not only loved him, but admired him. He might act like a tyrant and an old-world patriarch, but maybe his concern really was for his son's future.

It must be difficult to always get things right as a parent. After wasting so many years with a man she didn't love and who treated her like his possession, it was too late for Kiah to ever find out for herself.

The meal progressed as before, with laughter and family stories being retold for Kiah's benefit. She could see Jack relaxing, chatting to his brother, teasing his mother and Mel, joking with Angel and her cousins. All the time keeping her in his peripheral view and making sure to include her, make her feel part of his family.

After checking the time on his watch, Mr. Sullivan Snr. carefully stacked the empty plates in front of him and stood up. "I have to go," he said. "I'm expecting an important phone call from California in fifteen minutes." He turned to Jack. "But a word of advice, son. If you're contemplating another relationship, think through my offer. No woman wants to marry a man with no money."

And with a nod at the table in general, he strode off through the patio doors, presumably, back to his office.

Jack, lifting his chin to the sky, let out a frustrated snort, while Kiah's face flooded with heat. How typical of what she'd learned of Jack's father so far. Joseph Sullivan, powerful head of the Sullivan family, thrived on having the last word.

SIXTEEN

The following week at *Windsong* everyone was so busy, Kiah had little time for anything outside of riding track-work, grooming, walking horses to cool them off, organizing special feeds, cleaning stables and transporting horses to various tracks for trialling. She'd danced a jig of joy when Jet proved himself by scooting away and winning a 6-horse-trial by five lengths in fast time, at the local racetrack. Taylor, although coming close to parting company with the playful Jet on the way to the barrier, was effusive in her praise after the trial. Said she hadn't let him fully extend. And of course, Jet, playing off all the praise heaped on him, pranced back to the wash bay after the trial looking as though he was ready to go around again.

The only fly in the ointment for the week was that she and Jack only managed to spend three nights together. But the lovemaking was so tender, so intense, it almost brought her to tears. Made her want to wake up lying beside this man every morning, for the rest of her life. As for Jack, if his father's words about no woman wanting to marry a man with no money had troubled him, he didn't mention it. Probably desensitised to anything his father said by now. Anyway, it certainly hadn't put a dent in their lovemaking.

The following Saturday, after transporting Magnifico to Pine Ridge, one of the smaller country race-tracks, Kiah decided to let her hair down and enjoy the day. After all, the sun was shining, the country setting idyllic and although Magnifico was only competing against lesser horses, with minimum prizemoney to the winner, the whole exercise was to boost his confidence. Jack figured, after what the horse had been through, it was best to nominate him in an easy race before tackling the Kangaroo Downs Cup.

Magnifico wasn't racing until the third event on the programme, so after settling him into his stall and making sure his dark chestnut coat gleamed like rich silk, Kiah left him with Belle, his handler for the day, to become familiar with the noises and distractions of his surroundings and went hunting for food.

Most of the smaller country tracks only raced once or twice a year so the locals usually made a celebration of the occasion. There was a bouncing castle and pony rides for the children and lots of gaily decorated food stalls to promote local produce. It might be a little early for lunch, but with a mere slice of toast hastily coated in vegemite for breakfast, five long hours ago, Kiah's steps quickened as she came closer to a stall with the large *Hamburgers R Us* sign out the front. The smell of frying onions and hamburger meat made Kiah's taste buds perform exuberant cartwheels in anticipation.

"Kiah? Kiah Stanton?"

Kiah stopped, heart galloping so quickly it would beat the favourite in the next race. She knew that voice. She'd heard it in her sleep many times over the past seven months. She'd even imagined the man behind the voice nailing a gutted rabbit to her caravan door, before Cockroach put his hand up for the grisly act.

On the balls of her feet, she turned around slowly, poised to beat a hasty retreat if her questioner tried to trap her in his web. Throat dry, she had to push his name out through what felt like chunks of cement. "Connor?"

It was Senior Sergeant Connor Preston. Richard's best friend. The man who'd threatened her when she told him what happened in the bathroom the day Richard died. Accused her of being a spiteful, ungrateful, lying bitch. A harridan. A cock-teaser. Not worthy of being the wife of a man of Richard's status. A man who daily put himself in harm's way to protect the innocent. A hero. A leader of men.

A fictional man Kiah didn't know…

"I heard you were into the racing scene now and I've been trying to catch up with you."

Kiah, eyes never leaving his, took a step back. "I have nothing more to say to you, Connor. And if you continue to harass me, I'll-I'll…" What? Ring the police? He *was* the police. Breath rasping in her throat, mouth dry, she took another step back, ready to run.

"Please, Kiah. Don't go. I want to apologize for not believing you the night Richard died." Connor's voice was soft, rueful. He extended one hand. "Please. Can we talk?"

Not wanting any part of Connor Preston to touch her, she pulled away further. This was a trick. A ploy to soften her defences while he grabbed her and whisked her away to a jail cell. She looked for Jack but he was nowhere in sight. He'd bundled Magnifico's owners, off to the bar for a drink and a catch-up. If she made a fuss, someone nearby might ring the police and that would play right into Connor's hands. She'd have to run and hide until the race-meeting was over, try to get word to Jack that Connor was out to arrest her.

Connor dropped his hand to his side. "Richard's mother told me what really happened the night Richard died. We were at a party and Beryl had too much to drink. Let it all out. Laughed. Thought it was a huge joke, how he used to beat you, control you, put the fear of God into you. And how the night Richard died, he handcuffed you to the towel rail and then blasted you with the taser. Got so angry and carried away while punishing you for…" He hesitated, chewed on his bottom lip. "I-don't-know-what…and that he had a heart attack and dropped dead leaving you still attached to the rail for hours before Beryl found you."

"Your *friend*, Richard, the hero, had cracked my ribs the day before — not for the first time — and even though he'd warned me he'd hunt me down and kill me if I ever left him…I'd had enough. I was leaving him that night." She glared at Connor, a prickly sensation behind her eyes forcing her to swallow and take a deep breath. No way was she going to cry or show any emotion in front of this man. "*That*, Sergeant Preston, is the 'I-don't-know-what' reason he was punishing me."

"I'm sorry, Kiah. I honestly didn't know what you were going through." His eyes studied the ground at his feet before he looked up. "You were very good at hiding it. Always the perfect host."

"It was easier to be a good host than suffer the effects of a punch in the stomach after you left."

"Kiah," Connor sighed and looked around. "Can we go somewhere and talk?"

"We're talking."

"Somewhere quieter?"

"Connor, I have a new life now. I don't care that you're sorry. If you'd taken time out from hero-worshipping your psycho friend and really looked at me back then, you'd have seen what was going on. There were enough clues for a kid of ten to have solved the mystery of why I barely spoke to you or any of Richard's friends. And under what tree were you born not to have wondered why I was rarely without bruises?"

"Richard said you were clumsy. His exact words, 'endearingly clumsy'. He said he was always watching out for you, but you were born with two left feet and a head that was forever in the clouds."

"And you believed him?"

"Why wouldn't I?" He paused, then let out a long sigh, eyes closed, shoulders slumped. "I'm sorry, Kiah. Looking back, I guess I should have known things weren't right, but…well, he was my hero as well as my friend. The cases that man solved, the dangers he faced, the medals he was awarded…I guess they clouded my judgement. I didn't *want* to see the truth." Connor ran a hand through his hair tousling it further. "But I do want to make it right, now. Come back, make a formal complaint about Richard, even if it's only divulging what really happened on the night he died. I'll back you up. One hundred percent."

Suddenly the burning anger Kiah had bottled up since that night, regularly stirring and poking it with a stick, died down, the embers glowed a final red, then turned to ashes. Connor was giving her the go-ahead to clear up the lies told by Richard's mother, to let everyone know Richard Stanton was nothing but a bully, a monster, a puffed-up psycho who thought he was above the law he was sworn to uphold. But did she want to? Did she really want to go backwards? She'd come so far since that terrifying night when, unable to move from the towel rail, scalp bleeding from being dragged bodily along the floor, nerves raw from the pain of the taser gun, she'd watched the life drain out of Richard's body. What would it achieve? Richard was dead. He couldn't hurt her or anyone else now. She hadn't woken screaming from a Richard-enhanced nightmare for months, not since Jack had shown her what a real, honest-to-goodness hug can do for a person's well-being.

So why drag the whole nightmare up again?

Eyes on the horses in the first race as they made their way out onto the track, sprightly, bouncy, eager to run their hearts out, Kiah shook her head. "No, it's too late now. The past is the past, and I'm happy in my new life. Happier than I've ever been. However," she paused to make sure she had Connor's full attention. "You can tell Richard's mother, from me, if she's not out of my unit by the end of next month, I might change my mind. Might even go to the National papers, and let everyone in Australia know exactly what her hero of a son was really like behind closed doors."

With that, Kiah nodded a curt goodbye to Connor, sniffed the air like a hound dog, and moaned when the heady smell of cooked onions infiltrated her nasal cavities. And then continued her march toward the large *Hamburgers R Us* sign.

*****

After downing his one and only drink for the day, Jack clapped Rick Tonsley, one of Magnifico's two owners, on the shoulder. "His price is too short for a bet, mate. Best to just sit here in the stand, enjoy the race, and cheer your horse on."

Jack had spent the last half hour with Rick and Jake, joining in their excitement, shouting them beers and filling them in on how close their horse had come to being harmed the night Cockroach broke into the stables. But these owners were what every trainer coveted. They never interfered — left all decisions to Jack. Paid up on time. And they were even talking about buying another racehorse for him to train.

"Time to make sure your champ's ready to race, so I'll leave you guys to it," he said. "See you in the winner's enclosure."

He spotted Kiah talking to Belle in the parade ring. The horse looked magnificent, eyes bright, mane and tail gleaming in the sun, all thanks to Kiah's grooming. His heart contracted as he gazed at the woman who looked even more magnificent than the horse. It wasn't just that she was beautiful, it was the way she carried her head, the way she quietly talked to the horse calming him down, the way her body moved when she stretched forward to flick a piece of forelock out from under the brow band. The way she smiled and waved when she saw him.

Jack had thought a lot about Kiah since his father's stinging finale the day of the family barbecue. Although his father's words angered him, on another level, they made him realize how much he loved this woman with the big heart. How much he wanted to have her beside him every day — and in his bed every night. And yes, his father had a point about no woman wanting to marry a man who couldn't provide for her, but with Magnifico in top form, odds on to win the Kangaroo Downs Cup, of which a third of the winning purse would go into *Windsong's* bank account, Jack could ask Kiah to marry him. Then, if she said yes, they could enjoy the highs and lows of training racehorses together.

Smiling, Jack strolled up behind Kiah and slid his arms around her waist. Then, with a light tug he pulled her closer and dropped his chin on her shoulder. "Ready to watch our champ win this race in a canter?"

She nodded, and as the seven horses engaged in Race 3 danced toward the gate ready to spread out onto the track, Jack and Kiah made their way down to the running rail to watch. This was Magnifico's final race leading up to the Cup. A hit-out to get him fully race-fit for the big one and to make sure he'd come away from the horrors of Cockroach, without losing his confidence.

The horse had done everything right since arriving at *Windsong*, two days after Kiah had driven a battered float through his gates with an equally battered horse inside. Magnifico could turn his life around. If he won the Cup, it would entice other owners to send better horses for Jack to train. Prove to his father that he could make a successful living by training horses. That he didn't need to work in the family business to have a healthy bank account. Yes, a win in the Cup would give him the confidence and the money to ask Kiah to marry him.

Jack's arm tightened around Kiah's shoulders. "For luck," he murmured, drawing her soft body closer. Head bent, his lips touched hers, then deepened.

Coming up for air, Kiah smiled up at him then leaned over the rail as the dark chestnut horse, coat gleaming in the afternoon sun, breezed past on the way to the barriers. "Best looking horse here today."

Jack smiled down at her. She looked so sweet wearing that green dress with the white spots — his racing colours — hair loose around her shoulders. Fair dinkum, he could cover the woman with sprinkles and lick her all up. "That's because I'm lucky enough to have the best and prettiest groom in the industry."

She punched him lightly on the arm. "Flattery will get you everywhere, Mr. Sullivan."

"Mr. Sullivan now, is it? That's not what you called me last night. I distinctly remember the words, hot, love god, and was there a breathy-sounding, sex-on-a-stick?"

A blush crept across her cheeks and she ducked her chin. Kiah was so cute when embarrassed. He squeezed her hand. He loved her, Angel adored her, and with a listed winner under his belt he could offer her more than the hard life of a battling trainer of bush horses.

Mind still on Kiah and the future, he turned his head to watch the field being loaded into the barrier stalls. Magnifico walked straight in, ears pricked, but the grey stallion behind barrier six decided the Troll-From-Under-the-Bridge lived inside his barrier. When two attendants linked arms behind the grey ready to hustle him forward, he reared and his jockey, evidently deciding it was safer on the ground than on the back of a thousand pounds of recalcitrant horse, kicked his feet out of the stirrups and slid to the ground. In the end, an attendant blindfolded the grey and led him into barrier six, quickly climbing out again once the jockey remounted.

"Locked and loaded." The voice of Johnny Gap, the local farrier, horse-dentist and gambler, boomed over the track's sound system. Gappy, as the locals called him, was never happier than when studying the form or tipping winners to his mates over a beer. The highlight of his year was standing in the broadcasting tower, calling at Pine Ridge's annual race meeting.

"They're off and racing!" His voice, oozing excitement swept across the grounds and could probably be heard in the main street of Pine Ridge. "Stardust jumped well from the inside but the favourite, Magnifico, has scooted across from the outside barrier like a cat with a cracker tied to its tail. He's already two lengths in front of Stardust and Pinocchio running together, followed by Chairman, Daisy Belle, Strike It Rich and last of all the big grey stallion, Witchcraft."

Jack gripped the rail, his fingers digging into the painted wood, heart galloping along with the horses. He could see his jockey's tiny green and white form sitting still and composed on top of Magnifico's back. Dillon was following his instruction to the letter, bouncing the horse to the front to keep him out of trouble. Good boy. Even from this distance Jack could see him take a light hold of the reins; no good letting the horse use up too much energy this early.

Kiah, jumping up and down, her hair swinging, let out a yell, blasting Jack's eardrums. "Go Mags! Keep going!"

Gappy's voice continued through the crackle of the loud-speaker. "Sweeping towards the home turn, it's still Magnifico in front by three lengths doing it easy. He's coasting along, his jockey hasn't even popped the question yet, followed out wide by Chairman storming down the outside but not making much ground on the leader, then comes Stardust, Witchcraft and…oh, no…Magnifico's slowing down. He's dropping back through the field. Bloody hell, Magnifico's pulling up…"

The air whooshed out of Jack's chest as Dillon gradually eased Magnifico into a head-bobbing trot then back to a walk and finally a ragged halt. This wasn't happening. It was a bad dream. Like he was up in the clouds looking down on the course and it was another race, another horse. Not *his* horse. Heart lurching through icy sludge, he watched Dillon slip out of the saddle, land with bent knees, then run his fingers gently down the chestnut's off foreleg. Had Magnifico merely jarred up in the run, or was it worse? A tendon? A suspensory ligament? Still seemingly inside someone else's body, Jack watched the jockey pat the horse on the shoulder, and then, head bent, lead his dashed hopes for the Cup and a life with Kiah, slowly past the grazing sheep on the inside of the track and towards the exit gate.

The whole time, his father's words kept repeating over and over like a never-ending loop of doom in Jack's brain… 'No woman wants to marry a man with no money.'

SEVENTEEN

Over the open half of the stable door, Jack watched the taillights on Magnifico's owners' car bob up and down as they hit the dip at the end of the driveway. Jake and Rick had listened to the vet's verdict in disbelief, figuring naively that horses were like wind-up toys and kept on racing until 8-10 years of age when they were retired and redirected into another sphere of their life. Show-jumping. Eventing. Dressage. Whatever. But not this. Not a twelve-month layoff after such a short racing career with only a 50/50 chance of their horse ever racing again.

Gone was their enthusiasm for the Sport-of-Kings. Gone was their interest in purchasing another horse for Jack to train. Instead, they were faced with enormous bills. There was yesterday's nerve blocks and ultrasound, ongoing vet bills, three months of stable rest followed by months of rehabilitation which included hand walking, treadmill, and hydrotherapy. All on the off chance that the suspensory ligament would heal slowly and not with stiffer, less stretchable scar tissue and could withstand another race preparation. Even then, there was always the chance of Magnifico losing several lengths, and not being competitive.

Their car's tail lights continued through the gateway then veered left onto the road before disappearing into the distance.

Holding onto the end of the lead rope and while Greg Channing, the vet, unwrapped the pressure bandage from Magnifico's leg, Jack let out a sigh that seemed to come from way-way down in his well-worn R M Williams boots. A sigh that brought a jagged lump to his throat, prickles to the back of his eyes. He'd failed. Things were looking pretty bleak not only for Jake and Rick, but for the stable too. Instead of bringing *Windsong Stables* out of the mire left by all the debts, doubts and innuendos after his uncle's suicide, he'd pushed the stable's name deeper into the mud by getting it once more in debt.

And then he thought of his staff. Dillon, almost in tears as he led Magnifico off the track. He'd stayed with the horse throughout the track vet's examination, and when even the 70-year-old country vet — his specialty 'cows and llamas' — predicted the horse would be off racing for up to 12 months, Josh had apologized. As though the horse's injury was his fault. If the stables closed down, what would happen to Dillon and Belle and Taylor and Olivia and Josh his other staff? What about old Steve? Who in the industry would employ a bandy-legged taciturn old track rider in his late 60s? And as for Jack, he'd rather go door-to-door selling vacuum cleaners than go back working in the family business. The job stifled him. Even the *thought* of those first twenty years of his working life made him want to throw up. He'd be no good to anyone if he became that man again.

No woman wants to marry a man with no money...

And there it was again. His father was right. How could he ask Kiah to marry him now when he was on the threshold of bankruptcy? After the suffering she'd been through in the past, she deserved a much better future than he could give her.

"Injuries always hit newbies the hardest." Greg said, breaking into the black cloud of Jack's thoughts. The vet finished fastening the ice wrap around Magnifico's right front leg, stood up, and stretched, one hand in the middle of his back. "I reckon, all prospective owners should be forced to attend a lecture before they commit to buying. Learn the realities of owning a race horse. Things like..." He shrugged, then reached into his veterinary bag. "A very small percentage of horses pay their way in racing, and, after colic, injuries to the suspensory ligament, which can finish a horse's racing career, are the most common." He tapped a vein in Magnifico's well-muscled neck and injected a dose of Phenylbutazone to reduce the inflammation and pain, then lifted his eyebrows in Jack's direction. "But of course, then there'd be fewer owners in the sport, so that's not likely to happen."

Okay, Jack felt sad for his two friends but also knew how risky it was from the other side of the fence. All the work that went into training a racehorse could be snuffed out in a minute. A second. He ran his hand up Magnifico's nose and scratched behind his left ear. The horse pushed against his hand, asking for more. Jack obliged. The beautiful low-flying chestnut had come such a long way since arriving at the stable, straight from the paddock, and looking to bite anyone who came within striking distance of his flashing teeth. Now his coat shone, his eyes were bright and he'd looked magnificent galloping out in front of the field before hitting a piece of rough ground. If the boys decided to stick it out, Jack would be right behind them, doing whatever was needed to bring Magnifico back to the track.

That's if *Windsong* was still a working racing stable by then.

When his uncle died three years ago, leaving the stable to him, the business had been in debt to the bank for half a million dollars. It had taken most of Jack's bank account to get *Windsong* freehold again. And he'd been getting there — but things had gone wrong in quick succession — slow horses, non-paying owners, more money going out than coming in. And now, the final blow, Magnifico's injury.

After seeing Greg off, Jack wandered through the stables giving each horse a final check, a routine task he always enjoyed doing at this time of night. Lofty had knocked his water bin askew again so he spent ten minutes realigning and refastening the bin to the stable wall while Lofty snuffled hot air into his ears and played with his hair. Goldie, one of his favourites, wanted a cuddle, and Jet, Kiah's horse, nosed in his pocket exploring for carrots. Jet had trialled well during the week and Jack was looking forward to preparing him for his first race. But unless he could pay the bills owed to the feed store, the farrier, the vet, the petrol company, and everyone else associated with running a racing stable, that wasn't likely to happen.

Lastly, he removed Magnifico's ice boots and made him as comfortable as possible in the deep straw bedding. As he was leaving, the horse nudged him in the back and let out a low mournful whinny, so Jack chopped a full carrot into thin slices, added it to a handful of bran and a scoop of lucerne chaff and tipped the mixture into Magnifico's feed-bin before running the bolt across the stable door.

Then, unable to put his talk with Kiah off any longer, he locked the feed room door and headed toward his office. He knew Kiah was in there working on the computer. When they'd spotted Greg's vehicle coming down the driveway, she'd offered to Google and research any alternative treatments for torn ligaments, while Jack and Magnifico's owners spoke to the vet.

The closer he came to the office door, the slower, the jerkier his steps became, until finally he was standing directly outside, barely able to breathe. In an attempt to stem the conflicting thoughts scurrying around in his brain turning his stomach to barbed wire, he re-directed all thoughts, once again, to his father's prophetic words. It was time. He couldn't put this off any longer. Pulling in a shaky breath, he placed his fingers around the door handle, determined to do the right thing…

But how could he? How could he break up, walk away from the only woman who'd made him feel alive again? The only woman, since his wife died, who'd made him feel whole?

Kiah was amazing. She was warm and loving and beautiful and funny. He loved her with all his heart.

He slowly twisted the door handle…and that's why he had to let her go.

*****

Kiah let out a low whistle. She'd been googling alternative treatments for torn ligaments without much success — unless plastering the leg with boiled seaweed and covering it with glad-wrap worked miracles — and then somehow found herself studying the stable's finances instead. She rubbed the tip of her nose and frowned at the figures staring back at her from the computer screen. It was late, she was tired, but no matter which way she crunched those numbers, *Windsong Racing Stables* looked to be in the red.

Bottom line — they needed more winners and more owners who actually paid their bills.

Deep in thought, Kiah chewed on her left thumbnail and pushed out a sigh. Okay, things looked pretty grim at the moment, but Jack would know what to do. He was shrewd. Smart. Capable. He'd sort it out. And if he asked her, she'd be happy to help.

First up, he needed to get more proactive with owners who were lax in paying their bills. A late fee if a month overdue and any trainer who was more than three months overdue — there were currently seven of them — should be sent a final reminder and a warning that if their account wasn't paid in full within the next five days, it would be passed on to a debt collector.

Then there was their lack of advertising. Maybe she could talk to Belle in the morning and ask her to redesign the *Windsong* website; eliminate the weeds, moss, and dusty cobwebs that invaded their current one. Belle could even do some of her social media magic and encourage new race-lovers to form syndicates. Blog on the everyday running of a racing stable. Highlight a different horse from the stable each week for their followers. The possibilities were endless. Not that Jack could pay her much, but Kiah knew Belle would jump at the chance to help.

The door swung open and out of the corner of her eye she watched Jack clomp into the office and toss his battered bush hat onto a vacant chair. Face pale, hair wild, he looked as though he hadn't slept for a week. She quickly logged off the stable's account, bringing the alternate seaweed remedy back up, before frowning at him. "You okay, Jack?"

He grunted and turned his back on her. Something had upset his applecart. She watched him yank open a deep drawer in the old-fashioned metal filing cabinet, a throwback to his uncle's filing system, select a file, and bury his nose inside. Almost like he didn't want to have a conversation with her.

Since Magnifico's breakdown at the track the day before, Jack had grown distant; almost like he was pulling away from her. Okay, she knew he was worried about the horse, but it was more than that. More to do with her. And yet she couldn't think of anything she'd done to upset him. In fact, she'd been nothing but loving and supportive. She knew how much Jack wanted to win the Cup, not only for the boost it would give to the stable's finances, but to prove to his skeptical father that he was good enough.

Kiah glanced at the time. 10.30pm. No wonder she was hungry. She hadn't stopped for a bite to eat since that hastily put together sandwich ten hours ago. She shut down the computer, stood up and stretched her arms in the air. Maybe Jack needed a cuddle. Nose still stuck in the file; his body language spoke of more bad news. Earlier in the day, one of his paying owners had rung to say he was shifting his horse to another training stable, plus goofy Lofty had somehow got his foot stuck in his waterer and while scrambling to get it out ripped off his shoe, including part of his hoof. Which meant he was out of action for at least six weeks.

"Hey, want me to make pancakes for supper? Banana and cinnamon…?" She walked across to Jack and wrapped both arms around his waist, leaning her head against his strong, muscular back. She loved this man so much, sometimes she felt like crawling inside his skin just so she could get closer. "Maybe we'll have time for a moonlight walk along the riverbank afterwards. That always relaxes you." She poked him with one finger. "Hey, your body feels stiffer than a starched shirt." When that got no reaction, she rubbed his back in soothing circles, an action that normally turned him into a soggy lump of jelly. "We could even pack up the pancakes and take them with us. Have a moonlight picnic under *our* tree." The spot where he'd opened up and told her about his wife, Bianca, and she'd been brave enough to tell him about the day Richard died. She snuggled deeper into his back, running her lips across the familiar dip between his shoulder blades. "Come on, what do ya say, Jack?"

Without turning around, Jack shrugged, bouncing her off him. "No time for that, Kiah. I have a stable to run."

Kiah stepped back, the rejection slamming into her chest like a heavy bag of oats. "I know that, babe, and I'm here to help in any way I can." She frowned. Perhaps there was more trouble in the stables and that was why he was acting this way. "Has something happened to one of the other horses?"

Jack slowly turned around. He shook his head, his eyes boring a hole in the faded blue and gold office carpet, as though he couldn't bring himself to look at her, to be near her. As though Magnifico's accident was her fault.

"Jack?"

He looked up, his eyes seeming to drink in her every detail, like he was storing it all for future memories. And then a shutter slammed down over his eyes and all emotion disappeared. "Kiah, we need to take a break. We're going too fast. You need to get out and see other men, to live, to see the world, before you settle down again."

Everything around her slowed down. It was like she was trying to process his words through a swarm of buzzing bees. "Slow down? Take a break? What are you talking about, Jack?" She could hear the squeak of disbelief, of confusion in her voice, but couldn't stop herself. "The night before Magnifico's race you-you told me you loved me, that we were like two halves of a stick drifting along in the river and we'd finally found each other."

His jaw tightened as a flush colored his neck. Almost afraid to look at her he stared down at the file in his hand and shrugged. "Heat of the moment."

Heat of the moment?

She opened her mouth, tried to speak, to tell him she loved him and there would never be anyone else, that she didn't want to go out and see other men because he was the one, the man she wanted to spend the rest of her life with, but his glacial words, *'Heat of the moment,'* hung in the air like the toxic stink of a clogged drain. Two nights ago, he'd told her he loved her and kissed her, and they'd made love until the sun peeped over the back paddocks; caressing, exploring, loving every part of each other's body, like they were the only two people left on earth. She'd given him her heart. And with those words — *heat of the moment* —he'd stomped on it, smashed it into a zillion, jagged pieces.

Was she such an unlovable person that men couldn't bear to be near her once they got to know her? Like Richard, who'd been all charm and gentlemanly manners until two days after their wedding when she'd burnt his toast and he'd thrown a kitchen knife at her?

"Why, Jack?"

Jack licked his lips, stared at the wall behind her.

"What changed? What did I do?"

Jack fidgeted with the file in his hand finally letting it fall on the desk. "Nothing," he said, still refusing to look at her. "It's me. I-I'm not ready for a relationship."

Kiah studied Jack's expression. It was like he'd dragged a mask over his own gorgeous face, the one she'd grown to love; leaving the façade of a man she didn't know at all. A man who couldn't even look at her. And the change sent chills snaking through her chest like a vine, strangling, compressing her heart. During her marriage, it had always been the coldness that got to Kiah more than the anger.

A memory washed over her like an upturned bucket of ice-water. Of another face, eyes devoid of emotion. A day in mid-December, when she'd gone against Richard's orders, thinking, if he sees how special the lounge room looks decorated for Christmas, he'll change his mind and get into the Christmas spirit. She'd even bought a bottle of his favourite wine, a nice Shiraz from the local Dan Murphy's store, and placed the wine and two glasses on the coffee table for when he arrived home. But the moment he'd pushed through the front door, she knew she'd gone too far. Eyes chips of frost, jaw tight, lips thinner than cigarette papers, he didn't speak, instead it took him only ten minutes to wreck every decoration she'd spent all afternoon putting up. Then, not only did he blank her out for the next two weeks, crashing into her as though she was invisible, he'd locked her in the bathroom for 24 hours on Christmas day.

It was then she knew, deep in her heart, that even though Jack was nothing like Richard, she could never live with another man who made her feel unworthy of his love. She wasn't the shadow of a woman who'd hit the open road the day of her husband's funeral. She'd left that woman behind at the gravesite.

"Silly me," she said, and snatched her bag from the desk before slinging it over one shoulder. "And here's me thinking you were one of the good guys. Turns out you're just as big an asshole as the rest."

"Kiah…please…I…"

Ignoring the pain on Jack's face, she tossed her hair from her eyes and strolled out of the office, taking care not to show how much her hand shook when she fumbled with the door handle, nor how her legs almost gave way under her with each step that took her away from the man she loved. She'd pack up and leave *Windsong* tonight. Couldn't stay. Couldn't see Jack in the morning, pretending nothing had happened, knowing how much he'd hurt her. She'd presented him her heart and he'd booted it out of the ball park.

The caravan door squeaked as she dragged it open, reminding her she'd never get to use the can of lubricating oil she'd bought from the local hardware store that morning. When she switched on the light, the new floral curtains at the windows smiled back at her. Curtains that still smelled faintly of Jack's new cologne — Alpine with a sprig of lemon — from when he'd helped her take the old faded curtains down and hang the new ones in their place.

His dragon-head toothbrush lay beside hers on the sink, his grey-blue sweater that matched his eyes was draped over the back of her chair, his muddy boots drying out under her table.

Jack Sullivan was everywhere.

Heat prickled behind her eyes and a heavy weight pushed against her chest, threatening a flood of tears. No…she wouldn't cry. Jack wasn't worth one damn tear. Not one. He'd said he loved her and they'd talked of a life together, the three of them, her, Jack, and Angel. She blew out a breath and closed her eyes. Angel. Oh, God, what was she going to tell Angel? How could she explain to the little girl she'd come to love like her own child, that her father was lower than the scum at the bottom of a toilet bowl?

She couldn't…

Dragging a suitcase out from the bottom of the wardrobe, Kiah began throwing everything she owned inside. She'd left her last life with only the clothes on her back — ugly black funeral attire that had ended up in a bin outside the Salvos — and she was leaving *Windsong* with not much more. Riding clothes, jeans, tops, a couple of sweaters, two pairs of shoes and a dress she'd bought specially for Magnifico's disastrous race.

And her most important possession of all…Jet.

After stashing her suitcase and loose belongings in the back of the Range Rover, Kiah hooked up the horse float and drove across to the stable block. It was all quiet at this time of night. Steeling herself, she climbed out of the car and made her way across the meticulously raked gravel, where shadows from the dim outside light danced beneath her feet. Overhead, a swarm of crazed moths threw themselves hypnotically against the bare light bulb. Was that what she'd been doing with Jack? Throwing herself at him? Misreading all the signals?

Inside, the building was quiet, warm, sweet-smelling, the contented snuffles and occasional stamp of a horse's hoof almost bringing her undone. She'd miss every one of these horses. And the people. Belle, Olivia, Taylor, Josh, Dillon, even grumpy old Steve. They'd all helped her become whole again. A snuffle from stable 10 told her Lofty was playing with his water bowl. Again. A tabby streak dropped from the hay loft, landing lightly on her shoulder. She ran her hand over Piglet's head, wished she could take him with her, but she couldn't, this was his home. She gently lifted the stable cat off her shoulder and pushed the tack-room door open, leaning in to snaffle her halter from the nearest peg.

A high-pitched neigh greeted Kiah as she opened Jet's stable door. "Shh, baby…it's only me. We need to move on, find somewhere else to live, okay?"

After slipping the halter over his head, she led her horse out of the stable and up the ramp into the horse float, where he immediately buried his nose in a hay-net full of lucerne. As long as there was food on tap, an unexpected late-night trip didn't faze him at all.

Then, with a last look at the place she'd come to think of as home; at the silhouette of the caravan looking small and abandoned in the light of the half-moon, at the shadowy horses dozing in the paddocks each side of the driveway, at the house where Jack would likely be under the shower, his beautiful naked body glistening in the artificial bathroom light as he prepared for bed — without her — Kiah let out a muffled sob, threw herself behind the wheel, and started the engine.

EIGHTEEN

Jack swiped a shaky hand through his hair and took a breath. He'd never believed hearts could actually break, but the way his heart was struggling to beat, the pain currently slicing through his chest, maybe it was true. An image of Kiah's face when he'd crushed her with his words of rejection, haunted him. Made him want to throw up. He crumpled into the kitchen chair and stared at his housekeeper, who stared right back at him. Her face like a thunder bolt waiting to strike.

"You *did* explain to Kiah *why* you wanted to take a break?" Marg said, her voice charged with the same razor-sharp chills that matched her eyes.

He blinked up at her. Not quite on her wavelength yet. "Er…explain?"

"Yes. Give her a reason for suddenly, out of the blue, whacking her with a break-up. Telling her you didn't want her anymore."

"But I *do* want her," he protested, hackles rising. "I love her. That's why I set her free rather than drag her into debt by staying with me."

"And you told her this? Let her decide if she loved you enough to stick with you through the bad times as well as the good?"

"Well…no…I—"

"After what that poor lass has been through, you up and rejected her, with no explanation?" Marg, hands on hips, lips in a thin angry line, stood, glaring down at him. "And now you sit there crying about how bad *you* feel. Moaning about how are *you* going to live without the woman you love. Yet you acted worse than her cold bullying husband."

"No, no, you're wrong, Marg. *I'd* never hurt Kiah. Like my father said, I can't expect her to stay with me when the stable's in the red?"

"But you *did* hurt her, Jack. Can't you see that? Rejection was all Kiah knew until she arrived here at *Windsong* and found people who cared for her and a man she thought was different. Now, once again, she's told she's not good enough. And by the man she loved and trusted." Marg shook her head. "How do you think that made her feel?"

"But I—"

"No buts. You did the unthinkable, Jack."

Jack closed his eyes; the confusion, the pain on Kiah's face when he'd spurned her, imprinted on his brain. "Oh, God, what have I done…?"

"Instead of feeling sorry for yourself, get your miserable hide out of that chair and go find her. Do what you should have done in the beginning and explain about your finances. Tell her you love her and the only reason you made such an ass of yourself was because you didn't want to bring her down with you." Marg shook her head. "Come on, Jack, I shouldn't have to put words in your mouth, just open your heart and let your love pour out."

Jack blinked at Marg, but all he could see was Kiah's face, her robotic movements when he'd coldly and dispassionately pushed her away. He slumped back in the chair. "She won't listen to me now. It's too late."

Marg slammed her hand on the table making the sugar bowl jump. "If she doesn't want to listen — and I don't blame her — get down on your knees, Jack. Kiss her feet, if that's what it takes. But do it. Now."

Jack skittered his chair away from the table and stood, hands fisted, breath heavy in his chest. Marg was right. He'd made a complete balls-up of things but Kiah needed to know the reason why he thought taking a break was the best scenario for her. Thoughts skittering, like rabbits across a paddock, he stared unseeingly at the floor. Why had he listened to his father? He'd never listened to the man before — why now?

"Go on!" Marg prodded him in the direction of the door. "And if Kiah's silly enough to forgive you, bring her back here to the house. There's a cottage pie in the oven. All you have to do is warm it up for ten minutes and then feed her. Poor girl's been working so hard beside you, caring for you, worrying about you after Magnifico's accident, she probably hasn't had anything to eat since that sandwich she slapped together at lunch time."

Jack reached for his coat on the peg beside the front door and stood there, unable to move. Marg was right and he'd been too blind, too self-absorbed, to see it for himself. Kiah had barely left his side since Magnifico broke down on the track. Making sure he ate, helping him care for the other horses, trying to keep his spirits up. Just being Kiah. And because he'd acted on his father's twisted words, he'd thrown all that love and compassion back in her face.

He wrenched the front door open, took the steps in one bound and set off at a run. One moment of weakness, one moment of self-doubt, and he'd risked losing the best thing that had happened to him in a long time.

As he rounded the corner and hit the path that led to Kiah's caravan, he could see the caravan was in darkness. He frowned. Was she asleep already? Been so upset she'd gone for a walk in the night air to calm down? Or was she tossing and turning in that narrow bed, where they'd made love so many times, maybe crying because he'd hurt her so badly?

The moment he came closer, he knew something was wrong. The caravan door was half open. Ever since that psycho, Cockroach, left his deadly calling card on her door, Kiah had locked up each night before going to sleep and if she'd gone for a walk, she'd have closed the door and locked it before setting off.

Heart slamming against his chest like wild waves pounding relentlessly against a rocky cliff, he placed one finger in the middle of the door and pushed it all the way open. "Kiah? You in there? Are you okay?"

When there was no answer, he climbed the three steps, dread turning his stomach to mush, reached up and switched on the light.

It took him a full minute to register what was staring back at him. Both wardrobe doors stood wide open and all that was left inside was one lone wooden hanger. Kiah's new red and black blanket, one he'd helped her pick out, was gone from her bed. And her two lovingly framed photos that she kept on the shelf near her bed were missing. One of Jack and Kiah together, both laughing as he carried her across the creek, and the other, a photo of her horse, Jet.

Legs threatening to buckle, Jack slumped down onto the top step, head cradled in both hands, a gasp of despair caught in his throat.

He was too late.

Kiah was gone…

*****

It was almost midnight.

Blinking away tears, Kiah forced her eyes to stay focused on the steady pool of brightness emanating from her car's headlights. Lights that plowed through the darkness on the other side of her windscreen. Lights that lit up the gray of the highway and the fast-moving scenery in her peripheral vision. Lights that took her further and further away from *Windsong*. And from Jack.

What would he be doing now? Her bottom lip wobbled and she sniffed. Would he be tossing and turning in his bed, blankets tightly wrapped around his body, thinking of her, missing her? Or would he be sound asleep, his dreams centered on his horses and upcoming races; Kiah already a distant memory?

Her shoulders slumped as she rounded a bend and straightened up for another long dark lonely stretch ahead. Here she was back where it had all started — letting the road take her wherever it led. But this time there was no whoopee, no fist pump, no sense of setting herself free. Only heart-ache.

Hands cold and shaky, she gripped the leather-clad steering wheel tighter. The fact that Jack had rejected her was like a sharp stick penetrating her heart, digging deep, stirring painfully. She sniffed again and scrubbed at her eyes with her fist as the road shimmered in front of her, the headlights picking out the painted white line that seemed to be judging her. Telling her over and over again that she wasn't enough.

But why? Was she born with a flaw, a defect in her personality that made all men want to hurt her? Cause their love for her to turn to dust.

She cricked her neck, which had become stiff and achy from holding her shoulders tense. Maybe it was time for a short break from driving. Her brain was muddled, confused, and she didn't want to run the car off the road and crash into a tree, not with her precious Jet happily chewing on his hay in the float behind her. She'd stop at the next all-night service station, fill up with petrol and treat herself to a strong black coffee. Anything to take her thoughts off Jack Sullivan. Off his soft warm lips, his gorgeous grey-blue eyes, his strong arms and the way she could just step into those arms and feel safe from the world; like coming home.

But not anymore.

Five miles on, she carefully pulled off the road into a well-lit *On the Run* 24-hr. service station and eased to a stop in front of a petrol bowser. Jet didn't move. She was so much better at towing a horse float now than the day she'd first pulled into the driveway of *Windsong* and discovered Jack Sullivan was the same hot guy who'd rescued her at the sale-yards. Okay, as well as rescuing her, he'd also tried to talk her out of buying Jet, but that was only because he cared for her.

But not anymore.

Kiah unscrewed the petrol cap and inserted the nozzle, letting petrol fill the SUV's large tank. Once again, her mind drifted to Jack's kind eyes, his cheeky grin, the way his touch electrified her. She shook her head to clear the vision. If she wanted to start a new life, she had to stop thinking about Jack Sullivan. She let out a sigh as she returned the pump to the bowser and stared at the bright lights radiating from inside the building.

She was so tired…

Ten minutes later, cradling a takeaway coffee, Kiah trudged back toward the Ranger Rover and shivered. She pulled the collar of her jacket up higher. An icy wind had sprung up out of nowhere. As well as a coffee to warm her up, she'd grab the red and black fringed blanket from the back seat of the car. She'd bought it from Hayes Haberdashery in Shadow Creek last month to brighten up her bed in the caravan.

Opening the back door of the SUV, mind reliving the day she and Jack had made love on that same red and black fringed blanket under their special tree, Kiah let out a gasp of surprise and blinked down at the face smiling tentatively back at her. "Angel?"

Was she hallucinating? Had the shock of Jack's rejection made her see things that weren't there? Kiah leaned in and poked Angel in the chest to make sure she was real, sending the little girl into giggles. What the heck was Jack's daughter doing on the back seat of her car dressed only in pajamas? She peered over her shoulder expecting to see Jack step out of the shadows, but there was no one there. Once again, she blinked down at the stowaway.

"Hi, Kiah." Angel's voice was hesitant but her smile didn't waver.

"What the heck are you doing here? Why aren't you home in bed?"

Angel's bottom lip quivered and her smile slowly slid off her face. "Are-are you mad at me?"

"No, no, darling, just confused." Kiah took a breath to steady herself. "And worried. Where did you come from? How did you get here?"

"I saw you packing from my bedroom window and knew you were leaving, so I snuck out and hid under a horse rug, in the float, so you couldn't see me."

"You've been travelling all this way in the float? With Jet?"

Angel nodded. "Bit smelly and bumpy and I felt a bit sick when you went round corners. That's why I climbed into the back of your car while you were in the shop." She took a big breath, her chin wobbly, but determined. "And I'm not going home."

Kiah closed her eyes, took a long deep breath, let it out slowly. What the heck was she going to do now? As much as she loved Jack's daughter, this was a complication she didn't need. And then she pictured Marg, going in to wake Angel for school in the morning and finding her bed empty. Marg would be so scared. And what about Jack? His sweet Angel missing — the little girl he'd brought up mostly on his own since his wife died giving birth to her. Of course, Jack would think the worst, imagine Angel in danger.

She put a finger under Angel's chin and tipped it up so she could get her message across clearly. "Sweetheart, I love you, you know that, but there's no way you can come with me."

"Why not?"

"Because your dad will be off his trolly with worry when he finds you gone, that's why not." Kiah's head swam. Should she ring Jack, tell him to come and pick Angel up? But then she'd have to talk to him, and what if he blamed her, what if he was cold and unemotional on the phone like he'd been when he told her he needed a break? Her hands fisted at her sides. Maybe she should just drive back to *Windsong*, quietly tuck Angel back into bed before anyone woke up, then set off on her journey again. "Look, Angel, hop in the front seat of the car with me and we'll talk about it. And bring that blanket with you so you can wrap it around yourself. You'll freeze in those baby doll pajamas and end up in bed with pneumonia. And then your dad will probably blame me for that too." She closed her eyes and let out a breath. "Geez, wish I'd bought a jumbo-sized coffee."

Once they were both settled in the front seat, Angel lay her head against Kiah's shoulder and sighed theatrically. "He's an idiot, you know, my dad. Even worse than Sam, that weird boy in my class at school who brings me flowers and then when I thank him, goes all creepy and pulls their heads off."

Kiah pushed back a grin. "I'm really going to miss you, sweetheart."

"Well, take me with you."

"I can't."

"But you're my best friend in the whole world."

"I am, that's true. But your dad is your dad. It's just different. He loves you to the moon and back, and he'll be sad and scared when he finds your bed empty. And so will Marg."

Angel shook her head. "No, they won't. I left a note on my bed telling Dad I was going to live with you."

"But how did you know I was leaving, not just storing stuff in my car?"

"Well…," Angel snuggled closer, the sweet smell of baby powder making Kiah smile. "I'd snuck downstairs, see, 'cos I was thirsty and wanted to get a bottle of cold water from the fridge. And that's when I heard Dad talking to Marg, and he was crying, and my dad never cries, not even when Fatso, my guinea pig, died. Dad told Marg he broke up with you because he had nothing but debts and you deserved better than him. That you'd been through enough bad stuff, and he loved you too much to drag you down again." She frowned. "And something about Grandpa, but I didn't catch that bit."

Kiah closed her eyes, swallowed a pulsing lump in her throat that was threatening to choke her. A single tear rolled down her cheek. Jack Sullivan loved her. In his lopsided, upside-down crazy way he thought he was protecting her by sending her away. She wiped the tear away with one knuckle and grinned. "Your dad really said that…?"

Angel nodded. "And Marg blasted him. Called him an idiot for letting you go. Said he didn't have the brains he was born with." Angel nestled closer, her eye lids starting to close. "Dad might be an idiot, Kiah, but *I'm* not letting you go. I'm staying with you."

"Oh sweetheart." Kiah hugged the little girl to her, stroking the softness of her hair, sniffing back threatening tears. Foolish, overthinking, protective, Jack, had acted, not out of coldness and a need to hurt her, but out of misdirected love. Breaking up with her was his way of saying, *I'll always put you first, I'll always look after you.* She gazed down at his precious daughter, snuggled so close they were almost one, and smiled. "Maybe…just maybe," she whispered, "I can do something about that. Maybe, neither you, nor your dad, needs to let me go."

And then her latent Warrior Princess persona kicked in; the inner strength that saw her face many obstacles since taking charge of her own life. She lifted her chin and threw out her chest. Yes, she'd accept Jack's explanation and apology, but boy, would she make him choke on humble pie first.

NINETEEN

Instead of creeping down *Windsong*'s driveway, lights dimmed, engine low, and sneaking Angel back into her bed without waking anyone, after opening the gate, Kiah revved the engine, switched her lights on high beam, turned the radio up to the max, and, laying on the horn, barreled down the driveway towards the house.

As she came to a halt amid a shower of gravel, lights came on inside and outside the house and two figures tumbled through the open front door onto the verandah. Marg, dressing gown on inside out, and Jack, hair standing on end, and still wearing the same clothes he'd worn the day before.

Instead of throwing herself out of the Range Rover, Kiah took a long calming breath, checked that her best friend was still asleep under the black and red blanket — Marg was right, this kid would sleep through an alien attack — then killed the music and switched off the engine. Warrior Princess fully in charge, she opened the car door, swung her feet onto the driveway and slowly and regally, stood. The rest of her life depended on what happened in the next few minutes, and she had to get this right. She loved Jack with all her heart, but he'd hurt her and she'd vowed never to allow anyone to hurt her again. Even though he'd had her best interests at heart, Jack was in the wrong. So, it would take a lot of groveling, a lot of sucking up to forgive him.

With a toss of her head, she sashayed toward the front of the car and leaned back against the bonnet, arms folded.

"Kiah?" Jack almost tripped over his own feet in his eagerness to bypass the verandah steps and reach her. "Oh, thank God, you've come back. I went looking for you, thought I'd lost you. I didn't know where—"

"That's far enough." Kiah held up one hand in the recognized gesture, *'come another step and you'll be eating dirt'*. As much as she was trying to distance herself from the man, she couldn't help running her eyes, like a hot tongue, over the way his muscles pushed against that crumpled shirt, the lines permanently creased around his mouth and eyes, indicating his penchant for kindness, for smiling, and yes, those beautiful soul-deep, grey-blue eyes, the eyes that had drawn her to him the first time she'd seen him at the sale-yard. The eyes that were greedily consuming her right now. Pushing down the desire to throw herself at him, kiss him senseless, Kiah cricked her head higher and drew in a deep mind-clearing, breath. "Sooo." Lifting her chin higher, she drew the word out as far as it would go. "I believe you have something you wish to tell me, Jack?"

"I love you."

"Not enough."

"I'm sorry, so sorry, Kiah, I didn't mean to hurt—"

"Yes, you did, Jack. How could you *not* hurt me by pushing me away, telling me you didn't want me anymore, that my love and care for you wasn't enough?"

"But I didn't mean—"

"Your exact words were… 'I'm not ready for a relationship. We're going too fast. We need to take a break.'" Kiah upped the volume of her voice with each statement. "And what about the blue ribbon of them all? 'You need to get out and see other men'. "She paused for effect. "So, Jack, what part of all that *didn't* you mean?"

Marg, who'd been listening, watching, as though witnessing her favourite soap on TV, let out a loud groan from the top step of the verandah. "Oh, Jack, you didn't? You wouldn't? How could you suggest sending Kiah out to test drive other men? Please, please, tell me she's joking."

Jack flung a look in Marg's direction. "I was trying to protect her."

"By telling her to see other men?"

"Well, I wasn't thinking straight at the time." He let out a breath heavy with frustration. "I meant she'd be better off with someone who could support her, give her a better life than I could." He frowned. "Of course,

I'd have to punch any guy who *did* look at her, but..."

Kiah gazed up at the sky, so vast, so full of mystery. At the eons-old stars, light-years from Earth. Both less confusing than the man standing beside her. "Jack, that doesn't make any sense."

"Kiah, I'm so much in debt, I'm close to bankruptcy. I might have to give up training racehorses and work as a door-to-door salesman." He licked his lips, held her in his gaze. "What I'm trying to say is, I can't support you in the way you're accustomed."

"Oh, Jack," Kiah let out a groan. "I live in a caravan. I work in a stable. I push a lopsided wheelbarrow around the paddocks picking up horse manure. *That's* what I'm accustomed to. And I love it!"

"But before you came here you—"

"Lived in a cage with a dangerous wild animal," she said. "A luxurious cage — but still a cage." Unable to keep her hands off him any longer, she placed a palm each side of his face, looked deep into his eyes and shook her head. "You listened to your dad, didn't you?"

He nodded. "I'm so, so sorry, Kiah. I should have talked it over with you, explained about my finances. Then let you decide."

"That's the only way forward, Jack."

Jack grabbed both her hands in his. "Does that mean you'll stay? You'll give me another chance?"

"Maybe." Kiah swallowed the smile threatening to break through. "But first, you have some major sucking up to do, Jack Sullivan."

"Yeah, Dad, you have some major sucking up to do."

Kiah looked down at the mini-me now standing beside her, back straight, arms folded. Angel had woken up and decided to make it a two-girl army.

"Angel?" Jack, momentarily confused, did a double take. "Where did you spring from? Why aren't you in bed?"

Angel's bottom lip dropped. She snuggled up to Kiah's side. "You broke my best friend."

"Broke?"

"Broke up," Kiah explained. "Angel heard you talking to Marg, saw me leaving, and unknown to me, decided to stow away in the back of the float under a horse blanket."

Jack's face went white. "She what?"

"'Cos you were being an idiot, Dad, and I-I couldn't let Kiah go. I knew you'd come looking for me, and-and then, and then you'd find Kiah and make up."

"Oh, sweetheart, come here." Jack's arms went around Angel and he hugged her to him. "I'm not angry with you, but promise me you'll never, ever, do that again."

Marg, hurrying down the steps, joined them. She cuddled Angel and kissed the top of her head, then blinked across at Kiah. "We didn't even know she was gone."

"Maybe that's a good thing, otherwise, there'd have been a major panic."

"Pandemonium is the word you're looking for." Marg threw a sideways glance at Jack before smoothing Angel's hair away from her eyes. "Right, little one, you and I are going to have a few words in the morning, but now, let's get you back into bed and leave these two *big* kids to sort themselves out." Guiding Angel up the steps, she spoke to Kiah over her shoulder. "Don't be afraid to push him, girl. And Jack, if you have to get down on your knees, lick her feet, then do it. Forgiveness for being an idiot doesn't come cheap."

Jack grinned at Kiah as Marg and Angel disappeared inside the house. "I'm quite open to licking your feet, you know." He looked down at her boots, then back up at her. "But first, I'd have to take your boots off."

"Naturally."

"And maybe, your shirt." He slowly undid the two top buttons, then flicked a finger at her jeans. "And these would probably get in the way."

A delicious warmth crept from Kiah's toes right up into her chest, and nestled there, alongside the sting of hurt. She let her fingers trace the roughness of Jack's way-past-five-o'clock shadow, the sharp prickles teasing the palm of her hands. She inhaled the smell of sweat and horses, and gazed into a face she never thought she'd see again. A face that looked back at her with such depths of love and total, whole-hearted, unequivocal remorse, it took her breath away.

A loud stomp of an impatient hoof and an ear-piercing, *what-about-me* whinny from inside the horse-float set Jack laughing. "Seems like the other man in your life is getting antsy."

"Males." Shaking her head, Kiah let out a mock sigh. "They're all the same — want everything done yesterday."

He smiled down at her, his eyes devouring her like she was his favourite chocolate bar and he intended to lick her slowly, make the deliciousness last. "I don't know about yesterday," he said, his voice barely above a whisper. "But there's definitely something I need to do right now."

"There is," she agreed, her breath catching in her throat as his eyes continued to feed on her. "And I believe it includes a whole heap of groveling."

Jack leaned closer and trickled his lips across the pulse in her neck, making her knees turn to melted toffee. "So," he said, his voice soft, husky. "Shall we settle the other love of your life in his stable, pronto, then begin the first step of my lifelong journey to forgiveness?"

"Mmm…" was all she could manage as his lips, barely-there, yet oh-so-hot, continued their exploration of the delicate skin on her neck, the lobe of her right ear and the freckle high on her right cheek.

He pulled away, momentarily, one hand still cupping the back of her neck, the other caressing her hair as though she was a rare diamond. "And to proving that I'll love you 'til my dying breath?"

Kiah moaned as Jack's lips closed over hers. She loved everything about Jack Sullivan. The way he laughed, the way he hugged, the way he made her feel complete.

Still moaning, she opened her mouth to let him in, not just into her mouth, but into her heart, forever.

EPILOGUE

Kiah tugged gently on the lead rope attached via a metal clip to Jet's race bridle. "Easy there, tiger," she crooned, unable to stifle a grin. "Save all that mad energy for the race."

It was two weeks later and thanks to everyone at *Windsong* contributing towards the fifteen-hundred-dollar late-entry fee, Jet, aka Party Pooper, had been entered and accepted for the Kangaroo Downs Cup. A bubble of excitement tangoed behind Kiah's ribcage. Her rescue horse was currently strutting around the parade ring, minutes away from competing in the main race of the day. After winning his latest trial by seven lengths, two tenths of a second faster than Magnifico's best time, the excitement at *Windsong* had blossomed; grown from an acorn to a full-blown tree of hope for the future.

"Love you, boy," she whispered, planting a kiss on his bony cheek. For a moment he turned his head and she could swear he winked at her. The sparkle in those deep brown eyes, so different to the dull, lifeless stare that had broken her heart when she'd found him at the horse sale eight months ago. Today, her 'rescue' horse wouldn't have looked out of place competing in a Championship Hack class at the Royal Melbourne Show. Belle had plaited his mane and forelock, while Olivia had performed her own creative art work, combing quarter marks and shark's teeth patterns across his hindquarters.

"Easy, easy boy…not long to go now." It was almost like Jet knew it was Cup Day and couldn't wait to get out onto the track as he danced up and down on the end of the lead. Unless, of course, he couldn't wait to see how high he could toss his jockey on the way to the barriers. Even with the work they'd put into him, Jet still couldn't be trusted not to show off his legendary, high-flying buck — just for the fun of it.

"You playing silly buggers, again, Jet?" It was Taylor, *Windsong's* five-foot-nothing stable jockey, her infectious grin lighting up the dimple in both cheeks. She gave Jet's neck an affectionate slap, before leaning in and whispering something in his ear. Pig Latin? Voodoo? Promise of carrots? Whatever it was, it settled him enough for Kiah to leg her into the saddle where she picked up the reins and slid her feet into both stirrups. Kiah breathed a sigh of relief…so far so good.

Once she'd unclipped the lead rope and Taylor let Jet stride through the open gateway onto the track, Kiah went looking for Jack. She spotted the love of her life, leaning against the outside running rail, looking all Hugh Jackman-ish with his strong jaw, dark hair, and twinkling eyes. He'd taken up a position not far from the finishing post and directly across from a family of recently-shorn Merino sheep, seemingly gathered together to watch the race from the centre of the course.

"You okay? Nervous?" Jack greeted Kiah with a welcoming smile before pulling her into one of his special, air-whooshing bearhugs.

"A little." How she loved Jack's hugs. It was like being wrapped in a warm cosy blanket with meditation music playing in the background. Cheek pressed against his chest, she listened to the steady *boom-boom* of his heartbeat, inhaled his unique Jack smell, sensed his overwhelming love for her in every breath, every caress. She tipped her head up at Jack and grinned. "Can you believe we're standing here at Kangaroo Downs racetrack, about to watch Jet take part in the Cup?"

Jack shook his head. "Eight months ago, I'd have said you were dreaming."

"And what a dream it's turned out to be." Her grin widened as she stepped away and gazed around her, suddenly hit by a sweet sense of belonging, of being part of the racing scene. The freshly raked dirt track, the Clerk of the Course in his red coat and white breeches, the lone bookie hovering over his board calling the odds, and the excited crowd. It seemed like the whole town of Shadow Creek had come to cheer Jet on. From the horse-feed guys, to old Mr and Mrs Turner from Turners Shoe Store on the corner of Murray and Hargreaves St. Old Mr Turner, appearing oh-so-dapper wearing his white suit and green shirt and tie — the stable's racing colours.

With butterfly wings twisting and batting in the pit of her stomach, Kiah watched Taylor sit tight to a playful buck as Jet passed them on the way to the barriers.

Please, Jet, be a good boy today...

"Come here, you." Jack gently took hold of her shoulders and turned her around to face him. "I have something important to ask you." He breathed in, as though to fortify himself, then, took both her hands in his. "I know this isn't the appropriate time...God, it's probably the most *inappropriate* time in history...but I can't wait a second longer." His eyes never leaving hers, he inhaled another shaky breath. "Kiah, darling, will you marry me? Make me the happiest man alive?"

Jack's voice, gruff, as though pushing the words through a clogged-up throat, made Kiah's heart sing. Jack Sullivan was the man she'd been waiting for all her life. Her other half. She squeezed his hand, sniffing back a tear. "Okay."

"Okay?" Jack's eyes widened as though not sure where to go from there. "Is-is that a yes?"

"Of course, it's a yes." She looked up at him, her eyes tracing his oh-so-familiar face, loving the high cheek bones, the kissable lips, the strong jawline; everything about him. "Win, lose, or even if Jet bucks Taylor off before the race starts, I love you, Jack Sullivan. I don't care if we have to live in a tent on the side of the road, it's you I love, not the stables, not the winning, not the money." On tiptoe, she reached up until her lips found his; soft, warm, and compliant. And when his tongue gently prodded her lips open and slid inside, sucking, tasting, causing heat to pool in the base of her stomach, Kiah moaned into his mouth. All thought of where they were disappearing in a cloud of lust.

"Dad! Dad! Dad! Did Kiah say yes?" Angel, dressed in cute lime-colored jeans and a white tee, skipped up to them, her face alight with anticipation while Olivia and Belle followed behind, hooting at them to 'get a room!'.

Reluctantly Kiah drifted down to earth and stepped away, noting the dreamy smile on Jack's face. A smile she knew mirrored her own.

"You don't mind, do you?" Jack said, his voice a little breathy. "I had to speak to Angel about us last night. And as you can see, she was all for it."

Before Kiah had a chance to respond, Angel, still dancing from one foot to the other, grabbed her hand. "Did you say yes, Kiah? Will you be my mum as well as my best friend in the whole world?"

Heart brimming with love for the adorable bouncing ball of humanity cavorting in front of her, Kiah pulled Angel into a hug, breathing in the sweet smell of lollypops and chocolate ice-cream. "Don't tell your dad, because he might get jealous," she whispered in Angel's ear. "But how could I *not* say yes, when the deal included an awesome daughter like you?"

"They're off!"

The Kangaroo Downs Cup had started. What with the excitement of a marriage proposal followed by a daughter proposal, she'd missed Jet's journey to the starting gate. Kiah leaned over the running rail, scouring the field. Where was Jet? Did he make it to the barriers? Or was he being held behind the stalls by the clerk of the course while Taylor scrambled back onto her feet?

"Go, Jet!" screamed Belle, blonde pigtails flipping up and down as she urged Jet on from the rail.

"He's in front…" Kiah felt hot, then cold, then hot again, and if she didn't breathe soon, she'd pass out, miss the race, and forever be kicking herself.

"Not yet…keep a hold of him…don't let him use up all his juice…" Jack, squeezing Kiah's hand so tightly her fingers lost all feeling, was attempting long-distance telepathy to convey his instructions to Taylor.

"Jet! Jet! Jet! Jet!" The chant went up from Belle, Olivia, Angel and now Josh, who'd joined them on the rails. Gathered in groups around the track, Jet's fans from the little town of Shadow Creek, joined in the chant. "Jet! Jet! Jet! Jet!" Bottom lip trembling, Kiah fought back tears. This beautiful black horse rounding the home turn three lengths in front of the field and preparing for the run home, was the same downtrodden, emaciated horse she'd spotted in that dirty stall at the saleyard. The horse that fought back when confronted by even more mistreatment in the form of an ugly vicious horsemeat dealer. Jet wasn't beaten then, and he wasn't going to be beaten today. When the favourite, Petrol Guzzler, drew up alongside, challenging him for the lead, he dug down even deeper, found extra power, and with one last surge, crossed the line in first place.

Her amazing horse, Party Pooper, aka Jet, trained by her gorgeous fiancé-of-three-minutes, had won the main event on the programme, the Kangaroo Downs Cup.

Once the all-clear signal came through, Kiah, swamped by laughing, back-patting friends, pulled away to climb the presentation dais steps, her hand still firmly wrapped inside Jack's. As the winning owner, she was to be presented with a highly decorative silver cup, a blank plaque on the bottom waiting for the words, 'Party Pooper', and the current year, to be inscribed.

Her grip on Jack's hand tightened when she spotted Olivia, nose ring glinting in the afternoon sun, proudly parading the horse of the hour around an eye-wateringly green, artificial lawn in front of the dais. Jet, arching his neck like a prima donna, was busy informing his adoring fans of his greatness.

Kiah's heart bubbled over, threatening to drown the dignitaries of the day in happy tears. She thought back to the day of Richard's funeral. Eight long months ago. To that last-minute wrench of the Range Rover's steering-wheel which had culminated in this moment. A change of direction that had taken her out onto the open road and into a life full of firsts — a horse of her own, real friends, a little girl who needed her, and the courage to discover her own self-worth. But best of all, to this funny, kind, big-hearted man standing beside her. Jack Sullivan. A man whose hypnotic grey-blue eyes were currently ogling her lips as though they were banana and cinnamon pancakes, and he couldn't wait to feast on them.

From the Author

Dear Readers,

I've been writing humorous mysteries now for thirteen years, ever since *Untreed Reads* published *Chasing Can Be Murder* way back in 2010, so I thought it high time I changed genres. *Hoofbeats at Windsong* is the first book in my *Shadow Creek Romance* series. I hope you enjoy reading all about Kiah and Jack's journey to love, and, of course, the star of the show, *Party Pooper*, better known in the stables as Jet. If so, why not pop over to Amazon, or whichever online store you bought this book from and leave an honest review? Reviews are like dessert for authors — with a cherry on top. In fact, they are part of what keeps me writing; knowing you'll spend time with the people I create and fall in love with on their journey to 'the end'.

If you'd like to catch up with me on Facebook, go to: https://facebook.com/JuneWhyteBooks. Or to check out my website, go here: www.junewhytebooks.com

I'd also like to acknowledge and thank those who have helped me on my writing journey. My beta readers, Bev and Nancy — you're my backbone, my flag wavers, love you both. June Diehl with her oh-so-brave dog, Franklin — always there with positive suggestions and encouragement. Robyn and Wendy — I can whip off an email with a writing question and the answer pings back same day. Traci Andrighetti, my muse, my writing guru — always so generous with her time and knowledge. And finally, K.D. and Jay Hartman of *Untreed Reads* who've been with me since day one — without you, I wouldn't still be writing today.

Thank you.

June Whyte

*****

For those who haven't yet read *Doggone It!* (the third book in my *Gumshoe Chicks* Mysteries) I've included the first chapter, just for you.

Read and enjoy…

Doggone It!

ONE

As much as I loved my life, sometimes it felt like a car crash waiting to happen. So much to do and so little time…

Meat defrosting for tonight's barbecue? Check.

Kayla's fairy wand glued back together and drying on kitchen table? Check.

Advertisement sent to all new hydro-bath clients offering a free nail clip? Check.

My two 'Gumshoe Chick' besties babysitting Kayla the Cute and Jake the Joker so I can handle Penelope in the show ring? Check.

I let out a sigh and scratched behind my ever-patient greyhound, Penelope's right ear while watching the effervescent teenage-handler of a Bedlington terrier, young, carefree, so unaware of what hurdles lay ahead in life, set off around the show ring.

Today's dog show was our biggest event of the year. Being an active member of the Ladies Kennel Club, I'd spent the morning setting up show rings and organising coffee and sandwiches for the judges before actively taking part in the show itself.

Intent on presenting Penelope to her best advantage, I glanced down to make sure her back legs were exactly square, just as a flashy silver-backed dog brush skimmed my head and landed with a thud on the manicured grass, right under Penelope's nose.

I let out a startled gasp. Penelope didn't bat an eyelid. My unflappable black-and-white greyhound continued to stand proud, neck arched, body centred evenly over four strong legs. Miss Cool Calm and Collected, showing off her Best-in-Group assets in the line-up for Best in Show.

The irate, arm-waving men arguing on the other side of the show-ring fence directly behind me, however, were not so cool. In fact, the two poodle breeders, Stephen Channing, a bombastic bully, bedecked as always in gold chains and multi-coloured satins, and Chi, his normally sweet-natured partner, were becoming more and more heated by the second.

Hmm… trouble in Paradise?

While the winner of the Non-Sporting group, a twinkly-eyed brown and white bulldog, huffed and puffed his way around the ring, I peeped over my shoulder, loath to miss a second of round two in the fight of the century.

Chi, angrier than I'd ever seen him, stabbed at the air with one finger. "And what about *my* feelings, Stephen?" Another poke. "It's *always* about *you*."

"For the last time, Chi, you're delusional. I did *not* wink at the guy with the cute beagle." Stephen, his face fire engine red, stamped one knee-high booted foot. "And stop *throwing* things. You almost hit me on the *nose* with that brush, and you know how *easily* I bruise."

"In that case, I'll try harder not to miss next time," snapped Chi, hands braced on hips as he glared up at his flamboyant lover.

I couldn't supress my grin. Go Chi! About time he stopped taking Stephen's poisonous gaff.

Eyes widening in feigned disbelief, Stephen took a step back and shook his head which set off an overload of clinking gold rings in nose, lips and ears. "My, oh my! What's got into *your* boxer shorts today?"

"Your temper-tantrums and your cruel insensitivity. *That's* what's got into my boxer shorts today." A sharp right cross came out of nowhere, luckily only glancing off Stephen's satin-clad arm. Chi winced, rubbed his fist and sniffed. "Sometimes you make me *so* mad, I could…I could *kill* you." Shoulders slumped, Chi stomped off toward the brightly colored converted bus that transported their prize-winning poodles to the shows, week after week. "And I-I just can't take it anymore."

"Well, go live somewhere else, then!" sniped Stephen, throwing his arms around and crashing into a passing competitor, Corey Black, a meek little man in his mid-forties whose black miniature poodle rarely won a ribbon due to poor grooming — and the fact that the dog sometimes lay down and refused to move when asked by the judge to show his gaits. An occurrence that always sent Stephen Channing into a noisy and vicious bout of jeers and ridicule.

Corey, still off-balance from the unexpected collision, staggered head-first into one of the steel poles supporting the viewing platform. Blood oozed from a cut on his forehead. He clutched at the pole, swaying and blinking up at Stephen, who refused to even give him a sideways glance. Instead, the overbearing poodle breeder pouted, wriggled his booty and flounced along behind Chi, the clunky gold chains around his neck swinging with each step.

Chi spun around. "Why would *I* leave? It's *my* money that bought our property."

"Yes, but you put *Windswept Kennels* in *my* name…"

"Competitor number 38. Did you hear me?" The show judge, a tall thin bearded man in his mid-thirties, cleared his throat. He pointed at Penelope with a nod of his head, bringing me back to the task in hand. "Once more around the ring, please."

"Um…yes, of course."

Dodging Chi's sparkly dog brush, I set off, Penelope striding out beside me, my aim to show off her anatomically-correct body and smooth gait to the bearded judge and thereby win the coveted and final event of the day — *Best in Show*.

Not only was Penelope the gentlest, most loving greyhound in the world, she also knew her job in the show ring. She powered along beside me, neck stretched, muscles moving smoothly, each toe pointed before touching down on the grass.

All I had to do was keep up with her.

As we rounded the corner near the kennelling area and began heading back toward the other six Best-in-Group finalists, I encountered distraction number two. Yikes! In one of the kennels, my adventurous twenty-month-old son, Jake, was attempting to fit his head inside the mouth of a large German Shephard — *Champion Grimshaw I'm the King of the Forest* to be precise.

Oh. My. God. Where were my friends, Abi and Molly? They were supposed to be babysitting Jake.

I slid to a halt — as did my heartbeat.

One — the dog didn't know my son from a bar of soap.

Two —a bowl of fresh kibble had been placed under the German Shepherd's nose by his owner, who'd walked away, oblivious to what was happening.

And three — was that dog eying Jake like a juicy steak, tossing up whether the delicacy on all fours currently kissing him on the nose might prove tastier than the dry kibble in his bowl?

Just as I was deliberating between whipping through the gate or taking a shortcut over the fence, Abi and Molly, all arms and legs and yelps and white horrified faces, appeared one each side of Jake. Ignoring his highly vocal opposition, they snatched him up in the air and transported him bodily away from the dog's gleaming teeth and into his stroller.

"Sorry, Dana," mouthed Abi pulling an apologetic face at me as Molly attempted to strap Jake into his stroller while dodging flailing arms and legs and resisting his roof-raising vexed howls of protest.

My two best friends, Abi Truelove, who owned an upmarket canine boutique called, *The Pampered Pooch* and Molly Gibson, a best-selling author of rather raunchy romance novels, may have been successful in business but not having any offspring of their own, hadn't realized exactly how slippery a determined twenty-month-old boy-child could be.

Why had Peter, my husband, who was supposed to look after Kayla and Jake on show day — at home — away from danger — forgotten it was his day for child minding and put his hand up to work this Saturday? He knew how wired I got when I had to not only handle Penelope in the show ring, but also keep tabs on our two munchkins under the age of four. Last time this happened, Jake and Kayla had somehow smuggled a prize-winning Shih Tzu into the back of our car and the irate owner came close to having me arrested for theft. I refused to let Peter near me for three weeks after that little debacle.

But some men were slow to learn.

I looked down at Penelope. Penelope looked up at me. And I swear she rolled her eyes before trotting me proudly back to the other six dogs in the Best-in-Show line-up.

"Everything okay?" The judge, a twinkle in his eyes, stood waiting for me.

"You got kids?"

The upturned lips transformed into a wide-open I-know-where-you're-coming-from grin. "Five."

I rolled my eyes. "You have my sympathy."

With a laugh, he turned away and moved slowly along the line of dogs until standing in front of a beautifully turned-out white Maltese terrier, complete with dark eyelashes and a pretty pink bow. The judge shook hands with the dog's owner. "Congratulations. Your dog is the best-coated Maltese I've seen in quite a while." And with that he accepted a tri-colored *Best in Show* sash from a nearby attendant and handed the ribbon to the dog's owner.

Immediately the runner-up in the toy group, a rat-sized smooth-coated chihuahua, entered the ring attached to his owner, a flamboyantly dressed senior citizen sporting a scarlet beret and matching scarf. They affixed themselves to the end of the line-up ready to show off their wares to the judge.

The bearded judge studied the newcomer, asked the senior citizen to trot her dog around the ring once then moved back down the line, pausing firstly at the wide chested bulldog and then the lamb-like Bedlington Terrier until finally coming to a halt in front of Penelope. I tensed, moved her right back leg a miniscule to the left and chucked her under the chin hoping she'd flaunt her beautifully arched neck. Statue-still, Penelope radiated class and good breeding.

Finally, the judge turned to the attendant tagging him and asked for the blue and white satin ribbon with *Runner up in Show* printed in gold lettering across the front. With a smile, he handed the ribbon to me. "Your greyhound bitch is a lovely correct specimen of the breed and has a temperament to match. Congratulations."

Unable to control my delight, I gave a whoop, waved the sash in the air and grinned at my support team, Molly and Abi, who were yelling themselves hoarse, Kayla, one fairy wing drooping as she leaned over the fence waving and calling out, and Jake, who'd been coerced out of his tears with a bar of chocolate. When he saw me waving, he giggled and hurled Doggo, his much-loved stuffed toy, over the fence into the show ring.

"Best in Show is Mr. Graham Smith's Maltese terrier, *Australian*

Champion Austral Friendly Fire and Runner up is Ms. Dana Fox's greyhound, *Australian Champion Twinkletoes of Pettigrew*."

While Penelope cavorted along beside me, enjoying her moment of glory, I took off behind the ribbon-bedecked white Maltese terrier, for one final euphoric circuit of the show ring.

This was a first for Penelope and me and I intended to milk it to the max. Award-winning moments like this were what brought dog owners to shows week after week. Encouraged us to rise in the dark, get a load of washing on the line before daybreak, grumpy kids fed, even grumpier husbands out of bed, groom dogs until they shone and arrive at whatever showground was the pick of the week, just as the sun was stretching its golden rays.

I puffed out my chest, let off another whoop and threw my arms around my oh-so-adorable greyhound's neck. She was the star of the show, the Queen. I was merely her lady-in-waiting.

As I kissed Penelope on the nose and ruffled her soft ears for the umpteenth time, out of the corner of my eye I spotted Stephen Channing again. His pink satin shirt, tight-fitting white satin pants, glitter be-speckled boots and jewellery shop of clunky gold chains was hard not to miss. What was he up to now? One arm around the good-looking guy with the cute beagle, he leaned closer, laughing affectedly at something the other man was saying before taking a coy glance over his shoulder.

I looked around for Chi but couldn't see him at first. All I could see were tired competitors packing up after a long day at the show, eager to get home.

My eyes drifted across to the big rainbow-colored bus with *Windswept Kennels* emblazoned across both sides. And that's when I spotted Chi. The little poodle breeder was sitting hunched on a metal dog crate, shoulders slumped, hands dangling between his knees, a picture of misery.

He was watching Stephen laugh pretentiously at something his new friend said. And if looks could kill, both Stephen and Cute Beagle Guy would have been incinerated on the spot.

www.ingramcontent.com/pod-product-compliance
Lightning Source LLC
Chambersburg PA
CBHW060313310726
48976CB00007B/2317